JAGGED

JUSTICE

ROBERT E. KEY

Author's note:
This is a work of fiction. Characters, names, situations, and events derive from the author's imagination or are used fictitiously. Certain locations described exist. Any resemblance to actual persons living or dead, business establishments, organizations, events, or locales is entirely coincidental. Do not attempt the actions described herein under pain of criminal prosecution.

ISBN-13: 9781696784047

*Dedicated to the memory of my high school
English teacher,
Nell Marie Wylie (Miss Wylie)*

Contents

PERIOD ONE..1

1: The Desert..3

2: The Criminal Justice System 8

3: The Committee...13

4: The Prosecutor 22

5: The Beginning...29

6: The Child Molester 36

7: Ten Years Earlier 41

8: The K-Market Homicides 44

9: The Recruit..47

10: The Interview 51

11: The Vetting 58

12: Spousal Abuse...64

13: Half-Ass Actions..69

14: Problem Solved...75

15: Domestic Violence..82

PERIOD TWO...87

16: The Enablers 89

17: A Dangerous Vocation..95

18: The Transaction..107

19: Matricide 114

20: The Foul Mouthed Pedagogue 124

21: Domestic Violence Reappearance......................133

22: The Sermon 141

23: Iniquitous Clergy...144

24: Life on the Street...157

25: Street Extortion 161

26: Anonymous Lead 166

PERIOD THREE 173

27: Remorse...175

28: Hit Man 179

29: The Contract..191

30: "Double Homicide at Etta's Place".....................197

31: Press Curiosity 200

32: Deep Background...209

33: Unwanted Publicity...217

34: The Hookup..222

35: The Persuaders 226

36: Crack in the Façade...233

37: The Plant 238

38: "Vigilante Justice" 241

39: The Elk Hunt...244

40: Grief 250

41: The Contractors...254

42: The Parolee 260

43: Another Assignation 267

44: Unforeseen Tragedy 274

45: Post-Accident Inquiry 279

46: Suspicion 288

47: Conspiracy Continued 294

48: Infanticide 300

PERIOD FOUR 309

49: School Shootings 311

50: Justice Delayed 323

51: The Gambler 327

52: The Corrupt Prosecutor 333

53: Child Molestation 344

54: Search Warrant 352

55: Finality 356

56: Aftermath 365

57: Postscript 369

ABOUT THE AUTHOR 372

PERIOD ONE

1

The Desert

"Stillness, aridity, beauty, danger."

The sky was clear, the air hot and oppressive on a still, half-moon summer evening in the Sonoran Desert near Phoenix. The desert, noted for its dense vegetation, was studded with spiny plant life—mesquite, ocotillo, numerous cactus species, and the iconic giant saguaro.

The gunman was thirty-six years old, in excellent physical condition and confident of his physical prowess. He stood six feet, two inches tall at 190 solid pounds with sculpted muscles and "six-pack" abs.

Clad in heavy black denim trousers, black shirt, black baseball cap, shooter's gloves, hiking boots with soles modified to remove the tread pattern, and leather gaiters, he was reasonably protected against the spiny vegetation through which he hiked. His boots would later be placed in a plastic trash bag with other rubbish and discarded in a strip mall dumpster. The *Committee* deemed it necessary to avoid leaving any evidence of his presence during the operation.

Strapped on his back was a light-weight hunting rifle chambered for .270 Winchester ammo, equipped with a

Leupold VX Freedom scope that had been carefully sighted for targets up to two hundred yards. Decorated for expert marksmanship during a four-year stint in the Marine Corps, he was a skilled sharpshooter. Heavily sweating, he crept on hands and knees the final ten yards toward his objective—a low ridge overlooking the estate of his assigned target. The crawl left his knees raw and sore and he cursed himself for not bringing knee pads. He had hiked over two hundred yards through undisturbed desert battling cacti, thorny bushes, rocky terrain, and potential danger from venomous serpents to reach his destination. The hike required twenty five minutes since there was no trail and all he had to light his way was partial moonlight and a penlight flashlight producing only100 lumens of illumination. He was relieved not to have encountered any rattlesnakes—active this time of year, especially in darkness.

His colleagues on the *Committee* had carefully examined a USGS topographic map and aerial photographs of the area that yielded important details about the targeted property and desert to be crossed. Using binoculars from a prone position he was now viewing the sumptuous estate before him from an elevated vantage point. The property was accommodated with a huge terrace, lush tropical landscaping, and an elegant swimming pool shaped like a large banjo—circular with a rectangular neck allowing for lap swimming. Lap lanes representing banjo strings were painted on the pool's floor. *Very cool.*

The gunman spotted three security guards sauntering around the perimeter of the estate, wearing what appeared to be *Uzi* submachine guns strapped over their shoulders.

A noisy poolside party was in full swing with at least forty casually attired guests enjoying the festivities. Several bikini-clad women were batting around a beach ball in the pool and a four-piece band was playing loudly. Several couples were dancing to the music on the large pool deck. Perimeter misters emitted a cooling fog. A bow-tied bar tender was busy near the shallow end of the pool. *What a life this guy leads.*

Scanning the area, the gunman saw no sign of his target—Tomas Guerrero-Ochoa, a Mexican national who owned this large estate in Arizona where he resided most of the time. A Sinaloa drug cartel leader well known to authorities, he bossed a large criminal enterprise with operations including narcotics trafficking, money laundering, murder, kidnapping, torture, bribery, and extortion. Ochoa had been indicted and tried on criminal charges twice. But like John Gotti, the New York Mafiosi, had beaten the rap both times. His well-paid lawyers found technicalities that convinced the judge to dismiss the charge on one occasion and a compliant jury found him not guilty on the other. Investigations were continuing into other suspected illegalities involving Ochoa.

Surely he must be here, he never misses his own parties. The *Committee* had carefully researched the habits of Ochoa, observed his lifestyle, and through reliable informants had learned of this evening's event. After a wait of twenty minutes and a sense of growing frustration, the gunman spotted Ochoa emerging from the large house wearing a gaudy sport shirt opened to the waist, white trousers, heavy gold neck chain, and alligator-hide slip-ons. He was accompanied by a lovely, dark-haired woman dressed in a colorful robe. *Señor Ochoa, you've just enjoyed your last roll in the hay.*

Slowly the cartel kingpin made his way among the guests, shaking hands, joking, and embracing many with a kiss on both cheeks, mafia style. He was closely accompanied by a couple of heavies who the gunman judged were body guards.

The gunman dropped the binoculars in favor of the rifle scope. By this time, the party was even louder and Ochoa had worked around to the near edge of the pool with his back presenting a perfect target. His female companion chatted with guests nearby. At a distance of about ninety yards, the shot would be easy but the gunman reminded himself not to rashly pull off a round until the best opportunity was available. Two guests walked behind Ochoa blocking the gunman's view of his target. *Get the hell out of the way!* Momentarily, they moved on.

This is it he whispered. Working the bolt to shove a round into the chamber and fingering off the safety, he carefully put the crosshairs in the middle of Ochoa's back, now presenting a clear shot. Gradually pressuring the trigger causing a sharp crack of the weapon, he fired a 150 grain, hollow point projectile, striking its target squarely in the upper spine, blowing out the victim's chest. Ochoa pitched forward into the pool, dead when he hit the water, turning it bright crimson. Screaming and chaos ensued. Those standing near Ochoa realized where the shot had come from and dived for cover. But when no additional shots were fired after a few minutes, party goers sensed the attack was over.

Bodyguards pulled the bloody corpse out of the water and laid it on the pool deck. Most of the guests quickly fled the scene, not wanting to deal with EMTs and police when they arrived. The erstwhile security guards seemed to be in total confusion and were not about to head off into the desert to find the gunman fearing they too would be targets.

Remembering not to eject the spent shell casing from his weapon and quickly sanitizing the spot, the assassin made his way back to a narrow graveled road as quickly as the desert allowed. He climbed into a waiting SUV at the place of rendezvous and reached for a throwaway cell phone as the vehicle sped away. "The package was delivered," the assassin reported in a voice message to the *Committee*.

The rifle and scope were thoroughly wiped down and hidden in a pre-planned place a mile away about ten yards off the road where it could be retrieved later and disposed of. The assassin then used a large quantity of hand sanitizer and a damp towel to thoroughly scrub his hands, arms, face, and hair to remove GSR (gunshot residue) in the unlikely event they were stopped by police who might be searching for the shooter and randomly detaining suspect vehicles. Forty minutes later, he and his driver arrived back at the *Committee's* basement headquarters in North Phoenix.

The following morning, headlines across the nation blared: "Drug Boss Gunned Down at His Estate." Cable news networks led with the story.

2

The Criminal Justice System

"...it was the age of wisdom,
it was the age of foolishness, ... "

– Charles Dickens, *A Tale of Two Cities.*

The criminal justice system of the United States is regarded as a model of excellence throughout the world. Derived from the English legal system in which laws were established as a means for finding truth in the pursuit of justice, it protects the rights of the accused while ensuring due process. It is generally respected by a majority of Americans. The nation's founding document begins with "We the People." The United States Constitution incorporating the Bill of Rights comprise and exemplify the basic rights of American citizens, ensuring that law protects against arbitrary government power and serves to deliver justice.

On the dark side, however, the criminal justice system is seen by many as inconsistent, ineffective, and deeply troubled. In many jurisdictions, a low percentage of violent crimes are cleared by arrests, and when arrests are made, charges frequently result in probation, light sentences, or outright dismissal for lack of evidence. Law enforcement clears just over twenty percent of reported crimes. Fewer than half of those suspects are convicted. There is one murder in the US every thirty six minutes, yet over 200,000 murders remain unsolved every year. Overburdened prosecutors, crowded prisons, irrational rulings by presiding judges, and stacked juries frequently do not dispense justice consistently to crime victims or the public.

Convicted criminals with violent records are routinely freed from prison too soon and continue their criminal careers. Because of prison overcrowding and budget limitations, corrections authorities frequently have no choice but to release convicts before their sentences are completed. Such releases are intended to be limited to non-violent offenders, but mistakes in processing and outright carelessness result in dangerous felons being put back on the street. Quite predictably, they "offend" again. Victims, the general public, radio talk show hosts, police, and prosecutors are increasingly outraged and frustrated.

Local news reports detailed the long and violent record of a man who had stabbed three victims to death in Scottsdale and Tempe, Arizona, over a period of eight months. People wondered why the perp was not in prison. In urban areas, the public was aware of the increase in crimes committed in public; law enforcement seemed unable to stop them. Many felonies were reduced to misdemeanors, if indeed, suspects were prosecuted at all. Society was entering a post-legal era. If government fails its duty to protect citizens, they will claim the power to defend themselves and seek justice.

Moreover, our political system has been transformed from a legislative to administrative status. The Constitution forbids delegation of lawmaking authority to the executive branch, but this legal principle has been under attack for many decades. Government agencies are weaponized against innocent parties. Unelected bureaucrats, accountable to no one, are making and enforcing laws that trample on individual rights in contravention of constitutional protections. Another egregious example of government mischief is the seizure, without due process, of cash assets of anyone suspected of drug dealing or money laundering. Law enforcement officials often assume criminal activity and infer "probable cause" simply from knowledge of cash holdings.

THE *COMMITTEE* WAS FOUNDED in the basement of retired police detective Derek Overton. Its members did not initially refer to it by that term. It originally consisted of Overton, his friend, the owner of a large plumbing company, a next-door neighbor who was engrossed with Derek's stories about his career, and an assistant prosecuting attorney. The four regarded the word "offender" with contempt. They thought of an offender as one who calls you a "sonofabitch," thereby giving offense. They believed that criminals should be referred to as just that—"criminals," not by the euphemism "offender." They discussed and analyzed these cases at length:

Case – A child rapist with a previous record of molesting children in Oklahoma was sentenced to four months in prison and probation after exposing himself and fondling a thirteen-year-old-girl. Psychologists testified on his behalf and the judge agreed that he no longer posed a serious threat despite the rate of recidivism of such "offenders." Six months later, he was rearrested for violently raping a fourteen-year-old girl. The child's parents refused to allow her testimony and the rape kit went missing. The judge had no choice but to dismiss the charges without prejudice, meaning the case could be refiled if and when compelling new evidence was discovered. The defendant then relocated to Glendale, Arizona, a suburb of Phoenix where he lived a quiet, obscure life. But he was required to register as a sex offender. His presence was noted by law enforcement authorities and his neighbors were notified.

Case – In Los Angeles, a former star NFL running back and well-known celebrity murdered his ex-wife and her friend with a knife. Charged and tried for double murder, he was incredibly acquitted despite a mountain of evidence against him. The public was outraged. Jury nullification was blamed.

Case – In Phoenix, a wife beater was sentenced to only ninety days in jail and probation after repeated incidents of severely battering his wife during drinking binges. Neighbors told cops they heard and observed his violent behavior over a period of more than a year. The wife declined to press charges after the first couple of incidents, comforted by his assurances that he was sorry, begging her forgiveness, and promising that it wouldn't happen again. Then several weeks later, he broke her jaw and made raw meat out of her face. She managed to call 911 while he was threatening to kill her, but he fled before the police arrived and was not immediately located.

Case – A criminal who had been given clemency and freed from a forty-year prison sentence for murder in another state entered a coffee shop in Tacoma, Washington, and shot to death four police officers who were seated planning the day's activities. He was later shot and killed when resisting arrest. Several of his relatives and friends were charged with aiding his attempt to evade arrest.

Case – In Tucson, Arizona, a repeat "offender" (read thug) hijacked a car with a mother and two young children, drove them into the desert and murdered all three because he simply wanted the vehicle's wheel covers. He pleaded guilty and was spared the death penalty, sentenced instead to life in prison without possibility of parole.

Two of these crimes resulted in some measure of justice. The others caused the victims and their families to suffer without relief.

3

The Committee

"How can thousands of murders take place in Chicago without a national outcry? How can some call dope pushers who sell deadly substances 'non-violent criminals?' How can clergy continue to abuse children? How can people falsely accuse others for money or power, ruining lives?"

– Bill O'Reilly

Derek Overton organized the *Committee* with three associates and a mission to dispense justice when it had been denied in the most egregious criminal cases, and some not so serious but requiring measured reaction to balance the scales of justice. Their preferred clients were crime victims who had been deprived of basic fairness with punishment of the criminal, or lack thereof, in proportion to the crime they had suffered. Victims of crime did not know of the *Committee's* existence and consequently never sought to contact Overton directly or seek the service he provided. Cases attracted his attention typically through news reports, from confidential referrals, and from cases he learned of through contacts in the police department and in the county attorney's office—the latter an assistant prosecuting attorney who had become a member of the *Committee*.

TO SUPPLEMENT PENSION income, retired cops frequently hire on as security guards with firms providing armed protection to banks, shopping malls, sporting events, and entertainment venues. Retired detectives often pursue careers as private investigators, casually referred to as "private eyes" or "gumshoes." Their experience and knowledge of investigatory methods give them an advantage in the minds of clients over PIs without such experience. Derek became licensed as a Private Investigator by the State of Arizona. He found that a PI's work is much more detailed, demanding, and time consuming than a detective's efforts. After two cases that did not produce satisfactory results, he decided not to actively pursue this vocation.

He stayed in touch with former colleagues in the Phoenix Police Department, especially Detective Norman Willkie, an aggressive member of the homicide unit. The two frequently met for lunch at a small downtown café. They reminisced about former cases which resulted in favorable outcomes (arrests and convictions) and also many that did not. The latter were particularly galling to both men. Conversations analyzed what went wrong and what they could have done differently that could have made a difference. Suspects were often freed by trial judges on technicalities or, more often, light sentences were handed down that were not commensurate with the severity of the charges. Willkie harbored a gut-level hatred shared by Overton of every suspect he investigated and especially those he arrested. This sometimes adversely influenced his judgment and caused him to make mistakes during investigations that angered his superiors. Without initially revealing the *Committee's* existence, Derek regarded Willkie as a valuable source of information.

OVERTON WAS A native of Huntsville, Texas, where his father was a corrections officer at the Walls Unit of the Texas State Prison and his mother was an elementary school teacher. The couple moved to Arizona after the elder Overton retired from the prison system. Before moving to Phoenix to be near his parents, Derek earned a degree in education from Sam Houston State University in Huntsville. Two younger brothers also graduated from the same college and had become police officers in San Antonio where they lived quietly with their families.

His career goal was to become a public school teacher like his mom and teach civics at the high school level. After qualifying for a state teacher's certificate, he interviewed with several school districts in the Phoenix area but found himself disenchanted with low starting salaries and lack of opportunity for advancement in the public education system. On the verge of returning to Texas, he saw a recruiting notice in the *Arizona Examiner* newspaper inviting applicants to apply for admission to the police academy. Responding immediately, he was accepted and completed police training with distinction. He met and married Marjorie Hampton, also a cadet at the police academy. He was known as a good cop during his police career and was decorated and continually promoted through the ranks. After three years on the force, Marjorie decided on a different career course and went to work as an assistant with a security consulting firm in nearby

Scottsdale. She and Derek had one son, Ronald, usually addressed by his parents as "Ronnie."

Twelve years into his career, Derek earned the rank of Lieutenant in charge of the northeast sector homicide division. During his tenure as a detective, he investigated 321 homicides and solved 89% of them—a record he was proud of. In his final five years before retirement, he handled an increasing number of cases that stumbled in the prosecution phase and thus failed to hold criminals accountable. Justice was not delivered. He was angered by "offenders" who managed to slip through the system's prosecutorial procedures either because of weak prosecution or uncooperative witnesses.

He maintained a strict fitness regimen begun in his twenties, watched his diet and worked out regularly in the PD gym. Then nearing retirement and dealing with middle age, he began to neglect physical exercise, consumed too many calories, and found himself twenty pounds overweight, carried on a five-ten frame. Post-retirement, he was cautioned by doctors that he was at risk of developing diabetes. Retirement brought relief from his job stress but not to his growing wrath at the number of unpunished or lightly punished wrong doers he regarded as a cancer on society and who went on to "reoffend."

The *Committee* had no public face, certainly no business identity or phone number, and no internet or social media presence. It existed in total anonymity. Members did not think of themselves as vigilantes and did not use that term in conversation. The term *"Committee"* resulted from casual reference by its members. They kept no records, no meeting minutes, nothing in writing. All purchases of guns and other equipment were made at gun shows in distant cities using cash only, thereby avoiding a paper trail of purchases. Nothing was entered on computer hard drives. Members did not maintain any social media accounts, even personal ones. They did not communicate by text messaging, only by brief cell phone conversations using throwaway "burners," frequently replaced. For all practical, legal, and obvious purposes, the *Committee* did not exist. Like jurors in a criminal case, they were cautioned by Overton not to disclose or discuss their activities with anyone including relatives and friends. "Loose lips sink ships," he said.

Meetings were held in the basement of Overton's home in North Central Phoenix. Basements were rare in Southern Arizona. Slab-on-grade was the typical construction method for most residential structures; therefore, Overton's basement provided a very private and secure venue for their deliberations. It also served as his "man cave"— walls decorated with sports mementos, movie posters, and Native American paraphernalia. His favorite item was a signed, framed picture of Babe Ruth, obtained at a garage sale several years earlier from a homeowner who was unaware of its value and sold it to him for a mere $50. He later had it authenticated and appraised at $2,250. He became obsessed with Ruth's legendary career and having researched his life in detail, could recite his professional statistics and awards from memory. Of particular interest was the "Curse of the Bambino" that descended on Boston after the Red Sox traded Ruth to the New York Yankees where he established his fame. Overton frequently regaled members of the *Committee* with his knowledge of the baseball icon, causing them to groan with boredom.

Overton possessed an entrenched commitment to absolute justice and saw himself and the *Committee* on a sacred mission. He tried to instill a sense of the avenging angel among his colleagues. "What we do is righteous," he frequently reminded them. He regarded the *Committee's* mission in two parts: First, its operations halted specific criminal behavior, and second, when applied peremptorily, avoided lengthy trials that many times ended unsatisfactorily for victims of crime. From his professional experience, he had gained an astute knowledge of criminal investigation techniques with the commensurate ability to avoid leaving evidence in the wake of the *Committee's* operations. He knew most criminals were incredibly stupid. They regard themselves as much smarter than the dumb cops who investigate their crimes. This is their weakness and the cops' strength. Overton exploited this fact in planning the *Committee's* operations.

Philip Maguire (Phil) was a successful plumbing contractor and was an avid outdoorsman outside of work. His company provided subcontract services for numerous builders. He pursued hunting and fishing with a zeal that resulted in his disappearance from home several days during every big game season, greatly to the annoyance of his wife, Dana. The couple had two daughters, Alice and Marie, both away at college. Elk hunting was his first love and he relished the prospect of bagging the ultimate bull that would be recognized by the Boone and Crocket Club as a record trophy. He had hunted several seasons in Alaska and killed every large game animal in the state except polar bear, a protected species. He became enamored with bow hunting and had taken two trips to South Africa to engage in guided hunts of horned animals to be harvested with bow and arrow. Trophy heads adorned the Maguire home. His wife and daughters found this distasteful and were embarrassed when trying to explain them to visitors.

One cold November day he was a member of an elk hunting party led by an expensive guide in Wyoming. During conversation in camp, he offered an observation that a powerful rifle in the hands of a marksman could be used to "do a lot of good" in criminal justice. The hunting guide suggested he join the local Elks Club where he might find like-minded friends when he returned home.

Stephen Lee Simmons (Lee), a Marine and Overton's next-door neighbor, was a six-foot- two-inch, powerfully built man who jogged daily and regularly worked out at his gym. He maintained an upright bearing and military-style buzzed haircut. As a member of the 1st Marine Logistics Group he had received training in the marksmanship program at Marine Corps Base Camp in Pendleton, California, "The West Coast's Premier Expeditionary Training Base." His instructors recognized his potential talent and rapidly advanced him through the program. Ranking first in his group, he earned the Distinguished Marksman Badge and Distinguished Pistol Badge. After two tours of duty in Iraq and an honorable discharge from the Marine Corps, he entered Arizona State University in nearby Tempe, earned a degree in marketing, landed a good job with a pet supply company, and married Janet, his high school sweetheart. Janet gave birth to Daryl, a robust lad with great interest in athletics, especially football, as he reached his teen years. Lee quickly became friends with Derek after he and Janet bought the house next door.

Over beers and backyard barbeques, they shared political opinions and discussed how to solve society's problems with unconventional methods. With his wife and son, he took frequent weekend trips in his red Dodge Challenger "muscle car," a possession he was inordinately proud of.

David Baumann (Dave), assistant prosecuting attorney, was a native of Winslow, Arizona, with a shy personality, slim build, angular features, deep set blue eyes, and a constantly glum expression. After graduating *cum laude* with a degree in history from the University of Northern Arizona in Flagstaff, he went on to earn a law degree from the University of Arizona in Tucson, finishing fourth in his class. In his late twenties and unmarried with few friends outside of work, he became enamored of conservative politics and briefly considered running for a seat on the county Board of Supervisors. With a need for friends and social interaction, he joined the Elks Club near his home. During his time with the county attorney's[1] office, he was assigned mostly to minor cases and became frustrated with limited resources available in the criminal justice system to adequately deal with the problem of crime.

Time and again, suspects were routinely undercharged at the direction of his superiors, given probation for serious offenses by the courts, or had charges dismissed for lack of "compelling" evidence. It appeared that the county attorney's primary objective was to clear as many cases as possible as quickly as possible. This was understandable given the

---

[1] In Arizona, criminal prosecutions are the responsibility of an elected official known as the county attorney; in other states this official is referred to as district attorney, and in others, as state's attorney.

volume of cases and limited office staff. "I wish there was a way to create instant justice," he confided to colleagues in the office. "Just issue a contract on these thugs and watch as the scales of justice are balanced." His associates smiled and rolled their eyes at this lame attempt at humor.

4

The Prosecutor

"The First Duty of Society is Justice."

A lexander Hamilton's words appear above the entrance to the South Tower of the Maricopa County Superior Court building. Succeeding county attorneys all agreed, "Those words perfectly describe the work our prosecutors conduct every day on behalf of the public to hold wrongdoers accountable for their actions."

This is stated on the official website of the county attorney's office:

"Our mission is to hold criminals accountable for the crimes they commit and to ensure that the rights of victims are honored and respected throughout the criminal justice process."

AS ONE OF almost 250 attorneys who handle over 35,000 criminal cases annually in a metropolitan area of four million people, David Baumann, subsequently known to his colleagues on the *Committee* as "Dave," was regarded by his superiors in the Maricopa County Attorney's office as something of a nerd, but also as a competent prosecutor. After three years with the department, he found himself still assigned to misdemeanors such as traffic offenses, DUIs, bad checks, and non-felony domestic violence cases.

Website descriptions of the county attorney's work were impressive and necessary for public consumption, but David wasn't sure they consistently validated his or his fellow attorneys' work. So many cases, so many charges dropped for lack of evidence, so many cases pleaded down to lesser charges, and so few convictions relative to the number of original complaints. David understood and respected the system, but a sense of deep frustration affected him. He felt prepared for more serious assignments involving major felonies.

Three years out of law school and unmarried, he lived alone in a one-bedroom apartment near downtown. His only socializing was Friday afternoon drinks after work with two or three office buddies who were also bachelors. They usually discussed current cases, sports, and some of the more attractive women in the office. His best friend was Felix, his cat, who greeted him at the door each day when he arrived home.

SEEKING TO EXPAND his circle of acquaintances outside of work, David joined the Elks Club where he met Derek Overton one evening over drinks at the bar. Derek was familiar with the prosecutor's office from his time with the PD and was acquainted with many of the attorneys there. But Dave had joined the office after Derek's retirement so this was their first encounter. Derek was very interested in the young man's work with the prosecutor's office and engaged in a lengthy conversation asking numerous questions about case details and the effectiveness of prosecutions.

"As you probably know, cases are submitted to our office by city police departments and the sheriff. We follow up with our own investigation to prepare the case for prosecution. That involves gathering additional evidence and interviewing witnesses and perps," explained Dave.

Derek replied, "I remember the procedure from my time with the PD. What kinds of cases interest you the most?"

"Frankly, I'm pretty bored with the crappy stuff I'm assigned. It's mostly low-level cases like traffic citations, hot checks, and some DUIs," Dave said. "I think I'm ready to take on serious felonies and I've expressed that desire to my superiors. They just say they'll consider it, but so far it hasn't happened."

"Sounds as if you are pretty frustrated with your role at the county attorney's shop."

"The crime that really bothers me is domestic violence against women. Our office doesn't take these offenses as seriously as they should. Too many assholes skate repeatedly when they beat up their partners, and punishment is either too light or entirely absent. It's infuriating."

Derek detected exasperation in David's voice and sensed the possibility that he might be recruited to assist the *Committee*. "What if there was a way to deal with wrongdoers who commit that type of crime and others of a more serious nature?"

"I'm not sure I know what you mean," said Dave.

"You could provide information anonymously to someone who is able to dispense remedies when the criminal justice systems fails to do so."

"That would violate office policy and could get me in a lot of trouble."

"Just a thought. Forget about it."

DEREK REALIZED David could be a rich source of intelligence, potentially valuable in identifying targets for the *Committee's* crosshairs. He sat down with Dave in three more "chance" encounters at the Elk's Club and carefully advanced the idea of independent actions to right perceived wrongs when it was possible to do so without personal risk or retribution. Derek knew he had to establish a level of trust between himself and Dave for this to bear fruit. Their conversations were wide ranging and grew increasingly intense when the topic of domestic violence came up. Derek encouraged Dave to talk about his work and his vexation at not being assigned to handle more serious cases.

"There may be a way for you to effectively deal with criminals outside of your regular duties," said Derek cautiously. "I'm thinking of a way to apply remedies when the criminal justice system fails to do so. You might call it 'direct justice.'"

Derek plunged ahead, knowing that he was about to take a risk in disclosing his idea to an attorney in the prosecutor's office. But he detected something in Dave's demeanor and language that suggested he could be trusted.

"Would you consider providing assistance to a group I'm thinking of organizing that dispenses direct justice?"

"What do you mean direct justice?"

"It's where criminals, arrested or not, unindicted or indicted, and other wrongdoers who have not been held accountable for their actions are made to pay for what they've done by certain means, usually physical in nature."

"You mean vigilante justice, don't you?"

"You can call it that, but 'direct justice' is a better term."

"What assistance are you talking about?'

"If you could provide information about unresolved cases or not-guilty verdicts by juries when the facts clearly support a finding of guilty, that would be useful," said Derek. "You wouldn't have to be involved in correctional actions, just furnish the information that justifies it. I'm talking about information that enlarges what is already known publicly, or background on cases that were not resolved satisfactorily. You wouldn't be expected to disclose protected information about current prosecutions."

"I don't know... that might violate office policies. By the way, how are you connected to this organization?"

Derek attempted to establish credibility in Dave's mind by exaggerating the existence of an organization. "It's not really an organization in the formal sense. We're just a couple of guys who are discreet and super careful about what we do. We deal with criminals when the justice system fails to do so."

Derek went on, "I have connections inside the PD and we could use someone who can provide timely information from your perspective. There's minimal risk. The professional approach we take to each operation and the results would be effective... and rewarding. We wouldn't take action against anyone who wouldn't have it coming."

OVER DRINKS THE following week, Derek introduced Dave to Phil Maguire. The three discovered much in common with opinions concerning criminal justice. Soon, Saturday evenings found them in the Elks Club bar discussing cases Dave described. The information Dave brought to the group was a violation of office ethics, if not a violation of law, but Dave's professed outrage at men treating women badly trumped his loyalty to office policy. If his boss had discovered that he was disclosing details of cases under consideration or actual prosecution, he would have been fired immediately.

ON A CHILLY monday morning in February, the deputy county attorney called David into his office and informed him that he was to be assigned henceforth exclusively to both felony and non-felony domestic violence cases. Dave was initially shocked but quickly realized this could be a step up in his career. Many of these crimes were very serious in nature – causing injury and hospitalization, even death to the victim. He could strongly relate to this as he himself was a victim of beatings as a child at the hands of his stepfather, Hector Ramos, who roughed him up regularly for minor misbehavior. He hated the man for frequently hitting his mother, causing bruises to her face and arms. When his mother called the police after the first incident, Ramos was arrested, convicted of a misdemeanor and given probation.

A second incident resulted in his mother being transported to the ER, then spending three days in the hospital recuperating from busted lips, cracked ribs, and multiple bruises delivered by Ramos in a drunken rage. He pleaded guilty to felony assault and battery charges. Prosecutors asked for and received extended jail time. The couple soon divorced and Hector was seen no more, to David's great relief.

Arizona law defines domestic violence as a violent incident that occurs in the home between family members—as between two spouses or others in a relationship who reside together or who live apart, perhaps divorced but sharing a child. It can also happen between a father and son or daughter, mother and child, or between an adult child and his elderly parent. Most often it explodes between a couple living together whether married or not. The woman is usually the victim. Occasionally, weapons are used or property is damaged, and the abuser often causes injuries using physical force, leading to need for medical treatment of the victim.

5
The Beginning

*Vigilante – a member of a volunteer committee organized
to suppress and control crime summarily (as when the
processes of law enforcement are viewed as inadequate);
broadly, a self-appointed doer of justice.*

– Merriam-Webster

Derek invited his neighbor Lee Simmons to the Elks Club as his guest. During socializing at the club, they engaged in conversation with club members Phil Maguire and Dave Baumann about a number of topics including sports, their respective backgrounds, and the crime rate. Dave summarized several cases his office had prosecuted in the last five years, usually with success but sometimes not. Phil related several stories about his big game hunting avocation and elaborated on the properties of hunting rifles he used.

They shared a strong opinion that justice was not uniformly dispensed in some instances of criminal misconduct. "Wouldn't it be great" if justice could be applied on a highly selective basis when the opportunity arose and an operation could be conducted in relative safety with minimum risk. Overton presented the outline of a plan he had in mind to take action to do just that and suggested the formation of a committee to review various cases to determine what, if anything, could be done to redress selected situations. The others agreed, not really thinking about the direction the group would ultimately take... the use of measured action to achieve "effective justice."

DEREK INVITED THE group to his basement for drinks and private conversation the following weekend. He spoke forcefully of his belief in justice denied and the need to dispense punishment through measured action where it had not been applied to wrongdoers.

"What do you mean by measured action?" inquired Phil Maguire suspiciously.

"I'm talking about direct personal contact with wrongdoers and applying punishments ranging from forceful oral reprimand involving threats of follow-up to physical consequences, to the elimination of certain assholes when it's called for in the most egregious cases," said Derek. "The purpose of such solutions is twofold. First, they remove the threat such criminals pose to society and stop further crimes, and second, they prevent lengthy trials that are costly to the public purse."

"So you're talking about murder, right?" demanded Phil.

"I'm talking about taking out the worst of the worst who have not been held accountable by the criminal justice system," replied Derek. "There's a drug cartel boss who lives in luxury here in this metro area. This guy poisons people with illegal drugs, bribes public officials here and in Mexico, tortures and murders enemies or anyone getting in his way.

He's skated twice after criminal court trials. I say he should be taken out."

"Exactly how would that be done?" inquired Lee.

"You're the expert marksman, Lee. If we can get you within rifle range of this guy's home, you could take him out with one shot from a protected sniper's position. Look you guys, I know that sounds pretty extreme and would require meticulous planning. I've given it a lot of thought and I've studied aerial images of the area where he lives. I'm convinced it can be carried out with minimum risk. His name is Tomas Guerrero-Ochoa and he fits my description of the worst of the worst. He first came to our attention when I was with the PD and you wouldn't believe the shit he's done and is accused of."

"I wasn't involved in his prosecution," said Dave, "but I remember a lot of office talk about the case. Our prosecutors were in total disbelief when they failed to get a conviction."

"I eliminated plenty of bad guys in Iraq without a shred of personal guilt and I think I can do the same here when the situation demands it," said Lee.

"Beyond that," Derek continued, "there is a need to take preemptive action when something comes to our attention that's resulted in severe injury to innocent victims and will likely continue unless it's stopped. I'm referring mainly to domestic violence. Look Phil, if you have reservations about all this, you won't have to be involved in any operation unless you want to."

"Fair enough, but I want assurance that my opinion will be considered before we undertake anything."

"Absolutely," said Derek.

Derek continued: "I think it was F. Scott Fitzgerald in one of his novels who said 'There are no second acts in American life.' He was wrong. This is my second act, hell it's all our second acts. What we do should be regarded as blameless. We will do what needs to be done to disable and eliminate cancer from civilized society. Can we get rid of all of it? Of course not, but we can do what we can and God willing, justice will be delivered in the cases we take on."

After three subsequent meetings, the four agreed on the *Committee's* mission, general procedures, and affirmed Overton as their chairman and leader. They adopted the use of first names for all conversations. All operations would be undertaken only with three affirmative votes. An evaluation would be made of the practicality of taking each case or not before planning an appropriate response. General agreement was reached to consider action against individuals suspected of crimes such as production and distribution of narcotics (but not against end users), sex crimes, assault and battery (especially against women), burglary, manslaughter, murder, animal cruelty, and chronic disruptive behavior that consistently harmed persons, groups, or organizations. They were not quite sure how to define the latter of these, but were sure they would recognize it when they saw it. They further agreed that certain crimes were beyond their reach including kidnapping, prostitution, and all white collar crimes such as fraud and embezzlement. Also excluded were DUI and other traffic offenses, disorderly conduct in public places, and hate crimes.

COMMITTEE MEMBERS WERE aware of other organizations referred to as "vigilantes" such as the "National

Citizens Neighborhood Watch – Securing the American Border," otherwise known as "Minutemen." Supporters called them patriots, critics called them racists. Both President George W. Bush and Mexican President Vicente Fox called them "vigilantes," though they didn't fit the description of such groups whose function was to apprehend and punish those deemed guilty of wrong doing. It was the "apprehend and punish" that didn't apply to this group. Their stated mission was to assemble at the border, observe, and report suspected illegal border crossers to the authorities. The Minutemen, with over 1,000 volunteers at one point, were active in a vulnerable 23-mile stretch of the border with Mexico between Douglas and Naco, Arizona. They had a legal right to do what they were doing; nevertheless, public opprobrium and political opposition severely hampered the group's effectiveness and they eventually splintered into several subgroups with limited resources.

AT A LOCAL church gathering, an elderly deacon inveighed against The Minutemen, calling them vigilantes, racists, bigots, and a few other epithets.

"Excuse me," a parishioner raised his hand. "Vigilantes are those who seek to apprehend, detain, and punish suspected law breakers. The Minutemen do none of that. They only observe and report illegal border crossers. George Bush called them vigilantes. He was wrong about that and so are you." The deacon muttered something about right-wing extremists and remained silent for the rest of the meeting.

"THAT'S NOT WHO we are," Derek told the *Committee* emphatically, referring to The Minutemen. "Those dimwits attracted way too much publicity which finally worked to their extreme disadvantage. Far better for them to have quietly worked with the Border Patrol surreptitiously out of the media's sight. Our operations must be totally anonymous at all times with zero mistakes and not a hint to anyone about what we do."

Outside of the basement they communicated only by means of prepaid cell phones with limited minutes known as "burners." When minutes were running low, *Committee* members simply disposed of them and replaced them. Ever-changing phone numbers posed a problem, but each user developed a method of registering all necessary numbers in their phone. New burners were purchased with cash at various office supply stores, drug store counters, and airports by members who wore disguises with fake mustaches, dark sunglasses, and hats shading their eyes. They did not use stores' parking lots, preferring instead to park a block or two away and walk to avoid CCTV[2] surveillance of their vehicles. They also used portable surveillance camera jammers that were effective up to 100 feet. They took every possible precaution to protect identities.

Derek was a highly organized professional who used his extensive knowledge of investigative techniques and law enforcement methods to avoid potential identification and arrest. He was super careful in his research and examined each venue for an operation in minute detail. He was highly skilled at forestalling physical evidence. With the use of nitrile gloves, operatives never left fingerprints at a scene nor

---

[2] Closed Circuit Television

any other indication of the *Committee's* presence including DNA, CCTV images, or physical evidence such as shell casings. They chose locations to avoid or minimize the presence of eye witnesses.

6

The Child Molester

"The only thing necessary for the triumph of evil is for good men to do nothing."

– Attributed to Edmund Burke

Thirty-five year old Jason Higgins lived in a rundown mobile home park in the Glendale, Arizona, in the Phoenix area, having relocated there from Oklahoma City fourteen months previously. As a registered sex offender, this was his third place of residence since moving to the Phoenix area.

Arizona state law requires law enforcement officials to notify the community when certain sex offenders move into their jurisdictions. Notification is required when offenders are released from prison or who relocate from another city or state. He was classified as a Level 3 Sex Offender - a high risk to the community with a history of predatory sex crimes, convicted of a dangerous crime, or diagnosed as a serial predator. His name appeared on the Dru Sjodin National Sex Offender Public Website (NSOPW), named for a twenty-two year-old college student of Grand Forks, North Dakota, who was kidnapped and murdered by a sex offender who was registered in Minnesota. On July 7, 2006, President George W. Bush signed into law the Adam Walsh Child Protection and Safety Act. This act included "Dru's Law" which changed the name of the National Sex Offender Public Registry to the 'Dru Sjodin National Sex Offender Public Website.'

Higgins' first two Glendale neighborhoods had been notified of his presence and did not welcome him into their midst. Instead, he found sticky-back notes on his door several times saying things, like: "Get the hell out, you're not wanted here," or "Take your dick elsewhere." On a couple of occasions, he found cardboard boxes weighted with rocks in his front yard with similar messages written in large letters. In the mobile home park, his neighbors, though aware of who he was, were not friendly but neither were they hostile. He was able to live in relative obscurity.

He had a record in Oklahoma of molesting children and had served four months in jail for twice exposing himself and fondling a thirteen year-old girl. The court required him to undergo sex counseling and therapy. At his post-treatment hearing, psychologists testified that he no longer posed a threat despite the rate of recidivism of such offenders. Six months later he was rearrested for violently raping a twelve-year-old girl, sending her to the hospital for extended physical and psychological treatment. The child's parents declined to allow her testimony at trial and the rape kit went missing. The judge had no choice but to dismiss the charges without prejudice, allowing the case to be refiled if compelling new evidence was discovered. Higgins walked free and then moved to Arizona, intending to start over and build a new life.

At a height of six feet, he allowed himself to bloat to 260 pounds on a diet of fast food and a six pack of beer each evening. Entirely bald with a bushy beard, nasty scar below one eye, and heavily tattooed arms, his physical appearance was rough and intimidating. Neighbors avoided him. Owning a rusty twelve-year-old Jeep Wrangler, he found a part time job delivering newspapers on a route near his home. In that subdivision of modest single family homes, just one in six homeowners had a paid subscription to the local daily. Only four of the addresses on his route subscribed to at least one of the three leading national dailies, The *Wall Street Journal, New York Times*, and *USA Today*. To supplement his meager income, he sold newspapers on street corners generally between 8:00 a.m. and noon each day after finishing his delivery route. His employer, a publishers' distribution service, became aware of his background after hiring him but reluctantly decided to give him a chance in view of the difficulty of recruiting and retaining dependable paper carriers.

ALICIA ALVAREZ WAS a beautiful fifteen-year-old high school sophomore who resided with her parents in one of the homes on Higgins' newspaper route. She was in the first bloom of womanhood with swelling breasts, long light-brown hair, bright blue eyes, clear skin, and slender body. Her parents deemed her too young to date boys, though several had asked her out. Higgins noticed her on several occasions on her way to board the school bus as he delivered the paper to her home. He began to time his delivery to coincide with her departure from the house and always greeted her with a cheery "Hello, how are you today." After several of these encounters, he offered her a ride to school in his jeep. "The bus makes a lot of stops to pick up kids so I can get you there at least fifteen minutes early."

She politely declined two of these invitations, but on his third try and since he was so friendly, she foolishly accepted. *Why not? He's the neighborhood "paper guy." Right?* Instead of driving directly to school, he diverted to a strip mall parking area, stopped and started stroking her bare arm. "You and I could have a lot of fun if I can pick you up after school. You know... foolin' around."

Horrified at his suggestion, she jerked away, leaped out of the Jeep and ran the rest of the way to school. Her friends and teachers noticed her distracted demeanor and asked if anything was wrong. "I'm fine," is all she would say. Arriving home that afternoon and badly shaken, she told her father what had happened. Appalled that his daughter would place herself in that situation, he delivered a stern lecture that left her in tears. In a rage, he called 9-1-1 and the newspaper delivery service who promptly terminated Jason Higgins' employment. Since no crime had occurred, the only thing the police could do was send a uniformed officer to Jason's trailer park and warn him of the consequences of his behavior. His employer, aware of his status on the NSOPW, was ironically relieved that its employee had only propositioned the young girl. A physical assault would have resulted in a costly law suit by her parents.

The incident crossed the desk of David Baumann in the county attorney's office. He did some research and learned the following:

- Higgins had been sentenced in 1986 to twelve years for aggravated sexual assault in Kansas and was paroled in 1995.
- Sentenced in 1997 to five years for attempted sexual battery in Arkansas. Paroled in 2002.
- Sentenced in 2004 to ten years for aggravated sexual battery in Oklahoma. Paroled in 2010.
- Sentenced to four months in prison in Oklahoma and probation after exposing himself and fondling a thirteen year old girl in 2011. Six months later, he was rearrested for violently raping a twelve-year old girl. The child's parents refused to allow her testimony at trial and the rape kit went missing. The judge had no choice but to dismiss the charges.

Why is this piece of shit being put back on the street to repeat his behavior over and over?

Now drawing unemployment benefits and forced to move yet again to another sleazy trailer park, Higgins was observed sitting alone on a park bench for long periods of time. On his final visit to this location, a stranger approached and sat down beside him. After several minutes of casual conversation, the man arose, stepped behind the bench, deftly threw a loop of $1/8^{th}$ inch woven wire cable around Jason's neck, pulled it tight, and locked it into place. Jason struggled to free himself of the garrote for twenty seconds before passing out and collapsing on the bench, dead. The stranger disappeared. No witness observed the incident. Police investigators were unable to piece together enough evidence to identify a suspect.

7
Ten Years Earlier

Frustration: *Being upset or annoyed because of inability to achieve something.*

Lieutenant Derek Overton was pissed. He had been promoted to lead the department's northeast sector homicide unit five years earlier and it hadn't gone well. Several of his detectives had bungled investigations resulting in delayed arrests and in two cases, the judge dismissed charges for violations of suspects' constitutional rights. Overton had been called on the carpet by the assistant chief of police on two occasions and was required to provide written reports on the status of training for detectives. He complied with this after delivering tongue lashings to his subordinates. Morale in his unit was low.

Overton had graduated from the police academy with high marks and had attended numerous training sessions on various policing techniques including criminal investigations. Each case was different, requiring not only skills in gathering evidence and interviewing suspects, but also a talent for dealing with victims and their families. "Cultural sensitivity" was part of every officer's training. From this experience and his time with an Hispanic partner, Derek developed moderate fluency in Spanish, written and spoken. As a native of East Texas, he retained much of the southern drawl from his upbringing including "ya'll," "right smart" (a lot) and "dreckly" (directly, or soon). This was a source of amusement and joking by his fellow officers who sometimes made fun of his vernacular in a light-hearted manner. He responded with the claim that he spoke three languages, English, Spanish, and Texan.

He remembered his father's stories of dealing with inmates at the state prison in Huntsville, a component of the Texas Department of Corrections. The Walls Unit was the oldest prison in Texas, constructed of heavy brick walls, hence the name. Among its inmates in the past were famous outlaws and gunslingers. Some of the older cells had been preserved and were open to public tours. Many of the inmates were "corrected" or rehabilitated during their stay at Huntsville, earning GEDs, basic trade skills, or undergoing some form of religious enlightenment. Many others, however, were beyond redemption and resisted all efforts by the prison system to modify their character or behavior. Upon release, either paroled or having served their time, they went on to reoffend and landed back in prison. This was a source of enormous frustration to Derek's father. At home, he railed at length at the inability of the system to deter and prevent crime. This sank deeply into young Derek's psyche.

HIS CAREER AS a Phoenix police officer was interrupted with a report from his bother in San Antonio that his young daughter had been forcibly raped by an undocumented alien. This sent him into a rage causing his superiors to grant him a five-day leave. He returned to his home state to console his family and demand that prosecutors seek the maximum penalty against the rapist. The accused rapist eventually was tried, found guilty and sentenced to eight years in prison, a period of time Derek and his family deemed insufficient.

Upon his return to Phoenix, he continued to fume about the harm done to his niece and the need to "whack" her assailant. Subordinates under his command sympathized with him but worried about his professional bearing. It was starting to affect the way he approached suspects with harsh interrogations out of proportion to the crime under investigation. His personal rancor toward criminals grew markedly when numerous suspects arrested by his detectives were not sufficiently punished, either with light sentences involving probation or outright dismissal of charges.

Adding to his emotional distress was the passing of both his parents who had preceded him in moving to the Phoenix area and encouraged him in his police career. He had handled arrangements to schedule their memorial services and interment in Huntsville at Oakwood Cemetery, near the gravesite of Texas hero Sam Houston.

Reaching retirement, Overton struggled to keep a lid on his anger and avoid spilling his opinion to anyone who would listen. After a few days of idling around the house, he began to think about extra-legal means of applying retribution to perceived wrongdoers who escape punishment by the criminal justice system.

8

The K-Market Homicides

"Murder most foul...,"

– William Shakespeare, *Hamlet*

The Guerrero-Ochoa operation had been assigned to sharpshooter Lee and was their most complicated operation. The first two involved wife abusers who were severely roughed up and warned to cease harming their spouses. Both targets complied and no further abuses were detected. *Committee* members were under no illusion that the elimination of Guerrero-Ochoa would solve the illicit drug problem, but they decided to undertake the sanction as a test of their methods and a warning to the cartel that they could not simply do their business with impunity. Cartel bosses would understand there would be pushback from an unknown and mysterious force that could come out of nowhere to greatly complicate their operations. Besides, rival cartels would probably be blamed.

Talk in the basement turned to a horrendous robbery/murder that had occurred several days previously and was widely reported in local media. It became known as the "K-Market murders." Two thugs with bandanas covering their faces had entered a convenience store and demanded the clerk to hand over all money from the cash register. While one of them was pilfering beer from the cooler, the other was yelling and terrorizing the young female clerk and a nearby customer with a .45 semi-automatic. When the terrified clerk was slow to hand over cash amid rising tensions and more threats, the gunman pulled the trigger, sending a round into the girl's chest. Then he turned the weapon on the customer and fired two shots into his abdomen. Both were later pronounced dead at the scene. The assailants fled with several twenty dollar bills, a six-pack of beer, and a handful of candy bars for their trouble.

One other customer, hiding behind a merchandise rack, provided vague descriptions of the assailants, but was so shaken, she was unable to offer additional details.

Security cameras were inoperative due to lack of attention by store management. Police had no leads. No suspects were initially identified. Through exhaustive detective work including information obtained from informers and careful review of surveillance tapes from stores in the neighborhood, detectives were able to advance the investigation far enough to identify two persons of interest but not far enough to close the case. Grainy images from remote surveillance tapes showed both men wearing baseball caps, one with the distinctive New York Yankees logo. The suspects, a pair of unemployed white brothers, were career criminals with a record of several brief imprisonments. Detectives were unable to extract confessions and despite intense questioning, they both clammed up in separate interviews and requested lawyers. They were released.

OVERTON STAYED IN touch with former colleagues and three weeks later in a lunch conversation with his friend, Detective Norman Wilkie, he learned the identity of the suspects— Alex and Rodney Perez, two scumbag misfits with lengthy records of arrests, mostly residential burglaries, DUIs, and minor assaults. Wilkie said detectives were convinced they were the ones who had committed the crime, but had not been able to gather enough evidence to make an arrest. Frustration among the investigating officers was palpable.

"Can we do something about this?" demanded Derek at the next meeting of the *Committee*.

9

The Recruit

"Barring that natural expression of villainy
which we all have, the man looked honest enough."

– Mark Twain

A sense of common cause developed in a casual conversation between Derek and John Wayne (J.W.) Barrett, an ex-army ranger, veteran of the Iraq war, now employed by a personal security firm in Scottsdale. He stood six feet, three inches tall, and tipped the scale at a lean 220 pounds of muscle. Short blonde hair, steely blue eyes, and a well-trimmed mustache complemented his appearance. He was proud of his name and its derivation from the iconic actor. Derek and J.W. met one evening when they found themselves seated next to each other at the bar of Toby's Tavern on North Central Avenue, each nursing a draft beer. The place was pretty quiet that night and the conversation began with first name introductions followed by banter about the Arizona Cardinals who were playing a game being televised on the big screen above the bar. After a third round of beers, talk turned to occupations, families, and politics where they found uniformly philosophical agreement.

When J.W. learned of Derek's former life as a police detective, he was immediately interested and sought to point the conversation in the direction of criminal investigation techniques. As a security advisor, he protected the personal safety of his wealthy clients, often acting as bodyguard and confidant. Clients included senior level business executives, wealthy retirees, and slightly known celebrities who as "snow birds" spent winters in Scottsdale golfing and enjoying the sunny weather.

On one occasion, he observed what appeared to be a carjacking from fifty feet away in a shopping mall parking lot. A well-dressed woman placed several bags in the rear seat of a late model Mercedes sedan, then opened the driver's side door. As she was getting in, a long-haired, shabbily dressed thug ran up and climbed in alongside her. Before the woman could get the car started and in gear to back out of the parking space, J.W. arrived at the passenger side, shattered the window with his .45 semi-automatic Smith and Wesson, jerked the door open, and dragged the would-be hijacker out of the car by his hair that hung well below his collar. Caught completely by surprise, the thug dropped a six inch hunting knife and was cold cocked with a smashed nose and split lip resulting in a bloody face.

"What the hell do you think you're doing, shithead?" J.W. demanded. "You think you can kidnap a woman, steal her car in broad daylight, and get away with it?" Thoroughly shaken, the hijacker mumbled something unintelligible before peeing in his pants. When cops arrived on the scene a few minutes later, having been summoned by a couple of nearby shoppers walking to their car, J.W. immediately showed officers his employer's ID and license to carry. He described what happened in detail, adding that the guy had threatened him and the car's owner with a knife, hence the need to deal with the threat with physical force. The thug was transported to the nearest hospital where he was treated while handcuffed to a bed, discharged the following day, and immediately jailed where he faced initial appearance before a judge and ultimately, arraignment.

J.W. related this story to Derek who listened with great interest, admiring the courage and quick action of his new friend in rendering assistance to a helpless victim. "I just reacted on instinct. It was obvious what was happening and I couldn't just stand by and watch."

Derek responded with a couple of stories about his experiences on the force.

He sensed that J.W. was a like-minded professional who might be recruited to join the *Committee,* based on his background and obvious inclination to deal with wrongful behavior when he encountered it. The car-jacking case was interesting in that J.W. acted quickly and without regard for his own safety. The thug might have had a gun he could have used in self-defense. But speed and the element of surprise on J.W.'s part were the effective elements in dealing with the situation. After a brief pause in the conversation, Derek steered the conversation to the topic of justice denied to victims in certain cases with which he was familiar and asked J.W. his opinion of what, if anything, could be done for the victims. J.W. was quick to express his desire to get his hands on criminals who had not been sufficiently held to account and stated they would pay in-kind if he had anything to do with it.

This was music to Derek's ears and after more conversation about weaknesses in the criminal justice system, he asked his bar companion if he might be interested in learning how he might participate in an effort to provide justice to crime victims and punishment to criminals.

"Maybe, but I would need to know more about what you're talking about."

Derek recounted the K-Market homicides and several child molestation cases that had not been resolved satisfactorily. J.W. listened with growing shock as Derek detailed elements of each crime.

"I know that criminal suspects frequently slip through the cracks, but when something that serious happens, what can be done about it?" asked J.W.

"If you were made aware of an opportunity to speed things along with direct action against wrongdoers, would that appeal to you?"

"Damn right it would," said J.W. with conviction.

"I'm in contact with a group that undertakes to do just that. You seem to have the talents and attitude we're looking for but we need to know more about you and I hope you won't mind if we check you out just to confirm who you are. Don't worry, this will be done in absolute confidentiality to protect your privacy," assured Derek after noting the details on John Wayne Barrett's picture ID.

"No problem," said J.W. "Tell me more about your organization, and who is involved?"

"I'm afraid I can't tell you much more at this point," answered Derek. "If we decide to pursue a relationship with you, you will be brought up to speed on all necessary details. If not, you won't hear from us again. I hope you understand."

10

The Interview

"Why so much secrecy? Is it because we have no trust?"

A large delivery van with no side or rear windows arrived at a predetermined pickup point and J.W. was placed in an improvised rear seat anchored to the floor facing backward. "No offense," said Derek who was driving. Another person who did not introduce himself sat in the passenger seat. "I hope you understand the need for secrecy until all parties have arrived at an agreement concerning your possible role." Until he was thoroughly vetted and accepted, the *Committee* felt the need to obscure the meeting's location and other information about their activities.

After many turns, doubling back, and other maneuvers, the van arrived in the alley behind Derek's home. J.W. was ushered through the back door and into the basement where he was introduced to three other *Committee* members including the other van occupant. They were introduced only by first names: Phil, Dave, and Lee. J.W. knew Derek's first name but not his last. It would remain that way until he was trusted with membership on the *Committee*.

The large room was furnished comfortably with a conference table surrounded by six chairs on casters, several soft leather recliners, and small bar on one end with four stools. A large-screen, high-definition TV was mounted on one wall in front of an oversized couch. The room was equipped with an Arbalest Wi-Fi Bluetooth Jammer designed to prevent hacking into a wireless network, cell phones, bugs, or any indoor tracking technique. Absolute privacy from outside electronic spying was ensured. The *Committee* was super attentive to the privacy and security of its existence and operations. "No one can eavesdrop on us outside these walls," Derek had stated to his colleagues with conviction.

"We want to thank you for coming in and for tolerating the security procedures we imposed on you," said Derek.

"No problem," responded J.W. without smiling.

"You can think of this as an employment interview for a very unusual job, and we want to discuss your possible fit for our organization and your attitude toward some of the remedies we undertake against wrongdoers."

"I understand."

Derek began the questioning. "J.W. would you just talk about yourself, tell us something about your military background, your family, and the work you currently do."

"You bet, I'd be glad to," answered J.W. He then described in detail where he grew up, his age (thirty-three), his education (he held bachelors and master's degree in political science), and his military experience that included four years as an army ranger with two tours of duty in Iraq.

When he mentioned the name of his employer in Scottsdale, a look of incredulity crossed Derek's face. That was the same outfit where his wife Marjorie was still employed and nearing retirement. The name of J.W.'s employer had not arisen during their first encounter at Toby's. Derek was unsure how to handle this, so he remained silent.

A number of related questions were posed from other members who seemed satisfied with his responses. He was obviously a person of strong moral values and a strong sense of right and wrong.

"Do you have a wife and kids?" asked Phil.

"My wife and I divorced a year ago and she has custody of our two boys, but I see them often. My wife and I are not remarried and we have a good relationship."

"Any hobbies? What do you do in your spare time?"

"I'm a wanna-be musician. I play bass in a four-piece band on weekends. We have gigs in a couple of bars where the customers seem to enjoy us."

The discussion topic quickly changed.

"Would you agree that the criminal justice system in this country doesn't function properly at times?" asked Lee.

"Damn right, I would."

"And would you also agree that something should be done to apply punishment to those who have escaped legal penalties for committing serious crimes and other forms of bad behavior?"

"Absolutely!"

A series of questions explored his knowledge of weapons including handguns, rifles, ammunition, and explosive devices. His expertise on this topic was detailed and comprehensive. *Committee* members were impressed.

"You intervened physically in the carjacking incident. Would you hesitate to apply similar responses if you were convinced they were was justified?"

"Hell no, in fact I would relish it. Bad guys need to be hit hard when they are caught, either in the act or as soon afterward as possible."

Another hour passed with numerous questions intended to assess J.W.'s skills and his potential loyalty to the operation. At length, the key question was put to him by Phil. "If you were asked to carry out an extreme action by the *Committee* based on clear justification, would you be prepared to execute it?"

J.W. paused before answering. "If you're asking if I could eliminate a piece of crap from the face of the earth who doesn't deserve to breath the same air as the rest of us, hell yes, I would welcome the opportunity. I did plenty of that in Iraq ... and just recently, I sent a guy to the hospital when he approached my client with a knife demanding money and threatening him and his family. He was lucky I didn't send him to the morgue."

After another hour of questions and discussion, drinks and snacks were set out and a sense of camaraderie settled in to the satisfaction of everyone in the room. Derek again thanked J.W. for his participation in the interview and bade him goodbye.

"Be patient, we'll be in touch." The van, driven by Phil this time, returned him to the pickup location via a circuitous route.

"So what do you think?" Derek directed his question to the group. "I should disclose that he works at the same place as my wife and at this point, I don't know if that's a good thing or bad. Marjorie is aware of what we do though she's not an active participant and I don't want her to be."

"Didn't you know this before?" asked Lee.

"It didn't come up, I just learned about it and frankly don't know how to deal with it."

"Why would it be a problem?" Lee mused. "If Marjorie knows what we do, we should let J.W. know that she's your spouse and avoid any conversation with her at work about our endeavors, or any other type of contact for that matter."

Derek was still troubled, but let the matter go for then. "All right, I'll speak with Marjorie tomorrow to let her know that J.W. might be joining us and get her reaction. If there is a problem on that front, I'll bring it back to the *Committee.*"

"I like him, I like him a lot," said Dave. "He is obviously the type of person who would fit our need. But if we accept him, our number will grow to five members. Are we compromising security with another member and are we looking to expand even more in the future?"

"That's a valid concern" remarked Lee, "but we can start him out slowly with low-level operations to see how he performs. As for the future, we'll just play it by ear and go slowly."

Phil, who had returned from driving J.W. to the pickup point and had remained silent for most of the session, suggested that J.W.'s military experience was a definite plus and he could be relied upon to carry out assignments as directed.

"If we have initial consensus that he's acceptable," Derek said, "the next step to set up surveillance, observe his coming and going for at least ten days, monitor his contacts, and tap his phone with the technology we have, then reconvene here to make a decision." With that, the meeting broke up.

Nothing questionable or suspicious was discovered about J.W. Two weeks later, John Wayne Barrett was invited to attend a meeting of the *Committee*. The same van driven by Phil picked him up and used another twisted route to Derek's back alley.

When everyone was seated Derek said "We want you to join our group. Do you understand this is an extra-legal organization, we operate outside the law, and if any of us is ever arrested, let alone indicted, it's all over?"

"I totally understand and I'll do my best to meet your expectations."

Phil continued the protocol. "We go to extraordinary lengths to avoid detection in all our operations and we expect you to be super careful at all times. Always be aware of your surroundings and abort the operation if there's a hint that something isn't right. The last thing we need is a pain-in-the-ass innocent bystander who could tell the cops what happened. Same goes for surveillance cameras. They're everywhere nowadays, so we have to do one of three things to defeat them ... execute the operation out of camera sight, wear camo clothing that can't be identified, or employ surveillance camera jammers. Maybe all three at a time."

"Any questions?" asked Derek.

"What are the criteria for accepting a case?"

"Good question," Derek answered and then explained how cases came to their attention and how decisions were made to proceed with remedial action, or not. "We carefully review the facts of each case to understand exactly what crime was committed and how it was prosecuted, if it was at all. We discuss possible responses, and if they can be executed with minimum risk to ourselves. If a consensus is reached, we decide by majority vote to proceed with a specific action."

"These actions sound like they cost money, so where do you get financing to support what you do?"

"Another great question. We're self-financed at this point, but we need to find a source of outside funding to support weapons purchases, payments to infomers, and other expenses. We want to identify private individuals who want to see justice done when the authorities fail to provide it. Beyond that, I really can't tell you much more."

Derek continued. "We won't ask you to swear on a bible, but we need your word that you will never reveal anything about this group, its operations, and its personnel to anyone including friends, coworkers, or family."

"You have my word!"

Hand shaking all around and back slapping ensued followed by a round of drinks, then another.

"No more secrecy about this location," said Derek. "We'll give you a ride back and directions to this location. You'll be notified of our next meeting and how you will be assigned to an operation. We don't have anything definite at the moment, but a couple of situations are under consideration. We'll let you know."

J.W. was not initially told the full names of other committee members. He knew them only by first names. This was another element of security precautions the *Committee* took.

11
The Vetting

"More than employment, credit, and criminal records."

"**H**oney, do you know a guy by the name of John Wayne Barrett where you work?" Derek asked Marjorie that evening at dinner. "He's one of us now."

"Sure, he is one of our best agents. We call him J.W. He provides personal protection and driver services to our clients. They love him. What do you mean, 'one of us?' "

"We made him a member of the *Committee* and he's ready to take on an assignment."

"How on earth did that happen? Where did you meet him?

"I met him at Toby's over beers one evening. We just got to talking. He's an ex-army ranger and we exchanged war stories. After he told me some of his experiences as a bodyguard, I asked if he would be interested in looking at a situation where he might be able to apply his talents to dealing with bad guys. He responded favorably and we did a thorough review procedure which he passed with flying colors. We described our mission, and following a couple of interviews, we invited him to join us. He quickly agreed to come on board and I think he'll be a great addition to our group. He brings some unique skills we can use in the right set of requirements," Derek explained. "I don't know if it's a good idea that he knows you're my spouse. At least, not right now. So I'd like you to keep an eye on him, maybe engage him in casual conversation... try to learn what you can about him. We think he's trustworthy but that could change if something questionable arises. Just be very informal ... don't drill him with a lot of questions. We didn't tell him about the operations we've completed so he's still in the dark about the specifics. Our plan is to use him on one or two low level contacts to see how he performs before including him on anything major."

"This is a little scary," said Marjorie. "He's highly regarded around the office but I don't know him that well." After a pause in the conversation, she blurted—"Wait a minute, hold on! I just had a thought. I've noticed our HR person, Blanche, doesn't always secure her files when she leaves work for the day. It's very careless of her. I'm usually the last one out each day unless the bosses are dealing with a client on some issue. I think I can find his personnel jacket and have a look at its contents."

"Sounds like a plan," said Derek. "Just be careful you're alone and unseen doing this. Are there surveillance cameras in your office?"

"Oh yeah, there are, but I'm trained in their operation and I know how to disable them. It shouldn't be a problem."

"All right then, go for it and again, be damned careful."

Three afternoons later, Marjorie found herself alone in the office after everyone else had left for the day. She got up to use the restroom and then entered the small room nearby where the surveillance equipment was located. The cameras covered only the front portion of the office so there was no chance she could be seen moving from the restroom into the equipment room. She quickly disabled both cameras and walked back to the HR office to open the filing cabinet. The jackets were arranged in alpha order. She found the one titled "Barrett, John W." and removed it from its slot in the drawer.

Returning to her desk, she opened the folder and began to leaf through the pages. There was his résumé and employment application, several letters of commendation from previous employers, and the usual HR records showing dates of hiring and advancement, salary data, schedule of benefits, and days off. Performance evaluations were uniformly positive. *Nothing unusual here,* she thought.

Then the last sheet of the file grabbed her attention. It was a memorandum on a Maricopa County Attorney letterhead marked CONFIDENTIAL. With growing apprehension as she read through the document, she felt herself becoming light headed and almost toppled off her chair. Quickly regaining composure, she rushed to the copy machine, made a copy, and inserted the original back into the file. The file was returned to its place after which she restored the cameras to operational status. Time stamp data on the camera system hard drive showed a seven minute gap between 6:53 and 7:00 p.m. Digital data was automatically erased every 30 days. A month later, there was no record of the time gap.

Marjorie placed the folded copy in her purse and headed home after locking the office.

WAITING FOR MARJORIE to arrive home from work that evening, Derek had grilled filet mignon steaks, complemented with baked potatoes and coleslaw. Son Ronnie was away for the evening visiting friends. When they were seated for dinner, Marjorie said: "I removed J.W.'s personnel jacket from the file today after everyone was gone and you're not going to believe what I found. I combed through the whole thing and found nothing unusual until the very last page. Here is a copy."

"I'm all ears, Marj," said Derek between large bites of food. "This sounds ominous. Summarize it for me."

"It was a memo from the county attorney addressed to the president of our firm, and marked 'confidential' in very large red letters. It related his military and professional background at some length. Then it praised his service to the department as an unidentified informant in two cases involving former clients of our firm. They were both convicted of embezzling large sums from their firms and I assume it was on the basis of information J. W. furnished to the police."

Derek had stopped eating. "Does it say so, or is that your assumption?"

"The memo informs the reader that the information from J.W. was vital in the criminal investigation. Here, read it yourself."

Derek's appetite was gone. He got up from his chair with the copy and walked into the kitchen. He returned to the dining table a few minutes later to find Marjorie picking at her food. "I'm not sure what to make of this," he said. "It sounds like he provided a useful service to law enforcement while betraying his clients at the same time. It doesn't say if he testified at trial."

"What are you going to do?" she asked.

"Not sure just now."

Derek did not sleep well that night. He informed Lee of Marjorie's discovery the following morning.

"If we have a potential mole in our midst, we're screwed," said Derek. "We can't very well dismiss him from the team without arousing suspicion. He didn't mention this in our interview with him but he was obviously an important source of information in those embezzlement cases."

"Is there any way we can lay our hands on the case file? Dave can probably pull it from the county attorney's archives," said Lee.

"Great idea, I'll speak with Dave about it."

Three days later, Dave reported to Derek and Lee in the basement. Phil was not there, off on another hunting trip.

"He didn't testify at trial, but was interviewed on two occasions by our investigators. They noted he insisted on deep background status. He furnished information about conversations he overheard between the suspects and colleagues. He began to suspect criminal activity early in his contact with them and made it clear that he despised them for their abusive behavior toward him. They frequently found fault with his methods of personal security and snarled their unjustified complaints to him and his supervisor. After several months of this, the company terminated its engagement with them, but not before J.W. had gathered and documented information for later use in case it was needed. This included dates, times, and destinations of his trips with them, who they talked with, and notes of conversations overheard in the limousine. He had secretly taped four conversations that revealed incriminating information. So his motivation was not to rat out his clients from personal rancor, but to demonstrate his contempt for them and his desire to see them brought to justice. In my opinion, we have nothing to fear from him."

Derek and Lee were visibly relieved. Both relaxed in their chairs with smiles on their faces.

12

Spousal Abuse

"He sleeps with the fishes."

– Peter Clemenza, *The Godfather*

Alton Ferguson had a habit of beating up his wife. The childless couple had been married three years. All was peaceful and loving during the first years, then Alton lost his job and started drinking and taking out his frustration on Edie, his wife. Face-slapping escalated into face-punching, producing severe bruises and a bloodied nose several times. She called the police after one incident and sought medical treatment. Alton was arrested and spent the night in jail, but was released when she refused to press charges—an option available to victims at that time. Currently, victims do not have the option of declining to press charges. Criminal complaints are filed by the county attorney after reviewing the evidence against the defendant.

Like many victims of domestic abuse, Edie stuck by her man and hoped things would get better. They didn't. The abuse continued. Alton frequently cursed his wife when drunk, and physically attacked her with varying degrees of injury. Alton always apologized when he sobered up, begged

Edie's forgiveness, and promised it wouldn't happen again. She forgave him, but not really. She vowed to herself that one day she would leave him and be free.

Liz, Edie's next door neighbor friend, was aware of the couple's dysfunctional relationship and tried to convince Edie to seek help to no avail. One morning she couldn't help noticing her neighbor's messed up face and decided to do something about it. She was fond of Edie and could not tolerate the thought of her ongoing mistreatment at the hands of her shithead husband.

Liz's husband, Dan, had a thought. "Let me talk with Norm and ask his advice." Norman Wilkie was a college fraternity brother who was now a police detective. They had stayed in touch through the years.

After listening with interest to Dan's story of Edie's problem, Norman said, "I might know of a remedy to this situation that may be effective. It looks like steps are needed beyond just filing complaints with the cops." Norman related details of Alton Ferguson's behavior to his friend Derek. "This is something you might be interested in, buddy."

Several months previously, Derek had confided to Norm a general outline of the *Committee's* mission. Norm listened with interest and told Derek he would be as helpful as possible, but couldn't provide any confidential information related to an ongoing investigation.

Derek discussed the matter at length at the next *Committee* meeting to determine its worthiness for action. Research was conducted to confirm Alton's arrest record and discreet interviews of the neighbor led to a decision to accept the project. Detailed plans were made to apply a penalty to Alton Ferguson and deliver justice to Edie.

FOUR DAYS LATER, after emerging from a bar, Ferguson was seized in the parking lot about midnight and hustled into a waiting van. Being partially inebriated, he didn't put up much of a fight. Handcuffed behind his back and blindfolded, he was taken to an abandoned warehouse and made to sit on a stool under a bright light—all prearranged for the event. The blindfold was removed and he faced his abductors, three in number, all dressed in black with masks covering their faces. "What's going on?" he pleaded repeatedly and, "Who the hell are you?" Some minutes passed before any of the black-clad men spoke. It was a technique intended to increase the level of apprehension in Ferguson's mind. At length, one of them said, "We're here to discuss your treatment of Edie."

Alton Ferguson started groaning as he began to understand what was coming. "I never meant to hurt her and she always said it was her fault, and begged the prosecutor not to press charges," he burbled.

"It takes a genuine coward to beat a woman. Do you understand this? You hurt her and now it has to stop. You have to pay the price for hurting your wife and learn that if it happens again, you will disappear —permanently." One of the vigilantes yelled this loudly in Alton's face.

Alton listened to these words with wide eyes and a growing sense of terror. One of the blows caught him on his right ear and laid it open with blood pouring down this shirt. Screaming with pain, he attempted to stand but was shoved roughly back down. Several more minutes passed with no sound heard but the whimpering of the injured man.

"So now you know what it feels like, don't you?"

"Now listen carefully asshole. If you so much as touch Edie again to hurt her, we will know, we will find you, and you will be whacked. Do you understand?" Alton mumbled and nodded his head. "Don't think for a moment that Edie ratted you out. She knows nothing of this. We learned about you from another source so you know your behavior will come back to us."

Then, wearing leather workout gloves, they took turns pummeling his face, fracturing a cheek bone and causing multiple lacerations and contusions. A couple of sharp blows to his ribs broke two of them, causing additional trauma. Alton was in severe pain as evidenced by his yells and tears. Semi-conscious, he was placed back in the van and driven back to the bar, now closed. "Are we clear on the deal?" demanded one of his tormentors. Alton weakly nodded. He was dumped onto the rough asphalt surface of the parking lot. With a throwaway cell phone, a call was made to 9-1-1. Within minutes, emergency vehicles arrived and Alton was immediately started on an IV, given first aid, and transported to the nearest emergency room. The hospital called Edie and told her of his condition, but she decided not to appear for a while. When she told her neighbor what had happened, Liz just smiled benignly and offered to do what she could. Alton informed investigating officers that his assailants were white guys, one was overweight and had spoken with a southern drawl.

Alton slowly recovered from his injuries, his ear was stitched back together and his bones mended. He eventually found a part-time job and sought help from AA. The couple had several sessions with a marriage counselor. Her injuries healed but the emotional scars remained.

The marriage was peaceful for eight months, then Alton was fired from his job and started drinking again. A minor quarrel resulted in several body punches to Edie, sending her to the emergency room in critical condition with a ruptured spleen and bruised liver. Alton was sentenced to five years in county lockup for felony domestic violence. With early parole, he again took up residence with Edie who thought he was reformed and no longer posed a threat. But she was wrong. His bullying and abusive behavior continued and once again, he hit her hard enough to send her to the ER.

ALTON FERGUSON DISAPPEARED. Edie filed a missing-persons report but no evidence of foul play was discovered. Several days later, two miles off the coast of Corpus Christi, Texas, in dim early morning light, a sport fishermen thought he saw a container being lowered with a small splash from a boat about a hundred yards away. He promptly forgot about it. Alton Ferguson was never heard from again. His missing-persons case would go entirely cold after two years.

13
Half-Ass Actions

"The best laid schemes of mice and men."

– Robert Burns

Derek had not been feeling well for at least three months. He found himself fatigued and always thirsty. Drinking large quantities of water and iced tea did not relieve his thirst and caused him to frequently urinate. He felt numbness and tingling in his fingers and hands. Most alarming was blurry vision. Night driving became impossible.

"I can't be more than twenty feet away from a restroom," he complained to Marjorie. "What the hell is wrong with me?"

"Your doctor warned you about the possibility of diabetes after you retired from the PD, didn't he? You better see him and get checked out."

Following an examination involving multiple lab tests, Derek returned to the doctor a week later and brought Marjorie with him. The doctor told him he had high blood pressure and type 2 diabetes. Disease management involved regular blood tests to determine glucose levels and self-administered medications.

"You should carefully maintain a proper diet," warned the doctor. "I want you to lose weight and get some exercise. All this means a big change in your lifestyle." This left Derek in a mental daze.

THE REGULAR BASEMENT meeting had gone on for two hours of discussion with no clear consensus among *Committee* members. Several potential actions were discussed but were dismissed either for want of urgency or lack of strong evidence pointing to a suspect's guilt. The *Committee* strongly desired to avoid rashly initiating an operation if the evidence did not support it.

"Half-ass actions on some of these creeps don't work." Overton was speaking to his four companions. "When I was on patrol during my early days with the PD, we frequently got domestic violence calls. Dozens every year. We always carefully approached locations because we never knew what we would be up against. Most calls were fairly routine but I recall one in particular. He was a big guy, maybe two fifty, two sixty pounds, six foot three. His wife was a tiny little thing, a hundred pounds dripping wet. We were called to their home two or three times a month on a disturbance complaint. Usually it was just a shouting match, loud enough to disturb the neighbors who called 9-1-1. Then one night, he hit her hard enough to leave a nasty bruise on her face. A misdemeanor charge was filed and the guy was ordered by the court to enter a batterer's counseling program.

"First time offenders rarely go to jail. Anyway, one Saturday night a few weeks later, he messed her up really bad and sent her to the emergency room. My partner and I put him in the patrol car and instead of driving straight to the lockup, we detoured into a darkened alley, hauled him out of the car and put him in a kneeling position. I put my gun to his head and told him if he ever touched her again, I would pull the trigger next time. Asked if he understood, he weakly nodded.

"A month later, bailed out of jail, he killed her. So I say, half-ass actions don't work with these bastards. If we had done what we should have done the first time with Alton, Edie Ferguson would not have been hurt again. She would be okay today."

"By the way, how was your trip to Texas?" Derek asked J.W., who was now a full-fledged member of the *Committee*. J.W. nodded with a smile.

"Let's reconsider the K-Market case," said Derek. That crime was put aside earlier in light of Phil's discomfort with the status of the police investigation.

"These fuckers are walking the streets today," Dave reminded the group, "and the police are no closer to moving against them. Our office has reservations about making a reasonable-doubt case and won't move forward until the police are able to turn up additional supporting evidence."

"Where are they now and how can we even find them if we decided to take them on?" queried Lee.

"That's easy enough," said Dave. "They're living with their grandmother on North 36th Street and frequently go out drinking at a local bar. I learned this from the case file downtown."

"So how do we get at them and will this be a complete elimination of both guys?" asked Phil. It was a valid question since only one of the suspects had actually done the killing.

"I say we take them both out," said Derek. "It would be a service to society to remove these two scumbags from the world and would almost surely prevent future crimes."

After another thirty minutes discussing pros and cons, the *Committee* voted unanimously to pursue the operation subject to preparation of a detailed plan to ensure final success, safety of field operatives, and avoidance of law enforcement attention to themselves.

Face-to-face confrontation on the street with guns was out of the question, so a stealth approach was obviously needed. Lee agreed to lead the operation with J.W's assistance. Derek conducted surveillance of the targets' comings and goings from a dark-window van for two weeks. J.W. joined him when he was not on bodyguard duty with his employer. Unmarried, he was not burdened with the need for making excuses for his absence from home. They learned the two thugs were unemployed and rarely went out during the day. After 10:00 p.m., they regularly visited Etta's Place, a bar on Indian School Road. It was a sleazy place visited by neighborhood regulars and various citizens of shabby appearance and even shabbier behavior, though fights among patrons were rare.

WHEN HE KNEW the brothers would be there, Lee entered the establishment with his usual disguise, took a seat at the bar and ordered a draft beer. He immediately identified the two brothers from head shots Dave had obtained from the case file. The two were at the pool table with a couple of other bad-looking characters.

Nursing the beer and observing the brothers for an hour, Lee saw them heading for the door. He managed to exit the place after them and lingered while they got into their car and drove away. Following them home was easy. He carefully traced their route and noticed they parked in grandma's driveway about thirty feet off the street. A dense hedge partially obscured the walkway from the driveway to the front porch, providing an ambush opportunity.

The parking lot at Etta's Place presented a possible, though riskier, location for the operation. It was dimly lighted and at a late hour was occupied by only three or four cars, owned by late drinkers in the bar. Employees parked behind the building. No outside surveillance cameras were observed either at the bar or at businesses across the street.

THE NEXT DAY as Lee reported his findings to the *Committee,* a serious question arose. "Do we take these guys out under the nose of their elderly grandmother? Wouldn't that be a horrible thing for her to deal with?" asked Phil. After a brief discussion, it was agreed that the hit would not be applied at the house but at the bar. The operation was authorized for two nights later, provided the brothers visited the bar that evening.

Sure enough, the two emerged from the house at 10:45 p.m., got into their car, and drove away. Lee and J.W. observed this from a side street vantage point and followed them to the bar from a safe distance. If the brothers followed their usual habit, they wouldn't leave the bar until last call a little after 2:00 a.m. Parked at the closed and dark business next door, Lee and J.W. were prepared to do murder in the interest of justice if the circumstances were right. But the brothers walked out along with two other people. "Shit," breathed Lee. The risk that witnesses were present could not be tolerated, so the operation was scrubbed that night.

Two more dates over the next ten days ended the same way, leading to a decision to abandon the operation with the hope that police could gather enough evidence to nail the pair.

"I think we bit off more than we could chew with the K-Market case," groused Derek in the next basement meeting. "And it's a good thing it didn't go down. The level of punishment didn't strictly fit the crime since only one of the thugs pulled the trigger. After all, we're not murderers, just providers of justice who want to cleanse society of the filth that contaminates it." This rationalization was generally shared by the group.

Six weeks later still no arrests had been made. Two other convenience stores were robbed at gunpoint by two masked criminals, one of whom wore a baseball cap with the Yankees logo. Both store clerks had noted this fact and reported it to investigating detectives who disclosed it to media reporters.

"These convenience store robberies are still happening," said Derek. "And a clerk is going to be killed again if we don't do something."

The basement meeting was tense with anger and frustration at Derek's report of ongoing robberies. "How do we know it's the same guys?" asked Phil.

"The guy with the Yankees cap was identified at all three stores. It's got to be them," said Derek. "I say we go after them again, but our approach must be entirely different."

14

Problem Solved

*"The fault, dear Brutus, is not in our stars,
but in ourselves…"*

– Cassius, William Shakespeare, *Julius Caesar*

Domestic violence was the crime that most enraged *Committee* members—men harming women and children, especially children. Yes, women sometimes, though rarely, assaulted their male partners. However, the opposite case occurred most frequently. The *Committee* regarded physical attacks by a man upon a woman as anathema to civilized society. Males are generally larger and stronger than females and have a greater advantage in any physical confrontation; therefore, *Committee* members held the strong opinion that men have a duty to protect and defend women in their care and must not strike or otherwise harm a female except in circumstances of personal defense.

The thought of O.J. pummeling Nicole on multiple occasions, causing bruises and a black eye, infuriated them. "If the *Committee* had been active and had resources in Los Angeles at the time, that matter would have been taken care of before Nicole and Ron were murdered," Derek ranted.

"We should be very active in that area," said Lee. "Physical assaults, stalking, and verbal mistreatment are violations of a woman's body and mental wellbeing. We need to take action to teach a lesson to these creeps who can't control their impulses."

"Lee is absolutely right," agreed Dave. "Too many scumbags regard their women as possessions to be dominated and controlled. They do this with verbal intimidation and sometimes with their fists. It's especially bad when they're drunk or on drugs. According to the National Coalition Against Domestic Violence, one in seven women is a victim of domestic violence. Let's be bold and aggressive."

ON A RAINY evening, attention turned to an incident Phil had noticed a week earlier in an item appearing in the *Valley Viewer,* a weekly free publication. According to the story, cops had been summoned to a house in west Phoenix on a call reporting a violent fight between the occupants, a married couple with two small children. This was the third time either neighbors or the wife had called police. This time Joe Madsen had given his wife Rhonda a black eye and bloodied her nose, then proceeded to attack the older child, a boy of eight, causing several bruises. The child's screams alerted neighbors who called 9-1-1. Police arrived and Joe, the "offender," was arrested and taken to jail, charged with domestic violence, arraigned, and in due course released on bail. His employer was appalled but decided not to terminate him since this was a first-time occurrence and Joe was an excellent employee. Child Protective Services was notified and the children were promptly removed from the home, much to the shock and dismay of both parents. In a way, Rhonda was relieved that at least the kids were no longer in danger, but as a mother, her maternal instincts were to have her children with her, not with strangers.

The *Committee* considered these facts and decided to take retributive action.

"This kind of crap can't go on," Derek told his colleagues yelling with anger. "This shithead just beats up his wife when he has a couple of drinks and now he's injured his kid. He must be stopped. Do you all agree?"

"Yes, but is termination called for this time?' asked Phil. "After all, Rhonda was hurt during all three incidents, but not that badly. I think a serious conversation with Joe is in order, but not the ultimate sanction."

"Not seriously hurt?" shouted Derek. "Her nose was broken and her face was so badly messed up, she won't recover her appearance for months even if he doesn't hit her again. This will happen again and again unless we put a permanent stop to it!"

"But Joe is the sole breadwinner of the family with a pretty decent job. If he's eliminated, she will have no financial support. That's a factor we should consider," Phil offered with serious conviction.

"Let's have a man-to-man talk with him," suggested Dave. "It could be that a very stern warning with clear threats to his physical health will suffice."

"I really doubt it," said Derek. "Remember what I said about half-ass measures? They don't work. These assholes revert to form after time has passed and they think they can get away with it again, assuming they think, which they don't. So my position is to solve the problem with his elimination and then arrange to provide support for Rhonda from our resources."

"I don't agree" said Phil. "I favor Dave's suggestion. Let's confront him when he doesn't expect it and let him know in no uncertain terms that if he hurts her or the boy again, there will be hell to pay in the form of a painful whacking." Lee expressed his agreement with a "talk." Derek wasn't happy but finally went along with the majority.

A plan was developed and carefully reviewed by the principals. After a lengthy discussion, the *Commitee* decided to surprise Joe when he arrived at his car to return home after work.

AT FIVE THIRTY on a Thursday afternoon, Joe climbed into his Dodge Caravan after a tiring day of processing accounts payable for a local manufacturing company. His job wasn't physically demanding, but it drained his mental energy each day. Among his duties was the task of contacting past due accounts and making arrangements for payment. These conversations consistently put him in a sour mood that spilled over into his relationship with his family.

Slamming the door and settling in the driver's seat, he was immediately aware of the presence of a man who was hunkered down behind the front passenger seat. Also obvious was a large revolver pointed directly at his head. "Just be cool Joe and don't make any foolish moves like trying to get out of the car. We want to have a brief talk with you, so start the car and drive out of the parking lot as you normally do. No harm will come to you and we won't keep you very long if you cooperate," J.W. said.

"Who's we?" inquired a terrified Joe, "and what the hell do you want?"

"Never mind that, just drive where I tell you. This will all be clear to you soon enough," said J.W., who was clad in khakis and a plain baseball cap, large sunglasses, and a fake bushy mustache. With the use of an electronic jammer, he had disabled the surveillance camera trained on the parking lot and expertly entered the van with burglars' tools fifteen minutes previously. Joe was directed along back streets about two miles from his workplace and told to pull into an unused parking lot in back of an abandoned strip mall. He was instructed to remove the ignition keys and pass them back. Aware of the gun pointed at his head, he did so without question. Derek was waiting nearby out of sight and immediately opened the van's passenger side front door and sat down next to Joe. Similarly disguised, he began the conversation.

"Joe, you've been a very bad boy. Police have been summoned to your home three different times on complaints of domestic disturbance. What the hell's going on with you and why do you hurt your wife and kid?"

"That's none of your fucking business, and I don't answer to you," was Joe's hostile reply. Derek's sharp punch to the ribs quickly changed his attitude.

"Afraid that's not the case pal, we're here to teach you some manners and reform your behavior to ensure that you have a happy home and Rhonda isn't harmed again."

"How the hell do you expect to do that?" Joe asked defiantly.

"It's not us who will do it pal, it'll be you," answered Derek in a raised voice. "First, you'll let Rhonda know that your home environment will be stable, quiet, and free of violence from now on. You need to understand that real men do not hurt women, real men care for and protect their wives and girlfriends. Hurting a woman is the act of a coward no matter how provoked. But when you hurt your son, that's way over the line and what really got our attention. What kind of asshole does that?"

"I lost my temper and I don't know what came over me. Now the kids have been taken away by CPS and Rhonda and I don't know what do to. We're both devastated by this. We'll do whatever it takes to get them back." Joe's attitude had morphed from angry defiance to fright and now to remorse. He started to cry.

"We're here to help you clearly understand that hurting your wife and kid is unacceptable and any repeat of it will result in YOUR getting hurt... BAD... by us. You won't see it coming and you will go to the hospital for a long time. Now do you get it and do we have your absolute commitment to avoid hurting your family again?"

"Yes, yes, absolutely" was the weak reply.

"We will refer you to family counseling resources who can help you through this," said Derek. "They can help you with your home situation and get your kids back. They can also deal with your work challenges. You'll be contacted in the next few days, so be prepared to cooperate with their program. Failure to do so will not go well for you. Do not report this meeting to the police. Are we clear?"

"Yeah, I guess so," responded Joe.

"No guessing, dude. You need to be sure. Are you sure?

"Yeah, yeah, I'm sure."

You're free to go, here are the keys, drive carefully on your way home. And understand this—Rhonda did not report you. Your situation came to us from another source so any retaliation against her and we will know about it." The meeting ended. J.W. and Derek got out of the van and watched it drive off. When it was out of sight, they walked to a car parked nearby and drove away.

The *Committee* achieved its objective without further involvement, a result they were enormously proud of. The children were returned after six weeks of careful assessment by CPS and no other problems were reported from the Madsen household.

15

Domestic Violence

"Cruelty has a human heart, and jealousy a human face."

– William Blake, *A Divine Image*

A different set of circumstances came to the *Committ*ee's attention from Dave.

Anna Graves was being stalked and harassed by her ex-boyfriend, Max Gonzales. She was an attractive blond with brown eyes, slender body, and a bouncy pony tail. At twenty-five years of age and previously married with a small child, she was ready for another man in her life. Her relationship with Max began three months previously when they met at a bar. They started seeing each other a couple of times a week and after several dates she became aware that he was becoming very controlling and jealous of her time and contacts she had with anyone including family members and female friends. After one incident, when he discovered that she had met a girlfriend for lunch, a violent argument ensued when he accused her of seeing another man. He slapped her hard in the face, breaking her glasses and threatening to "break your neck if you go behind my back again."

This was a severe shock to Anna. She knew he had a jealous streak, but always assumed that it would subside as their relationship matured. She was genuinely fond of him until the slapping episode, but her opinion of him immediately changed to one of fear and distrust. Friends told her not to put up with that sort of treatment and urged her to dump him out of concern for her physical safety.

She informed Max they were all done in a voice message to his cell phone. That only enraged him. He pounded on her front door, demanding entry and shouting threats. Police showed up a few minutes later to find him belligerent and uncooperative. They cuffed him and sat him in the patrol car while they interviewed Anna. After a stern lecture he was turned loose with a warning not to disturb Annie again. That, of course, was not effective. Over the next month, he repeatedly cruised by her house slowly, sometimes stopping to glare at the front door.

She did not answer his calls so he took to leaving messages on her phone saying he was going to fuck up her life real good and threatening, "I'll catch you out sometime and bash your head in. A terrified Anna obtained a restraining order requiring him to stay a hundred yards away from her home and person. This worked for about a week but he was back at it again calling her from a throwaway phone threatening to kill her and her child at the first opportunity.

Overton learned of this from his friend Norm Wilkie and confirmed by his regular review of the police blotter and court records showing issuance of protective orders.

"This guy is clearly out of control and needs to be taken out," a greatly worried Derek told the *Committee* at a meeting in his basement. "And this needs to happen soon to protect Anna. No telling what he is capable of."

"No question we should take action immediately," agreed Phil. So a plan was developed and assigned to J.W. and Derek for execution.

AT 3:00 A.M. the following night, the apartment complex was quiet, no interior lights were on in any of the units and no one was seen in the parking lot. Max was awakened by loud knocking on his apartment door. Cautiously he opened the door as far as the security chain allowed and said "Yeah, who is it?"

His face covered with a bandana, J.W. burst through the door, easily snapping the security chain and shoving a groggy Max roughly back onto his bed. "We're here because of your shitty treatment of Anna. Do you think you can harass her and leave threatening messages on her phone and get away with it?" he demanded. Now fully awake, Max understood what was coming when J.W. delivered a sharp blow with an aluminum softball bat to his face, loosening several teeth and splitting his lips. The *Committee* deemed it necessary in all cases to ensure their targets understood why they had to pay a price for their misbehavior.

"Now listen carefully, asshole. No more contact with Anna. No phone calls, no harassment, no more visits to her door, no nuthin.' Understood?" Silence from Max. "Talk to me you sorry bastard. Get it?"

"Yeah, yeah, I get it," Max finally answered feebly, spitting blood.

"If it happens again, we won't be so nice to you next time. Understood?"

With that, J.W. produced a .22 caliber Walther hand gun with a noise suppressor and sent a slug into the left knee of Max leaving him screaming. Quickly exiting the apartment and climbing into a waiting SUV driven by Phil, he followed protocol by cleansing his face, hands, and hair with sanitizer. Using a burner phone he dialed Lee's cell number and reported, "The package was delivered." Using another burner, Derek dialed 9-1-1 to report gunshots at an address in northwest Phoenix. The pistol with silencer was wiped down and disassembled into several parts. Along with the softball bat, they were placed in black trash bags along with rubbish borrowed from a super market dumpster and deposited into multiple dumpsters several miles away. Driving at the speed limit, Phil returned to Overton's back alley.

Max was hospitalized for two weeks during which police detectives investigated the incident. No evidence was found leading to the assailants. Detectives were aware of Max's history and were not overly aggressive in resolving his case. In his statement to police, he reported that one of his attackers was a fat guy with a southern drawl.

Anna was not bothered again.

PERIOD TWO

16

The Enablers

"...money answereth all things."

– Ecclesiastes 10:19

The *Committee's* expenses were initially funded by equal contributions in cash of $1,000 each from the four founders and later in the same amount from J.W. when he had been with the group for a month. No bank account was opened, all monies were entrusted to Derek for safekeeping. He purchased weapons and other needed items, all cash transactions. He kept no financial records of any kind. They came to the realization they'd need larger amounts of cash from a reliable source at some point if they were to operate on a larger scale. That source proved to be a pair of wealthy real estate developers in nearby Scottsdale.

Russ Milam and Ben Moskowitz had become business partners ten years previously when each of them owned adjoining land parcels in a sparsely developed sector of Scottsdale. The twenty-acre property owned by Milam was zoned for residential use allowing low density single family homes. The other, thirty-one acres in size, owned by Moskowitz, was zoned for mixed-use commercial and medium density housing development. City government planners had made it clear that any development occurring on these parcels was to maintain the high quality of development in Scottsdale, an upscale community known for its opulence. Some would call it extravagance in its appeal to high net worth individuals. The businessmen met for lunch on several occasions at swanky restaurants and found common cause when both decided to proceed with development activities on their respective properties. They recognized the value of joint marketing and certain efficiencies of scale if production of both projects could proceed under single management. M&M Properties was thereby established as a corporation for that purpose with both partners owning fifty percent of the business.

The venture initially encountered substantial delays amid city review of site planning and architectural details. After a year of intense interactions involving design consultants, attorneys, and city representatives, leading to numerous design modifications, permits were issued and the project finally got off the ground. Since existing zoning was already in place, no public hearings were necessary and city council approval was almost pro forma. Considerable media coverage of the ceremonial ground breaking featuring the mayor, followed to the delight of the partners. The project named "Sun Gardens Scottsdale" took off and together with several other business endeavors throughout the "Valley of the Sun" added substantially to the net worth of both partners.

IT WAS DURING the development of Sun Gardens that Carlie, teenage daughter of Russ Milam, was invited to a party at the home of a family friend along with several of her girlfriends. The teenagers' indoor party went forward in the absence of the male host's parents and lasted late into the evening. Party goers listened to loud recorded music and consumed beers and shots of tequila pilfered from the home's unlocked liquor cabinet. Carlie at first refused to participate in the drinking, but not wanting to be isolated as a party pooper, eventually downed a couple of tequila shots and a beer. Recognizing her diminished situational awareness, two of the boys forced her into a bedroom, locked the door, and proceeded to kiss her and squeeze her breasts. "Come on, let's have some fun," one said, pawing at her clothes.

She had enough resistance to hold them off. Her virginity was preserved, but the boys, drunk and infuriated when their quest for sex was unfulfilled, proceeded to beat her with their fists. She suffered a broken jaw that had to be wired together, multiple bruises, and a split lip, leaving her face disfigured. The boys were arrested and brought to trial. The evidence was clear, they pleaded guilty. The judge, known as soft on crime, sentenced them to four years in prison, then promptly suspended the sentences with the observation that this was their first offense, and they were good students who came from good families. They walked free immediately, smirking at the Milam family as they walked from the courtroom. A devastated Russ Milam told his wife that he planned to contact someone who might be able to "put this thing right."

Russ was a client of the security firm where Marjorie Overton worked and in a casual conversation involving her and his assigned body guard, she stated that she was very happy when a couple of wife batterers had gotten what was coming to them when the criminal justice system apparently failed to do its job. There was something in her words that implied she knew something about what happened. Russ remembered this conversation after his daughter's misfortune and asked Marjorie to have lunch with him at his private club. Marjorie was suspicious of his motive, but agreed to the meeting.

She listened with interest to his telling of his daughter's traumatic incident and the unsatisfactory outcome. Most galling to her was the fact that the girl's face was badly damaged and possibly altered for life. She had already undergone several facial reconstruction surgeries. To his request, "Can anything be done, can you help me?" she asked for the names of the two assailants and told Russ she might be able to make a referral for assistance.

TEN DAYS LATER, the two boys were anonymously invited by text message to a nighttime meeting in the alley behind the first boy's home with the promise of "young girls ready to put out." Foolishly, they showed up, were invited into a large cargo van, and severely hammered with blackjacks[3] causing blackened eyes, broken ribs, shattered nose cartilage, lost teeth, and facial lacerations requiring multiple stitches to close. Both suffered severe concussions requiring lengthy hospital stays. "This is for Carlie Milam you shitheads. Let this be a lesson," one of their attackers yelled.

A large cargo van was seen exiting the alley intersection with the street, but the observer was unable to provide the make of the vehicle, let alone a plate number.

---

[3] A hand weapon usually consisting of a piece of metal (lead) enclosed in leather with a strap and handle.

The boys told police one of the attackers, a fat guy with a southern drawl, said "This is for Carlie." Police detectives appeared at the offices of M & M Properties the next day suspecting that Russ Milam had arranged some sort of pound-of-flesh vengeance for the attack on his daughter. Russ denied knowing anything about it which was true. He did not mention his conversation with Marjorie. No arrests were made. The matter was eventually dropped for lack of evidence.

Three days after the alleyway incident, Marjorie Overton found a large Tyvek envelope on her desk stuffed with U.S. currency, all old hundred bills. A note was enclosed with the words *"Thanks,.... . Russ."*

"It was delivered by messenger service this morning," a coworker told her.

Russ told his partner Ben Moskowitz the entire story—how his conversation with Marjorie over lunch led to action against the two young creeps who had violated his daughter.

"I don't know what she did or who she contacted, but I'm happy with the outcome. Those two young thugs paid the perfect price for what they did, and thought they got away with it. Their hospital stay will be longer than Carlie's."

"This sounds like a vigilante action, you know, people taking action to dispense justice when it's needed," said Ben. "Maybe we can support it with some level of anonymous financing."

"I just did that," responded Russ. "With ten thou to Marjorie. I think she'll get the money into the right hands. There will no connection with us. Plausible deniability will be in our favor in case anything ever comes back on us."

Over the next few months, packets of hundred dollar bills found their way to the committee via Marjorie. The money was used to purchase equipment and weapons, compensate informants, and fund other necessities.

Derek did not ask Marjorie for the identities of his patrons.

17

A Dangerous Vocation

*"There is no more dangerous occupation
than being a police informant."*

– Lt. Joe Kenda, (Ret.),
Colorado Springs Homicide Detective

Delray Sparks had served as an informant during Derek's days with the police department and the two had stayed in regular but infrequent contact since his retirement. Delray operated a small barbeque joint known as Uncle Pookie's in a Black neighborhood. Derek and his partner had lunched there two or three times a month and made it known to Pookie that information about criminal activity would be "appreciated." Delray (Pookie) was well known and respected in the neighborhood. He knew a lot of people who knew a lot of gang members. Over a period of several years, information flowing from Delray led to the arrest and conviction of six gang bangers involved in the drug trade on charges ranging from assault and battery to second degree murder. Several drug dealers were also collared and later convicted of possession with intent to sell. Delray was amply rewarded.

Delray's referrals developed other police informants.

Slender, with snow white hair and mustache, perfect teeth, and a small paunch below his belt, Delray was always smiling and jovial. Popular with his customers and adored by his employees, he was generous with down-and-out people who came in looking for leftover food. Every year, he provided Thanksgiving dinner free of charge at a local school cafeteria where he was allowed to use kitchen facilities. All who came were fed. Roast turkey, ham, mounds of mashed potatoes, dressing and gravy, salads, green beans and all the trimmings were served along with pumpkin and pecan pie, topped with whipped cream. Funds to finance the event were mostly donated by Phoenix area businesses and individuals, many not part of the immediate community but who wanted to support Delray's generosity. Of course, donations at the event were accepted at the door. Last year, he prepared and served forty-one turkeys and twenty-four hams with all the side dishes.Derek dropped by Uncle Pookie's for lunch one day about a year after his retirement. Delray joined him at his table and the two chatted about old times, the NFL Cardinals, and the weather (always hot that time of year). During the conversation Derek casually remarked that he would be interested in learning about any unusual "situations" that arose in the neighborhood.

"Hey, my man, ain't you retired?" inquired Delray. "Why would you want to know about goins' on around here?"

"I just like to stay involved and helpful to the police when I can. It's no big deal, but if you can feed me anything at all, I will appreciate it. So will the PD."

Delray remained silent for several minutes then got up to go into the kitchen to see how everything was going. Satisfied that noontime customers were taken care of, he returned to

Derek's table. Two young Black men seated nearby noticed the hushed conversation, called for the bill before they had finished eating, and quickly left the restaurant.

Nervously, Delray implied that he had knowledge about several shootings that had occurred in the last six weeks resulting in the deaths of three teenagers. Several twenty dollar bills were discretely passed under the table to support next Thanksgiving's dinner.

Gang activity was not an issue that appealed to the *Committee*, but this situation got Derek's attention since it involved seemingly innocent, young victims. Delray was obviously familiar with details of the crime and provided the names of two shooters: Jordy Nolan and Ladislaw Washburn. These two were in their mid-twenties and both had extensive arrest records dating from their early teen years.

Black-on-Black crime was out of control in many cities, Chicago being the worst case with over 600 homicides in 2017, a large majority of which involved Black perps and victims. The *Committee* knew any action they might undertake would be a drop in the bucket as far as reducing the overall impact of these types of crimes. Nevertheless, at Derek's urging they discussed the possibility of an operation to eliminate Jordy and Ladislaw.

That possibility was forgotten when three days later, Delray was shot dead in his restaurant in broad daylight by two masked gunmen who entered the premises and immediately opened fire with semi-automatic weapons. The restaurant, with a seating capacity of twenty, had only four customers who were terrified and all but useless in providing evidence to investigating officers.

"They had masks covering their faces. I think they were Black, but not sure about that, it all happened so fast," one of the customers told officers. The other three were of no more help. They obviously wanted nothing to do with the investigation, let alone provide any detailed information about the shooting. Crime scene tape secured the restaurant for the following week while investigators combed the property for evidence.

Over five hundred mourners attended Delray's funeral in his parish church that seated only two hundred fifty. The overflow crowd was accommodated on the front lawn by outdoor speakers rigged for the occasion. The service lasted two hours and featured speakers including the mayor and numerous business leaders. The fully robed choir sang *The Old Rugged Cross, Amazing Grace,* and other hymns with gusto. The eulogy was emotionally delivered by Delray's cousin. Delray was lavishly praised for his service to the community. Every speaker demanded justice for the crime that had taken their friend's life.

Back in Derek's basement, committee members were deeply shaken by these events.

"They saw you talking with Pookie and now you're a target, you get that, don't you?" warned Lee.

"Of course I do," said Derek, "that's why we need to let this go and let it cool down for a while. I don't know if they were able to identify me since I hadn't been there in over a year. All the employees were new since my last visit, so it's unlikely they know me by name or that I was with the PD."

SIX MONTHS ROLLED by. Derek mostly laid low by entirely avoiding Uncle Pookie's old neighborhood.

Following three more drive-by homicides, he decided to find out what he could about the crimes from his police contacts and from neighborhood informants whose identities Delray Sparks had furnished him. Wearing his usual disguise, he approached Rolando (Big Man) Hayes in a bar one evening with a promise of substantial monetary award if he could provide certain information about the events in the neighborhood. Rolando was a large Black man, six foot five, over 300 pounds, with a powerful presence and mildly threatening demeanor.

"Who are you, man?" he demanded. "Are you a cop?"

"Used to be, but no more," replied Derek. "You don't need to know my name. Let's just say that I'm a guy you never heard of, willing to pay well for good information," while flashing a roll of hundred dollar bills. "Let's continue this conversation in my car outside."

That got Big Man's attention and the two left the bar about five minutes apart. Big Man joined Derek in his van and the two drove to a deserted parking lot three blocks away.

"I need to know about the hit on Uncle Pookie and these damned drive-by shootings," said Derek.

"What's to know? The kids are dead, their funerals were several weeks ago, and the cops are trying to find out who did it," answered Big Man vaguely. "I don't know nuthin' about Pookie."

"I think you do and I'm willing to substantially enhance your personal income for some names. You can depend on absolute anonymity if you can tell me what I need to know today."

"What do you mean about enhancin' my income?" queried Big Man suspiciously. Derek quickly produced five one hundred dollar bills ('Bennies' as they were called on the street—hundred dollar bills with a portrait of Benjamin Franklin.)

"That ain't enough for me to take the risk, man. Word will get out that I talked to the cops and my life won't be worth shit."

"Will a grand protect you?" said Derek showing the big guy ten Bennies. "Just some names, that's all I need. Easy peazy, no sweat."

"What the hell do you want with names? What are you gonna do?"

"That's not your concern, Big Man. Let's just say that justice will be done. Now tell me who whacked Pookie." Currency changed hands and Big Man started to talk.

"Okay, but you ain't hearin' this from me, man. If word ever gets out... . " His voice trailed off. "The shooters were James Arneson and Levone Barcroft. They're Crips gang bangers and everybody's afraid of them. They pretty much control the meth and cocaine business in a six block neighborhood around Pookie's place. If anyone tries to horn in on their territory, they end up either dead or seriously hurt."

"How do you know them?" asked Derek.

"Hell, I grew up with 'em, went to the same school until ninth grade, then they dropped out and joined the gang. Word was, after several years, they were making big bucks as street-corner retailers. It must have been so, 'cuz they started wearin' Nike Air Jordans and gold chains. They have plenty of girlfriends they entertain at the Gold Showroom with expensive bottles of champagne."

Derek knew about the popular nightclub and its reputation as a hangout for well-heeled customers. "Where do they hang out, and what time do they normally do drug transactions?" he asked.

"You'll need to set up a meetin' with 'em, man. They don't just deal with strangers on the street. They did that when they first got started and got busted on a small marijuana beef. So now, they're careful about who they sell to and where deals go down. And they've graduated from half gram hits sold in night clubs to sometimes at least two or three ounces for customers with the bread to do business with 'em."

"Sounds like they're wholesaling the stuff. Are they always together when deals go down or do they operate separately?"

"They almost always work together for security and personal protection. One stands aside to keep an eye on the customers and watches for any sign of treachery while the other makes the sale. They allow only one or at most two people to approach them when the transaction takes place. It's a quick in and out... takes no more than sixty seconds. Buyers have to be ready to fork over the money in a hurry in exchange for the goods. If they hesitate for any reason, the transaction is terminated and no further contact is accepted with that customer. That's how cautious they are. They set up locations usually in side streets or alleys to avoid undue attention." Derek found this information from Big Man very helpful.

"I want to be introduced to them as a solid buyer with an interest in establishing a long-term business relationship, and I'm willing to pay a premium for high quality product."

"I'm not gonna be directly involved, but I'll see what I can do through a guy I know," said Big Man with some trepidation. "I'll let you know... lemme have your cell number."

Five days passed and Derek was beginning to think he was not going to hear from Big Man. Finally, his phone buzzed and he answered with "What's up?"

"Hey man, it's me. Show up on foot at the southeast corner of Bethany Home Road and 7th Avenue this afternoon at six. Don't be late." Click.

Derek was familiar with this intersection in north Phoenix.

He had to cancel a late afternoon medical appointment but deemed the introductory meeting more important. In his customary disguise, he drove past the intersection a couple of times, parked behind a convenience store there, and walked to the corner. At 6:00 p.m., his phone went off. A voice said "Walk east to 5th Avenue and wait."

Derek did as he was instructed. Five minutes later, his phone buzzed again. "Head south on 5th, walk to Rancho Drive and wait on the corner. A Black dude in a green shirt will contact you."

It was a hot spring day and upon arrival at the location, Derek was dripping with sweat. *This has better be good*, he thought.

Five minutes later, a young Black man who appeared to be in his mid-twenties with a heavy gold neck chain hung with a large cross and a bright green silk shirt pulled up and said, "Yo' man, get in, let's take a little drive."

"I'm not going anywhere with you, dude. I was told that you represent a serious seller. I'm a serious buyer so this is how this meeting is going down. I will walk back to my car at 7th and Bethany Home. Since you've walked me around the neighborhood on a hot day, that hike will take about ten minutes. Then you will get in *MY* car and we'll have a discussion. That is, if your boss is for real and interested in doing some business."

The kid, (as Derek later referred to him) a gofer for the two drug dealers, was not accustomed to this type of customer demand and hesitated to reply. After a nervous pause, he said "Okay man, I'll be there."

The kid called his boss, one of the dealers, and told him what happened. "Yeah, play along and let me know what happens."

Eight minutes later, Derek arrived at his parked vehicle, got in and gulped a bottle of cold water from a cooler behind the driver's seat. The kid drove up, exited his vehicle and got in the passenger seat of Derek's van. Derek ordered him to pull up his shirt to check for weapons. Satisfied that the kid was clean, he asked "What's your name?"

"Omar."

"Okay Omar, here's the thing. I'm interested in buying at least four ounces of high-quality coke from a reliable source. That's like thirty two 8-balls. I retail the stuff to high-end customers mostly in Scottsdale and Paradise Valley— nowhere near your turf. If the deal turns out well for both of us, I'll be a regular customer with an appetite for more product in the weeks to follow. Get it?"

"I think so, but how do we know you have the dough to cover that first buy? It's gonna cost you around four grand. That's forty bennies you know. We don't accept no smaller bills."

"Before the transfer," Derek replied, "I'll meet you a block away with a bag containing the money. You can count it if you want. If it checks out, we can proceed to the place of transfer. At that point, I'll trust you guys to deliver the product in two zip lock bags. Just be sure it's a full four ounces and not cut with inositol powder or anything else. We'll verify that later and if there's a problem with the quantity or quality, there'll be no more deals and you will never hear from me again, get it? Your bosses need to understand that I'm a serious businessman. Here's five hundred as a good faith deposit. It's yours to keep one way or another." To Derek, this was the cost of the operation subsidized by his wealthy supporters. If the deal didn't happen, it was just the cost of doing business.

"And Omar, remember these five C-notes. If we're able to continue doing business with your bosses, there will be something extra in it for you," Derek added,

Omar was visibly impressed and said, "We'll be in touch, keep your cell phone close. By the way, you got a name?"

"Just call me Jake."

Flashing a grin, Omar exited the van and drove off in his car, a late model BMW convertible. Derek, in that moment, smiled slightly, knowing he had tapped that very human trait—greed. And it would work in his favor.

Derek was familiar with the illegal drug trade from his days with the PD. Low level coke dealers usually sell in gram units. Very commonly, dealers at the bottom of the chain will sell a half gram of cocaine packaged in tiny Ziplock bags in bars or night clubs. They also sell "8 balls" or about 3.5 grams. The term "8 ball" is based on the fact that it's about an eighth of an ounce. Cocaine in these quantities is not of high purity, usually cut with inositol powder without the buyer's knowledge. It still gave a powerful kick. Of course, product degraded in this manner boosted the profit margin of the seller.

"This is an ultra, high-risk operation," cautioned Phil in the basement as Derek briefed the committee on his meeting with Omar. "If anything goes wrong, you could be a dead man. These guys don't fool around. And I don't like the idea of papering that guy with five hundred. Won't that raise their suspicion that something's not right about this arrangement?"

"I know, but I'm relying on their greed," said Derek. "I doubt that Omar will tell his bosses about the five bills. Instead, he'll tell them that I'm a straight shooting dude they can do business with. The first buy is a setup to gain their trust. They'll be anxious to score four large and if it happens smoothly, they'll be eager for the next deal. That's when the whack will happen. When we learn the location of the transfer, we can try to place a sniper in visual proximity, preferably at an elevated position so he has a clear shot." Derek had the procedure pretty much in mind. "And we'll have some leverage to determine the location so that it fits our plan for the sniper and the getaway."

This met with the approval of the *Committee*, except for Phil who was still dubious. "I still don't understand why we need to get involved with gang activity. They're killing each other without our help and the cops are so undermanned they mostly turn a blind eye to what's happening in those neighborhoods. Cops are helpless to stop the killing on the south side of Chicago, and Phoenix police face the same thing."

"The difference is," explained Derek, "my friend Delray Sparks got whacked. He was a good guy who didn't deserve it. I don't know how they got word that he was a police informant, but they did and now they have to pay the price. We need to deliver justice to Delray's family. What's more, if we can take those two slime bags out, the entire community will be better off." Phil seemed somewhat satisfied and shrugged his agreement.

18

The Transaction

*"The trouble with killin' a man whether he needs it or not...
you could hang for it."*

– Marshall Matt Dillon, *Gunsmoke*

Derek's cell phone buzzed four days later. The screen said "Unknown Caller."

"Bring four large in used bennies to the northwest corner of Ballinger Park south of the I-10. You know where that's at?" It was Omar's voice.

"I'll find it."

"Be there at six in the afternoon day after tomorrow. Me and another guy will meet you to count the bread. If it's all there, we'll tell you where to meet the bosses to transfer the goods. Come alone and don't be late."

Derek assembled $4,000 in hundred dollar bills and placed it in a quart size Ziplock bag in two bundles of twenty bills each. Lee drove him to the spot and dropped him off at the appointed time. He waited ten minutes and was beginning to think Omar wasn't going to show up when he and a companion drove up in his Beemer and parked along the curb.

Omar swaggered up to Derek with a grin. "Yo, what up Jake, got the green?"

"It's all here," said Derek, handing the bag over. Omar quickly opened it, thumbed through the bills, took out three of them and held them up to the sunlight. The meeting lasted not more than ninety seconds.

"Looks good," said Omar. "We need to be sure you ain't packin' heat. Put your hands on the hood so I can pat you down." Omar was satisfied Derek was not carrying weapons. "Now walk to the opposite corner of the park. James and Levone will be there with the goods. I'll call 'em with the news that payment's been made in full."

Derek did as Omar instructed. Two minutes later, the two drug dealers drove up in a metallic-red low rider with wire spoke wheels and whitewall tires. One of them got out of the car, approached Derek and handed over a brown paper bag with two Ziplocks containing white powder. "This is good stuff, man. It'll test at ninety-eight percent pure. Let us know when you need more, but give us at least a week," said James over his shoulder, walking back to the car. The meeting lasted thirty seconds. J.W., parked around the corner, observed the parting, then picked up Derek.

That night back in the basement, Derek reported to the *Committee*. "This is not good. Only one of them made the transfer, the other stayed in the car. We need them both together to complete the whack."

"If one of them waits in the car, then I can take him out from the street at the same time Lee is triggering the other," reasoned J.W.

Four ounces of white powder were flushed down the toilet.

Eight days later, Omar called Derek to offer more product and set up the next transfer.

"I need eight ounces this time, no less," said Derek. And I'll pay seven grand for that quantity. It should be cheaper in larger quantity, cheaper by the dozen you know, and I'm not gonna haggle with you. It's seven large or nuthin'. Are you guys good for it?"

"You got it." Omar spoke for his bosses. If they didn't go for it, he could back out of the deal. "Be at the same place this time at 9:00 p.m. day after tomorrow."

"Will I meet James and Levone at the same place?" asked Derek.

"Yeah, I think so."

The operation was planned meticulously with two gunmen assigned to the operation—ex-military guys Lee and J.W. Both had previously visited practice ranges separately in Tucson and Yuma to sharpen and ensure their marksmanship skills. Lee was armed with an AR-15 style rifle chambered for .223 caliber rounds and equipped with a muzzle flash suppressor—potentially helpful in obscuring their position in a nighttime operation. A lighter, more compact rifle was deemed preferable to the hunting rifle used by Lee in the previous Ochoa operation since the target would be at closer range. J.W. packed a Glock 17, 9mm Luger pistol with hollow point ammo for his part in the operation. It was equipped with a noise suppressor.

"What do we do about Omar after the cash changes hands?" asked J.W.

"Last time, he just drove away after he verified the cash," said Derek. "He'll probably do the same thing this time, but if not, we'll have to improvise. If he approaches the transfer point, he'll have to be taken out with the others."

"Okay, let's go over the plan again," continued Derek. "Timing is everything. If just one of them approaches me like last time, I will stand aside to give Lee a clear shot. There won't be much illumination, but enough from a street light to see the target. If both of them approach me, be prepared to take them both out. Lee, you have a semi-automatic weapon, so it shouldn't be too difficult. When you see the transfer take place, that's your cue to fire. Don't hesitate. J.W., you'll be parked about two hundred feet away with your motor running, lights off, passenger window down. When the gang's car pulls up, start creeping closer and when you see the transaction going down you will jam the accelerator to the floor, come alongside their car and pour lead through the open window at the driver when you hear Lee's shot. I'll be out of your line of fire and on my way to get in your vehicle so we can make a quick getaway. There'll be few, if any, park visitors or dog walkers at that hour, but if someone wanders by or hangs around, the operation will be aborted. I'll complete the transaction and we'll wait for another time. Clear?"

At 8:00 p.m., Lee deftly broke into the rear door of an empty house across the street and perched at a second floor window with clear line of sight to the transfer point. He had scoped out the house beforehand and was satisfied it was unoccupied.

At five minutes past nine, Omar rolled up in his convertible with the top down and motioned Derek to come over. He eagerly grabbed the bag with seven thousand dollars in it and started a quick count.

"Yo, you're beautiful, man. Looks like it's all here. I'll let 'em know and you can collect the product up the block like before." Derek did not respond, but turned and started walking to the transfer spot as Omar drove away. He had placed an additional $500 in the bag for Omar.

From his vantage point, Lee observed Derek as he approached the transfer spot almost directly in front of his perch. Derek paused and glanced over his shoulder to see if the drug sellers were coming. He didn't see a vehicle for another ten minutes and Derek began to think a ripoff had occurred. *Dammit, where are they,* he thought with growing irritation. A ripoff in the illegal drug trade happens when either money or drugs failed to change hands during the deal. This usually causes a violent reaction between both parties to the transaction.

After a few more minutes a red, low-slung coupe rolled up. Levone got out of the passenger door and sauntered toward Derek with two bags in hand. Just as he was within three feet of Derek, a large recreational vehicle approached and came to a sudden halt totally blocking Lee's view of the transaction. The driver must have thought a pedestrian was crossing in front of the parked car, hence the sudden stop.

'Who the hell is that?" demanded Levone, staring at the RV suspiciously.

"I have no idea," said Derek.

After a few seconds, the RV rolled on, exposing the drug deal starting to go-down. Derek made sure Levone's back was turned toward Lee's vantage point, offering a clear target. As planned, J.W. began his slow roll toward the transfer point. Derek stepped to one side out of the expected line of fire and to avoid any blood spatter. A shot rang out from across the street; Levone Barcroft fell dead in front of Derek. Three seconds later, J.W. pulled up, stopped alongside the coupe and fired four shots into the driver's side window. The first was deflected, another hit James Arneson in the head and two struck his neck and shoulder. He died immediately, drenching the car's interior with blood. Derek scooped up the bags carried by Levone, sprinted to the passenger side of J.W.'s car and got in. They sped off, turned left at the cross street, and made another left into the alley behind Lee's position to pick him up. The entire operation took only forty seconds. There were no witnesses. Neighbors in their homes nearby heard gunfire, rushed out, discovered the carnage and called 9-1-1. In minutes, emergency vehicles with flashing lights jammed the street, a crowd had gathered, and police struggled to deal with onlookers, TV cameras, and news reporters. Officers canvassed the neighbors but found no one with information about the crime. One bloody footprint was found near the body of Levone. Police criminalists later connected it to a size twelve Magnalite working boot, normally used by persons engaged in some form of physical labor.

"That was perfect," said Derek quietly. All three used copious quantities of liquid sanitizer on their hands, face, and hair. The AR-15 was later wiped down and sawed into pieces that were disposed of separately in doubled trash bags placed in six different dumpsters miles apart. The Glock was not destroyed but wrapped in a trash bag with other debris and placed at the bottom of a dumpster in an area of the city known for homelessness. This turned out to be a mistake.

Arriving home that evening, Derek noticed dried blood on the sole of his left boot as he removed it. *Oh, shit, I need to get rid of these right now.* He immediately bagged the boots and drove to a dumpster in back of a drugstore six miles from his home. The bin was almost full. *I was too damned careless in a big rush to get to the car,* he muttered to himself as he stuffed the bag into the midst of the other debris. Next morning, the rubberized floor liner on the passenger side of Lee's car was removed and deposited in a remote dumpster.

OMAR HAD DRIVEN away after collecting the money from Derek. He was grinning as he stopped at a traffic light four blocks away. Suddenly, two Black guys wearing dark sunglasses and plain baseball caps jumped into his open top BMW and told him to keep driving. The carjacker in the front seat pointed a large pistol at Omar and ordered him to pull into a small strip mall parking lot. "Now, get out and walk away."

Omar was stunned and terrified. "Ya'll won't get away with this," he yelled. "My bosses will come after you and you'll be dead men walking."

"Yeah, well that's our problem ain't it? You'll find this car in Greenwood Cemetery, dude."

At 2:00 a.m. that night, patrol cops saw a bright glow in the middle of Greenwood Cemetery located eight blocks from Ballinger Park. They found a late model BMW convertible totally consumed by flames.

Three days later, Big Man called Derek and said: "Hey man, I've got your half of the dough for you."

Family members, employees, and customers of Delray Sparks were quietly thankful that justice had been delivered. The illegal drug trade in Uncle Pookie's neighborhood was disabled and never regained its profitability.

19
Matricide

"Let the punishment fit the crime."

– Sir William Schwenck Gilbert

David Bauman was happy with his new role since many of his cases involved felony charges—a step up from the low-level cases he was accustomed to dealing with. One case in particular caused the victim, a frail elderly woman named Martha Bernitz, to be placed in permanent nursing home care after her son started a violent argument over the contents of her will. Her estate consisted of stocks, real property, and expensive jewels accumulated over a lifetime, all worth several million dollars. Her son, Reuben, had the clear impression that he was not a beneficiary of his mother's will.

Martha's relationship with her son had been contentious for years as a result of his gambling addiction and his repeated requests for money to support his habit. At first, she accommodated him with several hundred dollars every few weeks, then two or three thousand, accompanied with pleas to get professional help. A tipping point came during her stay in the nursing home when he demanded five thousand dollars to pay off a loan shark debt. She refused and informed him no more money would be forthcoming until he sought help to cure his addiction. "Reuben," she said, "the spirit of decency does not abide in you and I'm leaving my entire estate to the Nazarene church." Reuben flew into a rage and delivered a flurry of punches to her face. One blow broke her jaw. She was taken to the ER then to a stay in the hospital where she died three weeks later from complications of pneumonia.

David Baumann was assigned the case by the county attorney. He presented two charges to the grand jury, one for felony domestic violence, and one for second degree murder. The grand jury handed down an indictment for felony domestic violence, but declined to indict on the second degree murder charge, infuriating Dave.

Reuben made bail and was released from the county jail after a stay of ten days. The judge declined to revoke his bail after the death of his mother.

"It doesn't get any worse than this," Dave told the *Committee.* "A son abusing his own mother." The meeting in Derek's basement became highly charged emotionally as Martha's case was discussed.

"This cold hearted piece of shit took the life of the one who gave him life and now he's walking the street. It's not even certain he'll be convicted of domestic assault but the penalty for that is a tap on the wrist compared to what he really deserves," Dave loudly exclaimed with tears in his eyes. "My stepdad abused me and my mother and it has affected me ever since. I can't forget it and now it all comes back with the death of an innocent old lady."

"Why wouldn't the grand jury at least indict him for manslaughter?" asked J.W.

"Because I couldn't clearly relate his beating her up with her death. The official cause of death was pneumonia. Look, grand juries are sometimes hard to predict."

"I'm not clear on the grand jury process," Phil said. "Can you give us a quick seminar on what happens?"

"Sure," Dave said. "In a nutshell, there are two methods by which a suspect may face felony charges in Maricopa County. Either through a formal complaint filed by a prosecutor or through an indictment by a grand jury. When a crime has been reported to the PD or Sheriff's office, an officer arrives at the scene to interview the victim and any witnesses. He then prepares a report describing the crime. Police detectives and crime scene investigators will also respond if there is a need to gather additional evidence. In serious cases, a deputy county attorney may come to the scene to assist officers with legal issues. When their investigation is complete, the suspect will either be arrested or their findings will be referred to the county attorney's office for review by a prosecutor. If the prosecutor believes the report contains enough evidence that the suspect has committed a crime and conviction at trial is likely, the prosecutor will either file a direct complaint or seek a grand jury indictment.

"A direct complaint is a document prepared by the prosecutor which details the felony offense. A judge then reviews the complaint to decide if there is sufficient evidence to approve it and issue a summons ordering the alleged offender to appear for a preliminary hearing. An arrest warrant may also be issued.

"Instead of, or in addition to filing a direct complaint, a prosecutor may formally charge a suspect by presenting evidence to a grand jury. If the grand jury determines there is sufficient evidence that the suspect committed a crime and should be tried on charges, an indictment, or 'True Bill' will be issued. This is usually a slam dunk for the prosecutor. Someone once said a grand jury would indict a ham sandwich if told to do so by the prosecutor. Grand juries rarely fail to issue an indictment, or a "No Bill," based on testimony the prosecutor offers. Following a grand jury indictment, a judge will either issue an arrest warrant or a summons for the defendant to appear in court. Then, a complicated maze of procedures follows, including initial appearance, status conference, preliminary hearing, arraignment, pretrial hearings, and plea negotiations. If a plea agreement isn't reached, the case goes to trial. A lot of stuff goes on between these steps. It's all designed to ensure the defendant's rights are protected and all legal procedures are followed to the letter."

"Something needs to be done about Bernitz," said Derek. "If he violates the terms of his bail, he'll land back in jail beyond our reach."

"Fill me in," requested Phil. "What are the terms of his bail?"

"Good question," said Dave. "First, he must appear in court for all proceedings. Beyond that, he is limited in traveling only within the jurisdiction, avoiding the consumption of alcoholic beverages, and must check in with his bail agent regularly. He is required to maintain continued employment but since he hasn't worked at a regular job in years, that doesn't apply. Failure to comply with bail conditions is not an offense, but might lead to his arrest and surrender back to the court where he would be remanded to custody."

"Then we need to act decisively and soon," urged Lee. Following a brief discussion during which Reuben was reviled as the worst of the worst, not fit to breathe the same air as civilized people, the others agreed.

J.W. had vacation time coming and the following day was asked to monitor the daily routine of Bernitz, assisted by Derek. During the next five days, every move Reuben made outside his home was observed and timed. He shared a house owned by his late mother on South 9th street with a woman not his wife. He followed a regular routine. About seven each morning, he emerged from his front door to collect a newspaper from his porch. He didn't come out again until noontime when he got into his car and drove to Palm Shores Restaurant for lunch, sometimes with his live-in companion, but usually alone. Occasionally, he substituted a visit to Burger World for a fast food meal. After lunch, he slowly drove past his mother's former home on two occasions but never stopped. He parked at a local shopping mall and attended an afternoon movie one day. This was all very ordinary behavior and did not offer an opportunity for *Committee* action.

"It's fairly obvious this is gonna have to be a nighttime operation inside his house," said Lee.

Derek responded, "Not necessarily. His appearance each morning to get his paper gives us a chance. We haven't noticed any neighbors around at that time, so I think a carefully placed shot from a vantage point will be possible. There's a rundown vacant house for sale on 9th Street across the street two doors down. It has a second floor window that overlooks the street and I think it has a clear line of sight to Reuben's front porch. It would be an easy shot for Lee if we can find a way to get him into and out of the house."

Wait a minute," said Lee. "What's the address of his place on 9th?"

When J.W. recited the address, Lee said: "This is a crazy coincidence. That's across the street from a house I just bought. It's the one with the for sale sign. I know that neighborhood. My nephew Jacob and I bought the place with a plan to remodel and flip it for a profit. It's currently unoccupied and I can easily get in."

The issue was discussed at length—pros and cons, including the risk involved. In the end, the level of risk was deemed acceptable. So a "go" was authorized for two days hence. Lee immediately started preparing for the operation. He chose an AR-15 semi-automatic rifle chambered for .350 Legend cartridge, equipped with a sixteen inch barrel, 3x32mm scope, and noise suppressor. It was lightweight and highly accurate at a distance of two hundred fifty feet. The weapon had been purchased at a gun show in Fort Worth, Texas. A ten-round magazine was packed with hollow core projectiles, though ten shots would almost certainly not be required. Lee anticipated one shot would get the job done. To ensure proper operation and accuracy of the weapon he visited a shooting range in the foothills on the north side of Tucson. That particular range in the foothills was difficult to find and not well supervised. The range manager was totally indifferent to Lee's payment for an hour's worth of time and paid no attention to the customer wearing opaque sun glasses and a plain baseball cap pulled low over his eyes. It was therefore highly unlikely he could identify Lee if questioned by law enforcement officers, let alone tie him to the operation in Phoenix.

ON THE SCHEDULED morning, Derek dropped Lee off before sunup in the alley behind the vacant house on 9th and drove away with his lights off. Pulling a set of keys from his pocket, he opened the back door and climbed stairs to the upper floor with weapon in hand. He opened the window, removed the screen, and took up a position out of sight using a soft chair back to steady the rifle. The day dawned clear and windless, perfect for the operation.

The newspaper carrier tossed the day's edition onto Reuben's front porch at six fifteen. If Reuben followed his usual habit, he would emerge about forty-five minutes later to collect the paper. Lee was fidgety with nervous apprehension but calmed himself by sipping from a small thermos of hot chocolate. The thought of Reuben's treatment of his mother steeled Lee's resolve and absolved any second thoughts of what he was about to do.

Seven o'clock came and passed with no sign of Reuben. *The guy must have overslept or worse, isn't even at home,* thought Lee who, after twenty minutes, was ready to abort the operation. Then the door opened and out came Reuben looking for his paper. It lay about six feet away and as he was stooping to pick it up, a shot was fired. The bullet pinged off the brick façade behind him and harmlessly ricocheted away. *God dammit, the shot missed!* cursed Lee under his breath.

Reuben was confused for three seconds and then realized he was the target of a shooter. He turned to reenter the home when a second shot struck him in the neck. He fell to the ground bleeding profusely and died seconds later from massive blood loss.

"The package was delivered," Lee reported, using a burner after hurriedly exiting his sniper's perch and climbing into the waiting SUV in the alley. A large amount of hand sanitizer was used. Thirty seconds later, the vehicle was four blocks away. Police officers and EMTs arrived fifteen minutes later, summoned by a neighbor walking his dog and discovering Reuben lying on his front porch in what appeared to be a pool of blood. Reuben's girlfriend was blissfully unaware of the events on their front porch, sleeping soundly until police officers rapped on the door.

Crime scene tapes were put up and detectives canvassed the neighborhood but found no one with information about the crime. The street was jammed for hours with emergency vehicles and TV camera trucks. The story led the noontime news reports and was repeated with details that evening. No suspects were identified.

Lee worried that he had made one mistake. In his haste to depart the scene, he hadn't taken the time to replace the screen before closing the window. That omission would certainly lead investigators to the sniper's location where they might find usable evidence.

ANALYSIS OF THE crime scene revealed the direction and angle of the shot that killed Reuben Bernitz. Detectives located the sniper's nest on the upper floor of the empty house across the street two lots aside, two hundred fifteen feet away. The window screen had been removed allowing a clear view of Bernitz's front porch, but not replaced in the gunman's rush to flee the scene. Gunshot residue was found on a chair back and window sill. They also found clear finger prints on the knob of the interior door leading to the room in question and on stair bannisters and kitchen appliances. Prints were run through the data base of the FBI in Washington and were identified as belonging to Stephen Lee Simmons. He had been fingerprinted several times, first as a marine and later as an employee of the pet store chain. It was a definite match.

Lee had taken the precaution of using shooters' gloves made of synthetic leather after entering the room; consequently, no prints were found on the window or screen frame. However, several filaments of synthetic leather were found on the screen and were subjected to technical analysis with the hope that a match could be found with gloves in possession of a suspect.

DETECTIVES EASILY LOCATED the correct address and obtained a warrant to search the home of Stephen and Janet Simmons. Detectives McAvoy and Browning, accompanied by two uniforms, arrived at the house at 5:00 a.m. on a Friday, knocked loudly on the door, waved the warrant in Lee's face, and barged in. Lee was handcuffed and made to sit on the living room sofa. Janet was terrified. A three hour search turned up nothing, no gloves or anything else that might have tied Lee to the sniper's house.

Ownership of the house used by the sniper was found to be in the name of one Jacob Early who had purchased the property three weeks prior to the shooting. Questioned by detectives, he stated that it was an investment. He planned to remodel the home, expand the sun room, and eventually "flip" it for a profit. Asked if he knew a person named

Stephen Lee Simmons, he replied: "Sure, he's my uncle. He's helping me with the project."

"Records show that the purchase was an all-cash transaction. What was the source of your funds?" asked Detective McAvoy.

"Uncle Lee found the property and offered to go in with me to rehab it. We jointly financed the purchase. Me from my savings. He had a bank check at closing."

"But his name is not on the title. Why not? You say he financed part of the purchase?"

"He said he had some tax issues, and preferred that I serve as the sole owner. I didn't question him on it."

"Did he say why he wanted this particular property?" McAvoy asked.

"He said it looked like a good investment with potential for nice profit."

"The house was used as a sniper's perch for a homicide that happened last Thursday." This fact was not revealed to the public and was a shock to Jacob.

"How did the guy get in? Did he break in?" asked Jacob.

"There was no sign of forced entry so he must have had a key or one of the doors was left unlocked."

Lee's status with the investigation was downgraded from 'suspect' to 'person-of-interest.'

20

The Foul Mouthed Pedagogue

"...avoid profane and vain babblings...,"

– Timothy 2:16

Jeannie Marshall was a freshman student at Maricopa Community College. She and her friends Courtney and Marie bubbled with excitement as they registered for classes and talked about the fun they would have as college students. The three had played soccer in high school and sought to join the college soccer team. The girls lived at home with their parents and commuted by bus to the downtown campus. After a year in community college, they planned to enter Arizona State University in nearby Tempe.

Everything was rosy until their first class in second semester English literature taught by Roger Martin, a part-time instructor. Martin possessed mediocre teaching talents and was prone to lengthy off-topic sermons laced with profanity. Previous students thought his use of foul language was a device to compensate for his weak teaching skills. The very first lecture frequently included dropping the f-bomb in its various iterations. All the four-letter invectives and the "g-d" word found their way into his dialogue with regularity.

This was a shock to his students especially the three young women who knew the words but had never been exposed to them so carelessly. After the first class, Jeannie looked at Courtney and Marie and wondered what kind of situation they found themselves in.

"That's the worst language I've ever heard from one person," said Marie. "His cussing totally distracts from the subject and causes me to cringe wondering what will come out his mouth next." The girls continued to discuss Martin's behavior and thought the first class of the semester was an aberration. Maybe he was having a bad day after a fight with his wife.

But classroom tenor and tone did not improve during the next three weeks. Instructor Martin continued his stream of foul mouthed invectives inserted at times calculated to provide maximum shock to his listeners. Boys in the class also complained about Martin's behavior and several of them took the matter to the dean.

"He can't open his mouth without curse words, some of them really filthy. The girls are very uncomfortable and some are thinking about dropping the course," Will Roberts told the dean. "This college shouldn't tolerate this kind of environment in any classroom. It creates a negative atmosphere and damages the educational message of the course."

The dean readily agreed after several girls also reported his language and indicated that students had complained about Martin's language last semester after he was first employed by the college. Two parents also came to the dean and told him that it had to stop. The dean had a face-to-face talk with Martin soon thereafter and promised a threat of penalties including dismissal if he failed to clean up his act.

Matters immediately improved in the classroom with almost no objectionable terms heard other than "damn." This continued for almost a month when an issue arose during the study of Shakespeare's *Hamlet*. Charlie Abelson, who sat in a rear seat, opined that Laertes must have been gay owing to his obsession with Hamlet. The class snickered with amusement.

Martin exploded with anger. "That's just total bullshit and you are a fucking moron," he shouted. Having been personally attacked, Charlie got to his feet and advanced toward the instructor with fists clenched. "No one calls me that sir, and you will apologize right now or I will smash your face!" Three boys arose to intercept Charlie and restrain him from physically assaulting Martin. Several minutes of yelling ensued with most students taking Charlie's side. Finally things settled down, order was restored, and Martin mumbled an apology, not directly to Charlie but to the class. Again, Martin straightened up and avoided most of the offensive language for a couple of weeks. Not able to control his behavior, he once again defaulted to the use of vile language, apparently not remembering his conversation with the dean or the incident with Charlie. Students complained to the dean again. The dean had another talk with the instructor without lasting effect. Roger Martin's classroom vitriolic language was out of control. College authorities took no effective action. Students concluded the college was afraid to act decisively, fearing legal backlash from Martin on the basis of his first amendment rights. Four students dropped the class, unable to tolerate Martin's garbage mouth.

JACK MARSHALL, JEANNIE'S dad, was acquainted with David Baumann, whom he had met as a fellow member of the local Elk's Club and had become aware of his position as a prosecuting attorney.

Seeking possible remedies to the English instructor's behavior, Jack phoned Dave at his office. He told him of his daughter's experience with the English instructor. "Dave, what can be done about this? I guess he's not breaking any law, but is there any source of relief available? The guy is out of control and the girls are very upset. They love the subject matter but they dread going to class and are thinking of dropping the course altogether. He uses the f-bomb all the time, not to mention other expletives involving body waste and references to women as prostitutes. Several parents are circulating a petition among themselves demanding his removal but so far the college administration hasn't acted."

"I'm wondering why the college doesn't deal with this," replied Dave. "They're probably afraid of a lawsuit from the instructor. Let me think about this. No so-called 'teacher' should get away with that kind of behavior."

"THIS APPEARS TO be a sticks-and-stones situation with no resulting physical or financial damage to anyone," Dave reported to the *Committee.* "But students are tired of it. It appears that a more strenuous remedy is needed to reform his behavior."

Committee members had numerous questions. "How often does this happen? In every class? Are you sure those are the terms he uses? How long has he been an instructor at the college? Why hasn't the college done something?" These and other questions derived from the *Committee's* interest in cases involving abuse of women. To be sure, males were also unwilling listeners to instructor Martin's lectures, but it was the girls' distress that captured the *Committee's* attention.

THERE FOLLOWED A DISCUSSION by the *Committee* at their next meeting in the basement. "This guy thinks he is the coolest cat on campus and believes he can get away with that kind of language," said Dave. "And sure enough he has! College administrators have tapped his wrist a couple of times, students and parents have complained, but nothing has changed. He reforms for a while and then reverts to his old habits. The girls in his class believe his behavior amounts to sexual harassment but don't know where to turn for relief."

Phil was mildly interested at first and thought the whole thing might be blown out of proportion. "That kind of language is almost *de rigueur* among everyone today and if people don't like it they don't have to listen to it."

"That's just the problem," said Derek. "If they want course credit, the kids must attend class and listen to the lectures. They have no choice other than dropping the course, but why should they be forced to do that? They have a right to take the course without this kind of disruption."

Further conversation ensued and finally Lee proposed a solution. "His mouth needs to be washed out with soap."

The others grinned and wondered how this might be done. Lee continued. "Exactly how we have handled other cases—direct personal action! We confront the guy in a private setting, open his mouth, and use a brush with soap and water to literally scrub out his mouth. And then let him know in no uncertain terms that if he continues the use of profanity in his classroom, next time won't be so pleasant."

"Of course, this operation involves kidnapping and physical assault," said Phil. "Is this serious enough for us to take that kind of risk? I don't think so."

Twenty more minutes of discussion ended with a decision to observe Martin's movements over several days to determine if there might be an opportunity to "talk" with him privately. Unless that opportunity was available with minimum risk, there would be no action.

Derek undertook to perform this function since he was retired and had the time. In the next week, he found Martin's residential address, learned that he was unmarried, lived alone in a two bedroom cottage about two miles from campus, and walked his dog each evening at a small park near his home. He owned a car but took public transportation to and from work. He did not socialize with faculty colleagues or neighbors, and did not date anyone, at least during the time he was under surveillance. In short, he was a loner.

"Why are we even considering this?" asked Phil angrily. "Who cares if this guy has a potty mouth? It's a matter for the college to handle. We don't need to take the risk of personal confrontation to address this thing."

"It's a sign of cultural and social deterioration in society that language has been so corrupted that a college professor can get away with offending whomever he wishes, in this case, his own students," said Derek. "We hear these words every day on TV, in the movies, in casual conversation. It's pervasive and not likely to abate anytime soon."

"So let's make an example of this jerk and put an end to his profane diatribes," suggested Lee. "I'm in favor of a good mouth scrubbing. It won't hurt him, at least not badly and it'll be something he'll understand and remember."

With four in agreement, (Phil dissented), plans were made to conduct the operation. Martin would be approached on a pathway in the park near an alley where they could park a cargo van. Two days, later with no witnesses in view, he and his dog were greeted by J.W. and Lee in disguise at the planned location. "Hello, Professor Martin, how are you this evening?"

Shocked that these strangers knew his name, Martin said, "Who the hell are you and what do you want?"

"Just a little conversation about your pedagogy," said Lee as they quickly hustled him into the side door of the van parked a few feet away. Martin was so surprised he couldn't put up much resistance and found himself bound securely sitting on the backwards-facing chair in the van. The small dog was placed unhurt in the front passenger seat of the van.

"Now sir, you must answer for the foul-mouthed language you spout in your classroom. Your students are offended and you've been told by your superiors at the college to stop it and warned that some form of punishment will be applied. And still it goes on. Why?" demanded J.W.

"How the fuck would you know what I do and what business of it is yours?" shouted Martin.

"That's irrelevant to this conversation, sir. We just want to know why you use that approach to teaching and we're making it our business."

"I don't answer to you or anyone else and you're committing a crime by grabbing me and stuffing me into this vehicle. You can be damn sure I'll report this to the police," said Martin with his best faked authority.

"You do that, sir." A stinging slap on the face delivered by J.W. split his upper lip and caused Martin to gasp and utter a muted scream.

"Open your mouth, professor," demanded J.W., grabbing Martin's lower jaw and his forehead with nitrile gloved hands to force his mouth open. A bowl had been prepared with warm water mixed with shaving cream and a small, soft bristle brush. Derek soaked the brush in the liquid and proceeded to painfully scrub the mouth, teeth, tongue, and face of the instructor with generous amounts of the soapy preparation. This went on for two minutes after which Martin retched violently and threw up his dinner all the while struggling and yelling his distress.

"Understand something, dude. This is just a warning," J.W. shouted six inches from Martin's face. "You will cease the use of profanity in your classroom, is that clear? If we learn from our sources that it continues, you will see us again, and next time, it will not be so gentle. It won't be in this park, but at a time and place of our choosing and will come as a total shock to you. You won't see it coming and it will be severe, get it?"

Martin mumbled something unintelligible with his chin hanging on his chest. After Lee had determined no observers were nearby, Martin and his dog were released from the van and told to walk rapidly away from the scene without looking back. He did so and promptly called

9-1-1 from his cell phone.

"That was fun," said J.W. as they were driving away.

The uniformed officer who responded to the 9-1-1 call was amused by the complaint, having himself been threatened with similar punishment as a child by his grandmother. Police investigated Martin's complaint as a kidnapping and assault. The kidnapping element was reported to the FBI, but they declined to take an interest. The neighborhood was canvassed and park visitors were interviewed, but none were nearby at the time, so no usable evidence was discovered. In planning the operation, the *Committee* made sure no surveillance cameras were focused on the site. A fake license plate was used on the van.

Instructor Martin got the message. In his next return to the classroom, he was a model of polite decorum and spoke in a calm voice without invective. Students were astonished at the change in his demeanor and told him so. For the remainder of the semester, no further incidents of cursing occurred. He even formed friendly relations with students, socializing with them after class on several occasions. Classroom environment improved to the point where learning and appreciation for the works of the Great Bard of Avon actually happened.

21

Domestic Violence Reappearance

*"Violence and injury enclose in their net all that do
such things, and generally return upon him who began."*

– Lucretius

Emerging from the back door of his home at 10:30 p.m. in
suburban Chandler, Brian Stadtler caught a sawed-off
baseball bat full in his face, shattering his nose cartilage,
knocking out his front teeth, and splitting his lips. He went to
the ground screaming and bleeding profusely. Two large men
quickly muffled his cries with a heavy towel and dragged him
into the rear of a cargo van waiting in the alley. It was very
dark with no moon.

BRIAN AND MAGGIE Stadtler had been married twelve
years and had two children, a son age ten and a daughter of
six. The marriage was happy for the first six years but began
to go wrong when Brian started to throw frequent temper
tantrums and become abusive for no apparent reason. He had
fits of anger once or twice a month, soon escalating to two or
three a week. He would fly into a rage over the smallest issue.
"Why aren't the dishes done?" he demanded ten minutes after

dinner when the kids had left the table. His favorite complaint was the quality of her housekeeping. "This place is filthy, just look at the damn dust on the furniture. You haven't vacuumed the fuckin' carpet in over a week," he yelled. This was typical of his behavior which became worse as time passed.

Brian was a modestly handsome man, in good physical shape, and proud of the numerous tattoos on his arms and shoulders. The tattoos had been added over the years as he became increasingly addicted to "inking" his body. His favorite tattoo parlor was located in a seedy area of town. Twice a year like clockwork, he appeared to get a little more done. His preferred theme was fantasy creatures—dragons, serpents, mythical creatures, skulls, and satanic images decorated his arms, shoulders, and chest. Like many people who indulge themselves with tattoos, his habit started with a "bucket list" desire to get a tattoo. A small snake image was followed by an avalanche of other designs, all designed to attract attention to himself as a unique individual with weird tastes. He relished people gawking when he encountered strangers for the first time. Maggie did not like his habit and was embarrassed by it, especially when he wore sleeveless shirts in public. She confided to friends that his tattoos seemed to amplify his "macho" persona.

An innocent question intended as humor sent him into a rage on one occasion. She just asked, "Is that another tattoo?" after he arrived home from the tattoo parlor.

"Damn right it is, and if you don't like it, you can go fuck yourself!" This reaction sent her into the bathroom in tears. Other temper flare-ups occurred with increasing regularity. Shouting at Maggie and the kids turned into face slapping and forcing her shoulders against the wall, yelling with his face six inches from hers—in front of the kids. His son was the target of especially harsh treatment. After installed gym equipment in the garage, Brian required the boy to work out vigorously several times a week, calling him a pussy and cursing him when he felt the lad did not adequately exert himself. "You're gonna learn how to fight and defend yourself, boy." Boxing lessons sometimes resulted in a bloodied nose which Brian termed "the price of getting tough."

He spanked his daughter too hard with a 12" ruler for minor forms of misbehavior, raising welts on her buttocks. Maggie attempted to defend her children but this only further angered him, causing more violence against her. Feeling helpless, Maggie had been through hell for the last six months and finally decided to tell someone, though she feared if Brian learned of it, he would really harm her. On more than one occasion, he threatened to kill her. "This house is a fuckin' big mess bitch, and if you don't straighten it up, I'll kill you." She took to cleaning every day so the house fairly sparkled, but he still wasn't satisfied. Searching for something to criticize one day, he yelled "Look at the fingerprints on the lavatory faucets, why can't you do anything right?"

This was the last straw for Maggie. She sought advice from the pastor of the church she attended with the kids (Brian never went). The reverend offered an opinion that her husband's behavior derived from some type of mental disorder and advised her to call someone who could arrange a "fix" to her problem. He wrote a phone number on a small post-it note and gave it to her.

"Who will I be talking to?" she inquired.

"I don't have a name, but it's a contact for someone who may be able to help you in a very effective way," was all he said.

Next day, Maggie entered the number on her cell phone after Brian went to work. A recorded message said, "The number you have dialed is no longer in service." Perplexed, Maggie called her pastor to report the bad number.

"I'm terribly sorry. These things change frequently. Try this one." He recited another phone number.

After four rings, a male voice said, "May I help you?"

"Who am I speaking with?" she inquired of the man who answered.

"For good reason, I must remain anonymous. My name isn't important but perhaps we can help. Tell me about your situation"

The man noted the details she offered and asked numerous questions. "What would you like to have done to correct your husband's behavior?"

"He refuses to get counseling and I'm at my wit's end," she said tearfully. "I don't know what it will take. That's the reason my pastor suggested calling you."

"Are you willing to allow us to use any means at our disposal to solve this problem for you?"

"I think so, just don't kill him."

"That won't be necessary. Now what I want you to do is get out of the house with the kids today. I'll give you the location of a safe house. Don't tell anyone where you are. Take the kids out of school for a few days. Tell the principal that you have an ailing relative in another state. But leave the house as soon as you possibly can."

"What do you charge? I can't afford to pay you," pleaded Maggie.

"That's the last thing you need to worry about. We make no charge for our services."

Brian arrived home after work that afternoon and found the house empty. Calls for Maggie and the kids produced no response and he began to suspect she had left him, taking the kids. Boiling with rage, he called her parents and demanded to know their whereabouts. They knew she had entered a women's shelter that day, but her father expressed worry and half-heartedly denied knowing where she was. "Call the police and file a missing-persons report," he suggested and hung up. This remark told him they were lying, they knew full well where she was but weren't about to tell him. Angry calls to friends turned up nothing. He had no clue where she was. He was informed by the police department that they couldn't respond to a missing persons report until after forty eight hours had passed.

Brian went to work the next day but said nothing about his missing family. Coworkers sensed his glowering attitude but hesitated to ask him about it, knowing of his volatile temper.

At 10:29 that evening, the phone rang. "Walk out into your backyard," a man's voice said. "We know about your wife and can tell you where she is."

"Who the hell is this and what's up with the back yard?" demanded Brian.

"Can't talk on the phone, just come out."

Brian angrily slammed down the phone and walked to the back door. Seeing nothing, he opened it tentatively and stepped out. That's when it happened. Searing pain shot through his head and migrated down his back. His assailant was hidden behind a potted plant to his right, positioned to deliver a heavy blow directly to his target's face. Howling with agony, Brian was aware of two men muffling his cries with something soft. Now bleeding profusely, he felt himself being lifted and carried toward the alley. Unable to do anything more than struggle feebly, he was thrown into a waiting cargo van which rapidly drove off. The neighborhood remained quiet, no lights came one, and no one was nearby. The abductors felt they had succeeded in avoiding attention from potential witnesses.

With Lee driving, the van entered an abandoned, unlighted parking lot in a warehouse district twelve miles away and stopped abruptly.

The floor of the van had been carpeted with plastic film to prevent blood stains. Brian lay moaning for several minutes until finally J.W. said, "Word has come to us that you are mistreating you wife and kids. That must stop now. Get it?"

"Who the hell are you," Brian asked weakly, spitting blood.

"We defend those who can't defend themselves. We are in the business of educating assholes like you that you must change your behavior or pay a price. We want to help you, so here's what you will do, so pay close attention. First, you will apologize to Maggie for your behavior in a hand written letter and assure her that she and the kids will be safe when they return home. We'll give you a P.O. box number to send the letter. Then you will make an appointment with a psychiatrist who will examine you and provide a course of treatment to help you deal with your behavior issues. Whether this treatment works or not is up to you. But in any case, you will never again touch Maggie or your children in anger. If you do, we will know about it and you will be whacked, plain and simple. You will simply disappear. Is that clear? And finally, no more tattoos. See, real men don't hurt women, they protect them, and those tattoos don't really express your manhood, they only mark you as a gutless wimp."

"Now we'll drop you at the nearest fire station. The EMTs will give you first aid and take you to the ER," said Lee. "Your recovery will take a while, but it'll give you time to think about your future. And don't even think about reporting this to the police. The ER people will do that as they are required to, but you will simply say that you were involved in a fight and don't want to pursue the matter."

"Are we clear on everything?" demanded J.W. Without requiring an answer, he went on. "You will find an envelope taped to your back door. In it will be instructions for what you will do. Take them very seriously unless you want to see us again. If there's a next time, you will not survive it. "

The bloodied plastic film was folded up tightly and deposited into a nearby dumpster. Each page of instructions and the envelope was carefully wiped clean of fingerprints and surface DNA before being taped to the Stadtler's back door.

SIX MONTHS LATER, Maggie told her pastor that Brian had completely reversed the way he conducted himself at home. "It's truly a miracle," she said. "He treats me with respect. No more cursing or rough stuff. He's actually having some of his tattoos removed. The garage gym is gone and the kids are much happier. When he was released from the hospital, he started seeing a therapist. It sure worked. Thank you, thank you."

"God be praised," said the reverend with a smile.

22
The Sermon

"Talking and eloquence are not the same."

– Ben Jonson

In the basement, all five *Committee* members were present to review the latest operation.

"We'll keep an eye on Mr. Stadtler. If he falls off the wagon, we'll apply more stringent measures to ensure the safety of Maggie and the kids," Lee reported.

Conversation turned to the justification of what they were doing. This was a topic of ongoing concern for the group. Soul searching and guilt trips always followed each operation. Did we do the right thing? Did the punishment fit the crime? How much longer can we do this and continue to escape detection? "After all," said Phil, "we're committing felony crimes in response to other felony crimes, and some of them aren't even felonies. Kidnapping, physical assault, not to mention murder, aren't exactly some people's idea of criminal justice."

"Just look at what's happening nationally, especially in Chicago and Detroit," offered Derek, who, as co-founder of the *Committee,* also had the strongest defense of their reason for being. "The population of Detroit was almost two million at one time. Today, it's down to about 750,000. Population collapse resulted in almost 80,000 empty houses, many of which have been razed to create open space and prevent druggies from squatting in them. Ambulances refuse to enter some neighborhoods without a police escort because of the danger involved.

"City leaders had to make drastic budget cuts including a forty percent reduction in the police force. Crime skyrocketed. The rate of violence in Detroit is five times the national average and fewer than 10% of crimes are cleared by arrests. You're ten times more likely to be murdered in Detroit than in New York City. Another severe problem is forty-six percent of the adult population is functionally illiterate. The homicide rate in Chicago and Baltimore is out of control. Do we want that for our city? I don't think so. What we do is a stream of piss against a forest fire, but at least it's something. If we can deal with a few of the creeps who make trouble, isn't it worth the risk?"

"Action against violent criminals is one thing, but reactions to cursing in class or wife beating? Come on!" demanded Phil. "I think we have gone off the rails by spending resources on that type of operation, not to mention the risk involved."

"Women and children have to be protected," said Derek. "That's always been one of our guiding principles. No piece-of-crap husband or boyfriend should get away with beating up his female partner. It's true we can't possibly deal with every case, but we can make a difference when something like that comes to our attention and we can effectively confront it."

Derek's attitude was fortified by the recent national MeToo movement that arose following several well publicized incidents of sexual harassment and assaults committed by certain celebrities and politicians against women. He went on a rant.

"Unfortunately, those creeps are well protected in other cities. We would never be able to get close to them with our form of justice. And how can hundreds of murders every year be tolerated in Chicago while local authorities remain indifferent? Is it because a large majority of victims and perps are African American? And why are dope pushers who sell lethal substances called "non-violent" offenders?

"How can priests get away with sexually abusing children? These incidents are not just mortal sins, they are vile felony crimes, aided and abetted by the church hierarchy. Priests are male mammals with natural sex drives. They all have it, it's strong and it can't be tamped down by a stupid vow, no matter how solemn. Celibacy is unnatural and violates a man's basic, God-given instincts. Did you know that thirty-nine popes were married in the early centuries after Christ? And eleven of the twelve apostles were married. The Catholic Church did not officially ban marriage of its priests until the twelfth century. When the church comes to its senses and ordains women and allows priests to marry, this scandal will go away, or at least be greatly diminished."

"Thank you for that sermon, Derek," said J.W. "Now can we get back to a specific case?"

23
Iniquitous Clergy

"These are called the pious frauds of friendship."

– Henry Fielding

Reports of sexual abuse of children by clergymen had been in the news for many years. Religious believers and nonbelievers alike were appalled at the level of sex crimes committed by those in positions of trust. Especially atrocious was the scandal in the Catholic Church. A cascade of news reports implicated at first dozens, then hundreds of priests accused of hideous acts committed against young boys. A few girls were molested, but pre-teen boys constituted the great majority of victims. Especially outrageous were attempts by the hierarchy to cover up the scandal by simply moving offending priests from one parish to another where they could find fresh victims. It was revealed that several bishops and even one cardinal, a "Prince of the Church," not only were complicit in the cover up, but they themselves had engaged in unspeakable behavior with children and seminarians years before.

Catholics wondered if this was going on in modern times, to what extent did it happen in past times, even back to the earliest days of the church? When reports first emerged publicly, many parishioners rationalized that it was just a small number of errant priests and was not the fault of the church. As the scandal broadened and enveloped every diocese in the country, and when a grand jury in Pennsylvania reported that over 300 priests had molested more than 1,000 children in the state over a period of years, and when the five dioceses in New Jersey joined with more than 100 across the nation publicly naming more than 3,600 credibly accused priests, it was widely assumed that this was more than "just the priests," but represented the institution—the church.

Appalled at these revelations, large numbers of previously committed worshipers stopped attending Mass and many abandoned their faith entirely. Critics inside and outside the church strongly questioned the vow of celibacy priests were required to make at ordination.

REVEREND MICHAEL TURLOV was assistant pastor and youth director at Desert View Community Church in a tony neighborhood of Northeast Phoenix. It was a position he had occupied for two years following his graduation from seminary and service at a community church in Flagstaff for three years prior to coming to Phoenix. He was admired by parishioners and popular with youngsters who participated in many activities he planned and conducted for them. Twenty-seven years old and never married, he possessed a clean-cut appearance—medium height, not overweight, clean shaven, short haircut, no tattoos, and always neatly dressed. Young, single women members of the church found him attractive and came onto him in various subtle and not-so-subtle ways, but he avoided dating or entering into personal relationships.

As far as anyone knew, he led a private life with little socializing outside church. His unmarried status troubled the search committee and head pastor during the interview process, but he came with outstanding recommendations. A background check turned up nothing but a couple of traffic citations several years earlier. His credit record was clean.

He was always happy to accept invitations to family dinners—occasions that usually found him entertaining the children with various brain teaser games and adventure stories. Parents were delighted with his ability to relate to their kids. He was admired as a positive role model. During his second year at the church, he began offering counseling and tutoring services to boys and girls age eight to fourteen. He worked with youngsters who needed help with school studies or were troubled with various personal issues. Divorced or alcoholic parents, drug use, bullying at school, and academic struggles were among the problems that came to his attention. He had no background in psychology and was not trained in counseling methods, but his efforts seemed to produce positive results. Tutoring in math and science at the middle-school level was a specialty. These sessions were conducted one-on-one in his office, usually late afternoon and evening after church offices had closed and no other staff was present. He told students and parents this scheduling was best because the building was quiet and interruptions could be avoided.

Tina and Dale Shaw, ages thirteen and ten, were among his first clients. They had weekly back-to-back appointments. Near the end of his third session with them, "Reverend Mike," as he preferred to be addressed, hugged both in a too-tight embrace and slowly moved his hands to their posterior regions gently massaging their buttocks. Both kids tried to pull away but he assured them that the Lord approved of loving relationships between adults and children and they would feel better if they allowed him to explore their bodies. This led to gentle stroking of their arms and in Tina's case, touching of her budding breasts through her clothes.

Following this session with Reverend Mike, both kids were sullen and silent when their mother picked them up. Tina sat in a second-row seat behind the driver, and Dale in the rearmost seat of their seven-passenger van, as far away from his mom as possible. This was unusual since both kids always competed to sit in the front passenger seat.

"How did it go today," asked Marvella, their mother. Silence from the kids. "Did you hear me? How was your session?"

"Fine," is all they would say. But she noticed they were not themselves. Both kids picked at their food at dinner and said they were not hungry. Later that evening, Marvella heard Tina sobbing in her room. Knocking, then entering, she found her daughter curled up on her bed in tears.

"Tina baby, what is it? What's wrong?"

"I can't tell you. He said I couldn't tell anyone and if I did, God would punish me."

"Who honey, who told you that?" asked an alarmed Marvella.

"Mike.... at the church. Please don't make me tell," Tina pleaded.

"Honey, I'm your mother. You can tell me anything. I can see that you're deeply upset at something. What happened today with Reverend Mike?"

"I can't tell. God will send me to hell if I do. Mike said so."

Now horrified at what she was hearing, Marvella said: "Honey, that is not true. Our God is a loving God. He doesn't send children to hell on the word of a man. Now, I know something happened today and I need to know what it was so I can protect you."

"He touched me. I didn't know what to do."

"Touched you how? Honey, you can tell me."

"When we were almost done with the session, he was sitting next to me and started rubbing my neck. He said it would relax me. Then he got up and went behind my chair and rubbed my shoulders. And then... . and then his hands moved down to my chest and... ." Tina's voice quavered and trailed off.

"Did he touch your breasts? Honey, you didn't do anything wrong. You can tell me and nothing bad will happen to you."

"Yes, Mommy, with both hands, he started squeezing me so hard it hurt. He turned me around and started feeling my bottom. I knew it was wrong, but he kept telling me that God wanted this and I would feel better if I let him keep doing it. Mom, don't make me go back to see him again, I don't want to," wailed Tina, weeping. "He said this was part of God's plan to help kids grow up. We need to know the facts of life and he was only doing God's will."

Deeply shocked, Marvella was appalled and angered at what she was hearing from her daughter. "Is that all that he did? Did he touch you anywhere else?"

"No, I pulled back and moved away from him. He said not to tell anyone. If I did, God would punish both of us. He said, 'You wouldn't want that, would you?'"

"So he didn't touch you anywhere below your waist. Is that right? Are you sure?"

"His hands moved down to my waist, and then he squeezed my bottom until I pulled away. I'm telling you the truth."

"I believe you honey and don't worry baby, you won't have to see him ever again. Now what about Dale, did something happen to him?"

"He didn't say anything to me, but I could tell he was upset about something."

Marvella knocked on Dale's bedroom door. No response. "Dale, honey, it's Mom and I need to talk with you." Still no answer. She slowly opened the door and found Dale sitting on the floor by his bed. "Honey, I need to know what happened today with Reverend Mike."

"No... he said I couldn't tell anyone and if I did, God would punish everyone in our family." Dale started to sob.

"Honey, that's just not true. God doesn't punish anyone for telling the truth. Now, I know Mike did something to you and we need to talk about it." Her anger was rising, she knew it could not be obvious to Dale.

"He unzipped his pants and pulled out his ... thing."

"Do you mean his penis, honey? It's okay, you can tell me.

"Yes, he started rubbing it and then told me to rub it. He said it was God's will that I learn how to be a man. I thought it was wrong, but I didn't know what to do."

"Did he make you undress and did he undress?"

"No, he just pulled down his pants and told me to squeeze his... his penis. Oh, Mom, it was awful. He started rubbing himself and after a couple of minutes, some stuff came out and he pulled up his pants. Did I do wrong? Will God punish me?"

Now beside herself with fury, Marvella calmly assured Dale that God would not harm him or any of the family. "Did he touch you anywhere on your body with his penis?"

"No."

"Are you sure about that, because if he did, we will have you examined by our doctor."

"I'm sure, Mom, I'm sure."

"Okay, honey, I want you to take a warm bath, put on your jammies and go to bed, okay? I want you to put this out of your mind."

Worried that he would react violently against Reverend Mike, Marvella hesitated to tell Bert, her husband and father of her children, what she had just learned. But later in the evening, she decided he must know what happened. He sat mute and shocked as she related the story as told to her by Tina and Dale.

"That miserable bastard. We can't let the kids go back to another session with him. That's for starters." Realizing what had happened to his children and cursing the man who had harmed them, Bert started to cry with rage, holding his head in both hands. "Are you sure that neither of them were penetrated?"

"I persuaded both of them to tell me everything that happened and I'm pretty sure nothing like that happened," said Marvella.

"We need to be sure. Call Doc Spencer and make an appointment for him to examine both of them as soon as possible. He'll want to do blood tests or whatever they do to detect STDs. God, this is a nightmare! If we report this to the pastor, it's our word against Mike's and you know how popular he is with the congregation." Bert continued: "You know the other parents with kids in his program. Talk with the moms and ask them if anything unusual has happened to their kids." Both parents were in tears.

During the next two weeks, Marvella talked with three of the mothers whose children were involved in Reverend Mike's counseling program. She broached the issue by asking if they had noticed any difference in the behavior of their kids following the sessions. Two of the three said their children were enthusiastic about the program and said they had a really good time with Mike. A troubled expression crossed the face of Mary Ellen, the third mother. "Now that you mention it, my Jonathan has had four sessions with Mike for math tutoring and doesn't want to meet with him again. I couldn't convince him to tell me why not."

"I don't want to alarm you unnecessarily," said Marvella, "but you should know that both my kids were very upset after their last session two weeks ago. I managed to pry it out them that he sexually molested them. They said it was all touching and rubbing of private parts. I'm pretty sure there was no penetration of their bodies. Bert and I will not allow our kids any further contact with him and I think we need to report this to the pastor if you can manage to pull a similar story from Jonathan."

The following Sunday, Mary Ellen asked to speak privately with Marvella after services. "After many tears and much pleading from me, Johnny finally told me that Mike had pulled down his trousers and masturbated in front of him. Jerry is in a fury and I'm worried he will confront Mike."

As it happened, Marvella was a friend of Maggie Stadtler, who was also a member of the church with her two children and her husband Brian, who had started attending regularly after recovering from a physical attack. Maggie confided that the church pastor had given her the phone number of someone who could provide a solution to the abuse she was suffering at the hands of Brian. "They roughed him up very severely, but he got the message and the turnaround of his behavior has been remarkable."

"Could you give me that number?" asked Marvella.

"Absolutely."

Arriving home, Marvella punched in the number Maggie had given her. A male voice answered after three rings. "Good morning, may I help you?"

"I'm told you can help people who have a problem with bad behavior of someone they know. Is this true? Am I calling the correct number?"

"How did you get this number may I ask?"

"My friend, Maggie Stadtler referred you. She said you solved a problem she was having with her husband. Who am I speaking with?"

After a pause of several seconds, the voice said "You don't need to know my name, but we'll try to help. Tell me why you've called."

Marvella related the entire story of Tina and Dale's experience with Reverend Mike together with that of Jonathan, son of Mary Ellen and Jerry Butler.

"Perhaps we can help. What do you want done?"

"Reverend Mike needs to leave our church and never serve in any position involving children again. We hesitate to tell our pastor or report it to the police because the scandal would split our parish. Mike is quite popular and has many friends among our members. Most of them wouldn't believe these accusations and would take his side. From what the kids said, I'm not sure his behavior would rise to the level of a crime. We want to spare our children the pain of providing evidence in the event of an investigation or at worst, a trial. If he isn't stopped now, he may graduate to more serious molestations involving... God forbid, rape."

"Understood. Give us some time to review this matter and do some private investigating. I'll get back to you by the end of next week. In the meantime, don't let your kids get near this guy in a one-on-one situation."

"We've already made that decision. But please hurry. He may be doing this with other children in our church that we don't know about," pleaded Marvella.

"By the way, what you have described to me is certainly a crime. I'll be in touch."

DEREK OVERTON ASKED his police colleague Norman Wilkie to run a background check on Michael Turlov. It revealed a series of complaints of a sexual nature from two churches where he had been employed before coming to Phoenix. He had never been arrested. Instead, when his employers were asked to provide a reference, they falsely provided positive reports motivated by their desire to rid themselves of his presence before he caused major damage to the reputation of their churches.

At a regular meeting of the *Committee* in his basement, Derek was steamed. "Clearly, this guy is a pedophile. We can't let this asshole continue his behavior. He could step up his 'sessions' into something far more serious than what my caller described to me."

The *Committee* arrived at a quick decision to plan and conduct an operation designed to deal with Reverend Michael Turlov.

FOUR EVENINGS LATER, Mike answered a loud knock on his apartment door. Two men, dressed in gray sweats with bandanas covering their faces, forced him back into the room and slammed the door behind them. "We're here to have a little discussion about your contact with certain children at church."

"I don't know what you're talking about and you are committing a crime by busting in here like this," Mike yelled.

"Lower you voice and sit down, dude... listen very carefully. We know all about your fun and games with the kids who attend your tutoring sessions. So don't insult our intelligence by denying it."

Mike's move to reach his cell phone brought a hard backhand slap to his face from Lee, splitting his upper lip. "You can make that call after we're gone, but for now you need to pay attention. What we have to say is important to your future. So here's the deal. You can't have any further contact with children here or anywhere else, so this is what you will do. You will resign your position with the church effective immediately. You will provide an explanation that you were assaulted while walking home after dark and are in need of a change in your situation to fully recover. Then you will never again apply for or accept any position anywhere involving interaction with children. If you do, we will know and we will visit you again. If there's a next time, it will not be nearly as pleasant as this. Got it?"

With that, J.W. delivered a hard punch to Mike's face that resulted in a large bruise and puffed up black eye the next day. This was followed by a sharp blow with a blackjack to his right knee, not causing a fracture, but leaving the victim howling with pain. Pressing a large semi-automatic pistol to the center of Mike's forehead, J.W. whispered in his ear, "Your filthy behavior with kids stops now. Get it?" Silence from Mike.

"Answer me, punk, or we will hurt you where it'll do the most good."

"Yeah, I get it. Just don't hit me again," Mike whimpered.

"And one more thing. Do not contact any church member. You'll see us again soon if you report this to the police or fail to resign from your church position tomorrow."

NEXT DAY, MIKE limped into the pastor's study and laid a hand-written resignation on his desk.

"Oh Lord, what happened to you?" the pastor asked.

"I was jumped on the street last night by a couple of thugs. They beat me up and stole my wallet before I knew what was happening."

"Have you seen a doctor and reported this to the police? And why are you quitting? This makes no sense."

"I need time away from my job to reassess my career and heal, mentally and physically. I regret leaving you on such short notice, but that's the way I want it. Please understand."

"At least let me speak to our parish board before you leave. We might be able to work things out for you if we could understand your distress,"

"Thank you, but that won't be necessary," said Reverend Mike, as he headed for the door.

A bulletin was emailed to all parishioners:

> We regret to inform you that our youth minister, Reverend Michael Turlov, has resigned his position with our church effective immediately. Sadly, he was physically assaulted near his home two days ago. His injuries were not life threatening but did cause severe bruising to his face and left leg. He is leaving us for the reason that he needs time to fully recover from the emotional trauma of this experience. He has asked that we not provide any going-away event. We respect his decision and wish him the best in his future endeavors.

This message generated a flood of questions from church members, many of whom were upset and not satisfied with the explanation of Mike's sudden departure. The pastor could only repeat what he knew. A month later, an uneasy calm descended upon the church and the issue was eventually put aside.

24

Life on the Street

"Our life is but a span, and cruel death is always near."

– The New England Primer

Charles (Chuck) Singleton had been homeless almost three years. His life had spiraled downward after a divorce and loss of employment. Unable to find a job and without means to pay alimony to his ex-wife, he exhausted his meager savings and was evicted from his apartment. He had no choice but to enter a local men's shelter but soon couldn't tolerate the noise and confusion caused by other guests. So he hit the streets with a backpack and a few belongings. He returned to the shelter about once a week to take a shower and get a hot meal. A local church sponsored a free laundry program at a coin-op facility for people in need, so he usually had reasonably clean clothes.

His new vocation was collecting recyclables, mainly aluminum cans, which he redeemed for cash at a nearby recycling center. The best source of cans proved to be trash receptacles in local parks where picnickers deposited them. He found a shopping cart abandoned in a ditch and used it to transport his daily collection of goods. He learned to maximize the number of cans he could carry by depressing their sides and smashing them down to an inch in size. This, together with panhandling, produced enough income to support his drinking habit which was more intense after he became homeless. His beverage of choice was either Thunderbird or Night Train, two cheap fortified wines with alcohol content up to 18% (36 proof). Known as "bum wine" or "brown bag vino," they were originally marketed as sweetened desert wines, but quickly found favor with street alcoholics who learned they packed a quick buzz at low cost. Drinking allowed Chuck to partially escape from his circumstances. Shelter workers warned him about the dangers of alcoholism, but he disregarded their advice with the excuse "I can handle it."

One day in early summer he was rummaging through a dumpster behind a strip mall. He normally avoided this because of the filth and odor, but it sometimes yielded an unexpected treasure. He once found a child's bicycle in pretty good shape that he sold for ten dollars. This was enough to keep him in wine for two days.

But he needed another score and when searching through the rubbish, he pulled a black plastic bag from the bottom of the dumpster and felt something heavy in it. Ripping the bag open, he found used paper cups, wadded up newspapers and then... *what*? It was a pistol! *What the hell is this doing here? Someone must have had a good reason for getting rid of this thing.* Handling it very carefully, he found it unloaded. He didn't know much about guns, but he recognized it as a thing of value and possibly convertible into cash.

Word went out on the street that Chucker, as he was known among acquaintances in the homeless community, had a "piece" for sale. None of his homeless companions were interested but an inquiry soon arrived in the person of Carlos, a tough looking, heavily tattooed Hispanic guy who had heard of the item through an informant on the street. He approached Chuck without introducing himself and asked to see the gun, not totally believing what he had heard. Chuck didn't have it with him at the time but promised to retrieve it from its hiding place and show it to him at ten the following morning at an agreed upon location.

BOTH MEN SHOWED UP at the appointed time in an alley where they had some privacy.

"So whatcha got?" asked Carlos. Chuck gingerly removed the gun from a brown paper bag and handed it over. It was a .45 semi-automatic Glock.

"You stole this, right?" demanded Carlos. "How did you come by it?"

"Not stolen, found it in a dumpster," said Chuck. "In back of some stores. I go there sometimes to see what I can find. It usually doesn't pay off, but this time I got lucky. So what do you think? I don't have all day."

"I think I want it, how much are you asking?"

"Four hundred and that's a bargain. I asked around to find out what it's worth and that seems about right."

"I'll give you three hundred cash, right now. Take it or leave it, dude."

After a moment's hesitation, Chuck decided it best not to haggle and agreed. "But no hundreds, I want it all in twenties."

"Okay, no problem," said Carlos, peeling off fifteen twenties from his money clip and handing them over. "Thanks man, have a good day."

The transaction completed, Chuck went directly to the nearest MacDonald's and ordered two Big Macs, a large order of fries, and a chocolate malt. Afterward, he visited his favorite liquor store and purchased two 750ml bottles of Thunderbird wine. He usually bought it in pints, but this time he wanted to share a bottle with his cronies on the street.

That was a mistake. As he passed the bottle around in the park, he inadvertently exposed his roll of twenties. One of his "friends" observed this with interest. The next night, Chuck was beaten severely and relieved of his remaining cash. Four days later, he died in the hospital from a weakened immune system brought on by alcoholism complicated by the physical trauma of his wounds.

Such tragedies were not uncommon on the street.

25

Street Extortion

"Pay up or suffer the consequences."

Carlos Garcia was a member of Los Hombres Grandes, a street gang based in Los Angeles looking to establish themselves in Phoenix. Their primary activity was selling "protection" to small retailers owned by other Hispanics and Asians. They also marketed cocaine to anyone who could afford their prices. Carlos needed a weapon to display in full sight of his retailer clients to convince them to subscribe to his protection services. The monthly "fee" varied from $100 to $500 per business depending on several factors. This racket netted the gang upwards of twenty grand a month in one neighborhood of LA alone. If any small shop owner in Phoenix refused to pay or didn't pay on time, he might find the front windows of his business shattered or tagged with graffiti. It was better to pay.

Carlos methodically visited small businesses in south Phoenix during the next year offering his "protection" services. His initial approach was very friendly and professional, telling owners that a variety of bad actors including rampant teenagers and street thugs were active in the neighborhood and were committing everything from vandalism to muggings and armed robberies. His pitch was protection from these hoodlums. "You don't want these guys messing with you and we can prevent that." Of course, his fellow gang members were the ones doing these crimes.

He operated an effective shakedown practice, rarely threatening shop owners directly, but assuring them that their "protection" fee was worth the price. When owners refused to pay or were slow in remitting the extortion, they found themselves on the receiving end of vandalism including broken windows or vile graffiti sprayed on walls and doors. A couple of them actually called police to report the attempted shakedowns. This resulted in violent retribution sending Gloria Sanchez, a flower shop owner, to the ER with a fractured jaw and severe facial bruising administered by Juan, an operative of Carlos. He entered the shop at closing time one Saturday in a Guy Fawkes mask, demanded money and attacked her with a baseball bat. He was out the door in under three minutes. The flower shop had no surveillance camera and there were no witnesses so police were unable to pursue an effective investigation.

Neighboring business owners were appalled. Several felt that enough was enough and decided to take action to defend themselves and put a stop to the extortion they had been suffering.

The extortion racket had been reported to police when it began, but ensuing investigations so far hadn't yielded results, mostly owing to lack of cooperation from shop owners who feared retribution from the gang.

Police Detective Jake Browning was invited to a meeting in the back room of a dry cleaning establishment a few doors from the flower shop where those attending decided to conduct a sting operation.

The store's owner remarked that Carlos was due for his monthly visit the following Monday and would follow his usual pattern of asking how the business was going. "Any problems with the street?" he would ask and then demand payment of the "protection fee" while exposing the Glock in his waist band.

"Okay, here's what we'll do," said Detective Browning. "I'll get our technical people to set up surveillance equipment, at least two cameras, where they won't be noticed. Two of us will monitor the camera feed from this room. It's out of sight from the cash register. When he asks for payment, try to stall him as long as possible and keep him talking. Say something like 'I don't have the money now, just give me a couple more days. Tell me again what protection you provide.'

"This will likely cause him to raise his demand for payment and probably threaten you. At that point, we'll rush him and take him into custody. It'll be so quick he won't know what hit him. You'll need to duck behind the counter immediately when that happens in case he is able to grab his weapon. But keep him talking as long as possible. We will get everything he says on the record."

It worked out precisely as they had planned. Carlos entered the shop at eleven o'clock the following Monday morning, walked up to the counter and said "It's that time of the month again and I'm sure you want another thirty days of protection." After two or three minutes of back and forth hesitation by the shop owner and veiled threats from Carlos, Detective Browning and two uniformed officers suddenly appeared, immobilized him and placed him under arrest.

Informed of his Miranda rights, Carlos immediately clammed up and said he wanted a lawyer. The Glock was placed in an evidence bag and taken to the police lab for analysis.

The serial number was run through a review by the Bureau of Alcohol, Firearms, and Tobacco (BATF). A report came back saying the weapon was legally purchased by one Marjorie Overton from a licensed gun store in Dallas, Texas, two years earlier. A record check revealed the weapon was reported stolen by Marjorie several months previously.

Carlos was convicted of attempted extortion and sentenced to five years in prison. Other gang members made no move to replace him in the racket and eventually migrated back to Los Angeles. South Phoenix shop owners enjoyed their release from a serious threat.

FOLLOWING UP ON the stolen gun report, Detectives McAvoy and Browning found the address of Marjorie Overton and knocked on her door two days later.

Identifying themselves, Browning informed her the visit was routine and asked to come in. She invited them in. Derek was not at home.

"You filed a report some months back about a Glock pistol being stolen. It was found in the possession of a criminal suspect, and we need to know the circumstances of that theft," said Browning in a menacing tone.

Marjorie was shocked at learning the gun had been found and traced back to her. She knew she had to think fast.

"I bought the gun in Dallas during a visit there for personal protection here at home. I inadvertently left it in the car one day. The car was left unlocked and when I returned from shopping, it was missing. I knew I had been very careless."

"But if you placed it in your home for personal protection in your home, why did you have it in your car?' asked McAvoy.

Caught off-guard by this question, Marjorie didn't have a good answer. "I... I really don't remember."

"Do you have a permit for that gun?" asked Browning.

Marjorie was not intimidated by this question. "You should know as well as anyone that a permit is not needed to own a weapon in Arizona."

"Does the name Carlos Garcia mean anything to you?"

"Absolutely not, never heard of him."

"The gun was taken from him after an arrest for extorting shop owners in South Phoenix. When asked how he came to own it, he said he bought it from a homeless man who found it in a trash dumpster."

"NEVER AGAIN!" DEREK emotionally shouted to his colleagues. "Never again, can we dispose of an intact weapon. They must be cut into pieces and placed separately in the smelliest dumpsters we can find all over town. Totally destroyed. Throw some of the pieces into lakes and ponds. Remember that! This was a serious breach of our protocols and now the cops are in possession of evidence that comes back to us."

26

Anonymous Lead

"We know a subject ourselves,
or we know where we can find information upon it."

— Samuel Johnson

Sergeant Alex Fabens occupied a desk position in the homicide division of the police department. His job was to review current cases and provide analysis of evidence to detectives who were investigating specific offenses. Three homicides over the past year were committed by snipers using sophisticated weapons at distances ranging from fifty to one hundred yards. This obviously required careful planning and execution by expert marksmen with skills gained most likely in the military. These cases were eerily similar and Fabens was quick to point this out to detectives.

Tomas Guerrero-Ochoa was assassinated with a .270 Winchester round, Levone Barcroft with .223 Remington, and Reuben Bernitz was gunned down with .350 Winchester Legend probably from an assault weapon. Weapons were different in each case, but the *modus operandi* was almost identical. James Arneson was eliminated with a handgun in a simultaneous hit on Barcroft. These were all well planned and executed killings by professional assailants.

In each case, the victim was a criminal, or in the Bernitz case, someone who had committed a physical assault against his helpless mother.

In conference with Detectives Jake Browning and Alan McAvoy, Fabens stated the obvious.

"These hits were the work of a coordinated operation by highly proficient gunmen, sent to carry out the kills by someone in authority. Evidence at the scene was almost non-existent leading to the conclusion that a lot of thought went into the actions. These were professional hits."

"Our usual informants haven't heard anything on the street," said McAvoy. "We're not able to piece together anything that makes sense. The crimes were conducted in vastly different locations across the metro area and there seems to be no commonality except for the sniper aspect."

"Motivation seems to be getting rid of bad guys. You know, bad guys whacking other bad guys," said McAvoy. "Maybe we should just stand aside and let the snipers do our work for us."

"Very funny, Mac. If this kind of thing goes on, we'll have a serious problem on our hands," said Browning. "Right now, the only common denominator is the sniper thing. Maybe we need to develop more street 'humint'[4] to provide some usable leads."

A few weak leads from anonymous callers came in and were investigated to no avail. Nothing concrete came to their attention.

---

[4] Human intelligence.

A week later, McAvoy's desk phone rang. Without identifying himself, the caller said "You need to take a look at a retired homicide detective for those sniper killings."

"Who is this?" demanded McAvoy.

"Let's just say that I'm a concerned citizen who is worried about vigilantism." Click.

"That was an interesting call," McAvoy told Browning. "The guy said something about a retired detective who might know something in connection with the sniper killings."

"No kidding? What did he say?"

"That's it, just said take a look at a retired homicide detective."

"It's worth following up on. That's the first promising lead we've had."

Twelve homicide detectives had retired from the force over the past three years. Four had moved out of the state, two relocated to scenic Prescott, Arizona, and the remaining six still resided in the Phoenix metro area. Four others had resigned prior to reaching retirement age. One by one, their personnel records were examined to discover anything out of the ordinary. Nothing unusual was found, except in one. An interoffice memo in Derek J. Overton's file noted that he had expressed profane outrage on two occasions after defendants he had collared were found not guilty at trial. The memo noted "unprofessional conduct and disruptive behavior" in the presence of other police personnel. It went on to say that Lieutenant Overton had apologized. This occurred after he was placed in command of the homicide unit. No disciplinary action was taken.

"We can check cell phone records to trace his movements if we can get a judge to issue an order under SCA[5] rules," said McAvoy.

That proved to be a non-starter. Overton was not a defendant in a criminal matter; therefore, no legal access to phone records was possible. It would have failed anyway since he used burners instead of a standard cell phone.

McAVOY AND BROWNING interviewed each of the six local retirees in their respective homes. They made an appointment with a pretext: "The department is looking to provide more effective retirement counseling for our people and we'd like to get your input to shape that program. We need to get some background on homicide investigations to improve our training techniques." Each of the former detectives readily agreed to the meeting—eager to assist the stated objective. Interviews began with casual conversations intended to put the interviewee at ease. "How have you been? How is retirement treating you? How is the family? Are you playing any golf?"

After pleasantries and a brief period of small talk, the conversation turned to topics of police procedure and current cases under investigation.

"The department is reviewing our approach to interrogations. When you were interviewing suspects or

---

[5] The 1986 Stored Communications Act (SCA) protects electronic data from disclosure to unauthorized parties. However, a judge can compel carriers to provide information such as phone numbers called and answered, time and length of those calls, and cell towers the devices connect to enabling an approximation of the callers' locations short of issuing a search warrant.

witnesses, can you think of an example when you asked a specific question that was answered in a way that materially changed the direction of your investigation?" asked Browning.

Answers varied from "Can't think of any" to long, rambling discourses yielding little of value. Other questions centered on insights into evidence gathering and other minutia of homicide work. Gradually, talk turned to personal matters designed to ascertain how subjects spent leisure time. "Have you kept up your shooting range skills? Are you into hunting and fishing?" If the answer was yes to hunting, the obvious follow-up questions were "What type of hunting rifle do you prefer? Do you do any target shooting?" If the answer was affirmative, questions followed about locations, favorite ranges, and preference of pistols over rifles. None of the answers turned up any similarity to weapons used in the sniper killings.

Retirement counseling did not come up.

McAvoy and Browning interviewed the managers of all local shooting ranges with pictures of the six retired detectives without a single recognition.

The detectives reviewed their notes after each interview. "Overton seemed nervous and uncomfortable... some of his answers were evasive," said McAvoy. "And he rambled on too much. He seemed to be intent on throwing us off the subject."

"I think you're right. He's a retired cop... one of us. It's unthinkable he's mixed up in anything illegal. How do we process this?"

"We have no choice," said McAvoy. "We need to look at him more closely. Did you notice his southern drawl? I remember a couple of assault reports where the victim described one of the guys as overweight and had that kind of twang."

In the following days, the team canvassed neighbors, interviewed Derek's former colleagues, accessed his bank records, and reviewed his financial history. Derek was tailed for two weeks. Nothing unusual was discovered.

PERIOD THREE

27

Remorse

"Secret guilt by silence is betrayed."

– Richard Cumberland

Alone with his thoughts, Phil Maguire alternated between cold comfort with the outcome of the *Committee's* various operations and a sense of deep regret colored by guilt at the crimes committed in the name of "justice." He confided to Dave Baumann that the methods employed were risky in the extreme and sure to falter at some point, resulting in exposure of the *Committee's* existence and probably its members.

"We can't go on like this," he told Dave. "I'm going to propose a moratorium in our operations for at least six months to assess our overall approach and try to determine the status of investigation of the operations we've conducted to date. I have this terrible dread that we're on the cusp of making a huge mistake that will take us all down."

"I agree," said Dave. "The nonfatal punishments we've inflicted are deeply satisfying to me and effective in deterring adverse behaviors of the recipients. But killing is a very different thing. Regardless of how justified we think it is, we're going way out on a limb and at some point, it'll break off and we'll be in deep shit."

"I pray about this every day," said Phil. "I go to Mass weekly, sometimes two or three times a week. I confess my sins and receive absolution with acts of penance. My priest tells me God grants us discernment and the intellectual ability to determine greater goods and greater evils and to act accordingly. He is clear that murder is a mortal sin that merits eternal damnation unless it's forgiven in the sacrament of confession and absolution. A component of absolution is commitment by the sinner not to do it again. I haven't been the trigger man in any of our operations but I'm still complicit with knowledge and support of them. My priest advises me to give it up and to quit my involvement in this organization to redeem my soul."

"Are you saying your disclosed the existence of this organization to your priest?" demanded Dave.

"Only indirectly. I gave him no details, just the fact that I'm a participant with no direct role in killings or assaults. But don't worry, the confession is sealed."

Dave was shocked at Phil's rambling discourse. Deeply troubled by Phil's state of mind, he reported his concern privately to Derek.

At its next basement meeting with everyone present, the *Committee* discussed various matters at length including the risk of exposure. Derek expressed strong opposition to halting operations, even temporarily. "So far as we know, we're safe from official scrutiny and I see no reason to back off now."

"It's the 'so far as we know' that worries me," said Phil. "What we are doing is immoral."

"Yeah, but we're not monks hidden away in cloisters and this is not a morality show," replied Derek. "We need something to carry with us each time we go into the fight, something that drives us. That something is providing closure to victims."

Phil continued, "We know that retired police detectives, including you Derek, have been interviewed with the pretext of improving the department's retirement counseling program. We hear these conversations have turned to hunting and types of weapons used. Why would the interviewers be interested in the type of rifles used by hunters except to learn if there is any correlation with those used in our final solution operations? Maybe I'm being paranoid, but I'm worried that police investigations are creeping closer."

"When they visited me," said Derek, "the conversation was cordial and not at all aggressive. I detected no suspicion on their part about my personal life after retirement."

"But we don't know what conclusions they reached," replied Dave. "What if they get a search warrant for this house? What would they find in this basement?"

"Absolutely nothing," said Derek. "We keep no records of any kind and no weapons are kept here. Anyway, obtaining a search warrant requires probable cause and no judge will issue one in the absence of evidence of a crime. In any case, they know nothing about any of you. We need to stop worrying."

"I'm still in favor of suspending operations for six months just to see if there's any heat from an investigation," said Phil. "Let's take a break from all this, it's very stressful on all of us."

The next hour of discussion led to a decision to suspend operations for six months.

28
Hit Man

*"He is the last recourse in times when laws are so twisted
that justice goes unserved. He is a man who controls his
destiny through his private code of ethics; who feels no
twinge of guilt at doing his job. He is a professional killer."*

– Rex Feral, *Secrets of an Assassin*

During his detective career with the PD, Overton remembered three homicides among others that were never solved. Victims included two well-known businessmen and a high school science teacher. There were no witnesses in two of the cases, only the teacher's wife in the other. Usable evidence was lacking in all three. Investigators unearthed no strong leads. It all added up to the conclusion that these were professional "hits" executed by highly skilled contract killers. The crimes occurred six month apart and the *modus operandi* was similar in each case. Victims were shot with small caliber hand guns when answering door bells at home after 10:00 p.m. At this hour, streets were quiet and neighbors reported hearing no gunshots leading to the conclusion that silencers were employed. The killer acted quickly in each case.

Interviews with victim's spouses and friends revealed that each had a gambling addiction and owed over ten thousand dollars to local bookies who were also in the loan sharking business. They had all been threatened with physical violence unless payment was forthcoming. Two were severely roughed up outside their homes in broad daylight. Obviously, creditors had lost patience and decided to make an example of deadbeats who didn't pay their debts.

Derek couldn't help admiring the professionalism of the hit man (men?). They knew victims were home at that hour, walked up to the front door, rang the bell, pumped three hollow point slugs into the victims' chests when they opened the door, left no trace of evidence, and quickly walked away—all this in less than sixty seconds.

The teacher's wife accompanied her husband to answer the door bell and was standing about six feet away. Despite her shock at witnessing the murder of her spouse, she was able to provide a rough description of the assailant—average height and weight, probably white or Hispanic, in his thirties or forties, dressed in dark clothing with a black baseball cap—a description of at least half they young men in the region at any given time and therefore useless as evidence.

Derek described these events to the *Committee* and went on to illustrate the role of a hit man. Six months had passed since operations had been suspended and he was keen for the *Committee* to become active again.

"A contract hit man is an effective response when laws are unenforced or so warped that justice is not consistently served. If we could find and hire this guy or someone like him, we could lay off much of the risk to ourselves," he said.

"He's definitely a skilled professional who carefully plans his hits and knows how to avoid detection."

Lee was assigned the task of scanning ads in local shoppers, Craiglist, and adventure-oriented magazines to identify leads to potential "contractors." After a month of reviewing ads that said something like: "Problem solver," "Personal services provided," or "Have tools, will travel," he developed a list of three contacts that seemed promising. Ads contained toll free phone numbers, nothing more.

The first two numbers yielded a "number not in service" message. The third was answered by a refined female voice saying, "Thank you for calling, may I help you?"

"Yes, I'm calling about the ad you ran in *Adventure Today* magazine and I'm wondering if you might be able provide a solution to a personal problem I'm currently dealing with."

"That depends on the type of problem you are facing. Can you give me an idea of what it is?" the voice inquired.

"A guy owes me a lot of money and refuses to pay or even return my calls or emails."

"How much money are we talking about?"

"Eighty-five thousand dollars and it's now going on a year since he's made a payment," said Lee.

The line went dead and Lee thought the conversation was over, but his phone buzzed three minutes later. Caller ID showed a different number than the one he had called. He answered, "Yes."

"Hello, it's me again. Sorry about that but we have our procedures for screening new clients. I hope you understand."

"Sure, no problem."

"Eighty-five large is a lot of money. Are you looking to collect it all or part of it, or pursue another line of relief?"

"Collection would be great, but if that's not possible, I'm willing to consider other alternatives. Do you think you can help?"

"Perhaps. The next step is to meet with you to discuss the project. This is not a commitment to assist you, merely to examine the possibility."

"Are you local? I mean in Southern Arizona?"

"Yes we are."

"Fair enough. Where and when?"

"At Ralph's Bar and Grill on North Central Avenue at two tomorrow afternoon. Can you make it?'

"I'll be there. Who will I be meeting with?" inquired Lee.

"My name is Laura and I'll be wearing a light pink blouse. By the way, what's your name?"

"It's Jack," he lied. With that the line went dead.

Lee reported the details of the call to *Committee* members that evening. "This sounds like a good lead. She was very professional and not at all weird. She's probably just a contact person, not the one who will be doing the job."

"So meet with her and let us know tomorrow night how it went," said Dave.

RALPH'S WAS A well-known watering hole popular with many professionals who officed nearby. Lee took the afternoon off work, arrived fifteen minutes early, sat at a remote table, and ordered coffee. By 2:10, Laura had not appeared and he was beginning to think she was not coming when a stunningly beautiful woman in a low-cut pink blouse entered and walked up to his table. "Jack?" she inquired.

"That's me," said Lee, awkwardly rising and shaking her hand.

"Sorry I'm late, the traffic was murder."

"Would you like something to drink, coffee, or anything stronger?

"Coffee will be good." Lee waved the server over and placed the order.

After a minute or so of small talk, during which Lee couldn't help admiring her appearance and continually glancing at her cleavage, she said, "I need to know you're not wearing a wire. Would you mind if I do a quick electronic scan of your torso?" With Lee's agreement, she produced a small device from her bag and passed it over his chest, back, and waist as he was enjoying the upper regions of her chest and having unclean thoughts. Satisfied, she said "Tell me a little more about your problem with the debtor."

Lee managed to recover his concentration. "Before I do that, I need to know what kind of organization you represent. You are obviously the front person and you make a great first impression, but I want to know who I'm dealing with and something about your track record in solving problems."

"I represent highly skilled professionals who specialize in assisting clients to recover assets wrongfully taken, collecting legitimate debts, and otherwise providing remedies for other problems when either the client, bill collectors, or the authorities are unable to do so. We operate in total anonymity, I am the only person you will have any contact with, and you can be assured of successful results. Otherwise there is no charge."

"That sounds like what I'm looking for. Can you give me an example of a project you've done in the past?"

"I'm afraid that's impossible since client anonymity is absolutely guaranteed," she replied.

"That's exactly what I wanted to hear," said Lee, now concentrating more on what she had to say than on her bosom.

"Are your principals prepared to employ, shall we say, physical means to achieve an end?" inquired Lee cautiously.

"We can discuss that with specific agreement on the outcome you desire."

"It may be premature to ask, but what would you charge to collect eighty-five grand from this deadbeat?"

"To your knowledge, does he possess sufficient assets to pay the debt?" she asked.

"Absolutely. He owns numerous revenue-producing properties in the valley and I know for a fact that his stock portfolio runs to seven figures."

"In that case, our fee would be twenty thousand, payable only if we're able to collect. We would extract at least a hundred and five from him to cover our fee and you would net the original eighty-five."

"Speaking of a physical approach, in the event you are unable to collect the money despite your best efforts, would you be prepared to eliminate the problem altogether?" inquired Lee hoping she would catch his meaning.

"Again, we can discuss that if and when the time comes."

"I like what I'm hearing. Let me review our conversation with my people and get back to you."

"Fair enough, I'll text you a new number to call in a couple of days." She arose with a smile and walked out of the bar without shaking his hand.

DEREK HAD BEEN sitting at the bar nursing a beer when she entered. He recognized her immediately from the pink blouse. He paid his tab and left to sit in his car until she emerged after meeting with Lee. His objective was to get a make on her car and eventually identify her or at least the owner of the car.

When she emerged, she did not go to a car but started walking away. He realized that she had taken the precaution of parking elsewhere or possibly being dropped off at a location down the street and walking from there.

Very smart. These people know what they're doing.

He opened his car door, stepped out, and started following her at a distance of around a hundred feet. After two blocks, a new Jaguar sedan pulled up. She opened the door to get in. While she was getting into the passenger seat, Derek hauled out a small digital camera with electronic telephoto capacity and started snapping pictures. In Arizona, license plates are mounted only on the rear of vehicles and since the car was headed away from him, the view was perfect. He captured several high quality images, including one of her glancing backward, affording a frontal view of her face, a side view, and several shots of the license plate. The driver appeared to be a person with short blond hair, gender undetermined.

Very pleased with the photo results, Derek asked his former colleague Norm Wilkie with the PD to run the plate. The car's owner was identified as one Marcus Moretti, a resident of nearby Scottsdale. The woman was also identified. Her name was not Laura, but Deirdre Moretti, wife of Marcus.

Derek then performed a background check on both of them and found that Marcus had a record of extortion and mail fraud that had netted him millions before being arrested and convicted. Represented by a skillful criminal lawyer, he did only two years in prison and provided partial restitution to his victims. He was also a suspect in a hit job on a street drug dealer, but was not arrested. Deirdre's record was clean. They resided in a large home in an upscale Scottsdale neighborhood.

"These people are living well, where the hell is their money coming from?" mused Derek in his report to the *Committee* without revealing their last name.

"I think it's likely they're in the business of providing contract hits and if so, they would be a good fit with our operations," Lee said. "Let me meet with 'Laura' again and feel her out on the possibility of taking contracts on our two K-Market thugs."

With the *Committee's* approval, Lee punched the phone number used previously into his cell phone and tapped "Call." After four rings, a female voice said "Hello Jack, how can I help you?" It was Laura.

"I'd like to speak with you about doing a job. When can we meet?"

"Ralph's place is good, two tomorrow afternoon?"

"I'll be there."

SEATED AT THE same table at 1:45, Lee's phone buzzed. "Change of plans, Come outside and get in my car. We can take a little ride." It was Laura.

Lee got up, left a fiver on the table though he hadn't ordered anything, and walked out the front door. She motioned for him to get in the Jag. Wearing a tight fitting mid-thigh skirt, a sleeveless low cut top and elegant understated makeup, she was a stunner. Lee struggled to avoid gawking at her body, the shape of which was on full display. She was wearing a delicate perfume that he didn't remember from their previous encounter. Its aroma was so intoxicating that he began to feel slightly light headed. A few minutes later, she pulled into a strip mall parking area and killed the engine. The routine of scanning for a wire was repeated. "So what's up?"

"There's a small park a couple of blocks from here. Drive over there and we'll take a little walk. I don't want to talk in this car," said Lee, out of concern that it might be wired.

Upon arrival at the park, Lee produced a scanning device similar to one Deirdre had used. "Turnabout's fair play, right?" He enjoyed scanning the top of her bosom and waist as she leaned closer to him, smiling. She proved to be clean. They exited the car and started to walk a few steps.

"Okay Deirdre, let's cut the crap. I know who you are and I think I know the business you and Marcus are in. Forget the bullshit I told you the other day about a guy owing me eighty-five grand. He doesn't exist. That meeting was essentially an employment interview so let me cut to the chase. I need to eliminate two assholes from the face of the earth and I'm willing to pay well for the service. Interested?"

Deirdre stopped in her tracks, visibly shocked at being outed, but quickly regained her composure. "Maybe. Tell me more about the marks and where they can be found."

Lee described Alex and Rodney Perez, the two suspects in the K-Market murders but did not disclose that fact. He outlined their lifestyle habits and where they could be found.

"I'll provide pictures of the targets, descriptions of their car and home address. We know a bar they frequent. It should be very straight forward. There is one condition," he said. "They are not to be whacked where they live. It's their grandmother's house."

"Sounds doable," replied Deirdre who was now absorbed in the details. "If we accept this contract, when do you want this done?"

"ASAP or as soon as your team deems it practical with no risk."

"It's never without risk, but we are experienced professionals who know what we're doing. Our operations are carefully planned and expertly carried out. You will have no worries about anything coming back to you. In fact, I don't even know your last name and don't need to. The more anonymity, the better. Tell me, why do you want these guys eliminated?"

"You really don't need to know that," Lee replied brusquely.

He had no illusion that she had not checked him out as he had done, but her demeanor and overall tone had impressed him and he knew he was not dealing with ordinary street killers. Keen to learn more about the Moretti organization, he said, "There is a lot of risk associated with what you do. Aren't you concerned about getting caught at some point through a small mistake or someone informing on you?"

"As I said, I represent people who are professionals. We know how to avoid attention to our business and our personal finances. Our operations are meticulously programmed and carried out. And we are fortunate that the criminal justice system is so overwhelmed with details, crowded prisons, and the whole plea bargaining approach of prosecutors, so even if we are ever charged with a crime, we can be reasonably comforted that the law will be with us and not on the victim's side. Besides that, we have great legal representation."

"Let's talk about your fee," ventured Lee.

"It'll cost you twenty-five grand if we are able to do both at the same time," said Deirdre. "One at a time would be problematic since the first hit would put the other guy on alert, making him hard to find and eliminate. Fifteen up front and ten on completion of the contract."

"That's a lot of scratch for what seems to be a pretty simple job," replied Lee.

"If it were simple you'd do it yourself, wouldn't you?" she asked sarcastically.

"Okay, you're right. What type of payment do you need?"

"All used hundreds, unmarked of course."

"All right, I'll mull it over and get back to you. When I call, it'll be from a different number, not the one I've been using."

During the ride back to Ralph's, her businesslike demeanor changed. She told him how glad she was to have a new friend and how she enjoyed talking to him. Lee didn't know quite how to respond to this since their conversations had been all business. She was a very attractive woman who now seemed to be coming on to him. She complemented his appearance and his physique.

"Well, how about lunch sometime?" he asked awkwardly.

"Sure, I like conversations over lunch with interesting people. Give me a call soon."

As he was about to open the passenger door, she leaned over, smiling, and gave his left hand a gentle, prolonged squeeze, while providing a great view of her cleavage and pursing her lips slightly, said, "Thank you Jack, I'll look forward to seeing you again."

As the car drove away, Lee thought, *Is she flirting with me? What was that all about?*

29
The Contract

*"Whoever fights monsters should see to it that
in the process he does not become a monster."*

– Friedrich Nietzsche

Lee reported the details of his meeting with Deirdre to the *Committee.*

"If we decide this is a go, we'll need to approach our benefactors to provide the funds," said Derek. "Marjorie will know who to contact and how to explain it."

"So their names are Deirdre and Marcus. Do you know their last name?" asked Phil.

"It's best that we don't disclose that here. It's for your protection," replied Derek.

This seemed to satisfy Phil. Twenty minutes of conversation followed, with the others asking numerous questions answered by Lee to the best of his knowledge about the "contractors."

"It goes without saying that this is a verbal contract, nothing in writing," said Lee.

"How do we know we can depend on them to do the job without leaving any evidence? If they screw it up, our asses will be on the line," worried Phil.

"I'm the only contact they have and it will stay that way," said Lee. "They have no idea our organization exists and they know nothing about our operations."

"You learned the identities of 'Laura' and her husband pretty quickly," offered Dave. "Can we assume they have done similar research on who their client is, as well?"

"Maybe, but except for me, you're all protected," replied Lee. "How would they learn about us? Highly unlikely, so don't worry. Deirdre wasn't wearing a wire and I made sure I wasn't followed after both my meetings with her. Besides, I am relying on their greed to do the job successfully so that gives us an added level of protection. Their main interest lies in collecting the dough, not in knowing who their client is."

"So what's the next step?" asked Phil.

"Assuming we decide to place the contract with them, we will need to obtain financing from our source," said Lee.

All approved proceeding with the hits. Derek asked Marjorie to contact her source with a request for the funds. Next day, she phoned Russ Milam and asked to meet him for lunch.

"WE NEED TWENTY-FIVE thousand for an important operation in which street justice will be applied," she explained after beverages were served.

"May I know more about the targets?" he inquired.

"Two thugs who committed murder and are suspects in several armed robberies. The police are unable to advance the investigation far enough to make arrests, but we're confident of their identities. They need to be taken out before they do it again and hurt or kill someone else. That's really all I can tell you."

"That's enough. I'm still so grateful for your help with my daughter's attackers. That was your doing, right?"

Marjorie just smiled knowingly and looked away.

"You'll have the cash tomorrow. Let's meet again here, same time in the parking lot. Hundreds okay?"

She nodded with an expressionless face. "Sure."

"How will I know my investment has paid off?" he inquired.

"You'll see it on TV news and in the paper." They finished the meal and parted with a handshake.

THREE DAYS LATER, a courier delivered one hundred fifty used C-notes to Deirdre at an agreed upon location five blocks from her home. The benefactors had taken the precaution of collecting hundred dollar bills from six different banks.

The Morettis visited Etta's Place several times during the next ten days in disguises to thoroughly scope the layout, locations of exterior doors, type of customers, and existence of closed circuit television cameras. They found that rest rooms and the pool table area were not covered by surveillance cameras. This was a valuable piece of information that would greatly enhance the success of their plans. They identified the marks from pictures furnished by Lee and learned their routine of arriving at the bar after 10:00 p.m. several nights a week, but almost always on Fridays.

After completing their research and developing a meticulous plan, they decided to execute the hits the following Friday.

THEIR DRIVER DROPPED them off in the alley behind an adjoining building at 9:34 p.m. They entered the bar separately through the front door five minutes apart to avoid being seen together and perched on stools at the long bar several seats apart. Almost immediately, Deirdre was approached by guys trying to strike up a conversation and offering to by her drink which she politely declined saying, "I'm expecting someone."

The pool room had three tables at which Alex and Rodney Perez played separately with other customers, sometimes laying bets. Wearing a long sleeved blouse and tight fitting flesh colored latex gloves with nail polish in correct spots, Deirdre sidled up to Alex and offered to play a game of 8-ball which he quickly accepted. Had he noticed the latex gloves and asked about them, she would have told him that she had a silly aversion to germs. She previously observed him placing a glass of beer on a nearby table between pool shots. During their third game of 8-ball, Rodney laid his cue stick on the adjoining table and headed for the men's room, followed by Marcus. This was her signal to implement her role in the operation. While Alex's back was turned making a shot, she slipped a small packet of white powder resembling sugar into his beer. It dissolved immediately.

"Hey cowboy," she exclaimed, handing his half-full glass to him. "I'm buyin' the next round so drink up." Flattered at the attention of this sexy woman since she had earlier approached him, he grabbed the glass and downed it in several gulps. Within seconds, he began to feel nauseous and dizzy. Then he collapsed on the floor frothing at the mouth. She knelt beside him. "I think he's having a heart attack, someone call 9-1-1," she shouted as convulsions racked his body. Several bar patrons gathered around with concern and curiosity. She knew he was a goner from the fast-acting lethal dose of potassium cyanide she had placed in his beer. The spark of life was gone from his eyes.

While this was happening, Marcus approached Rodney from behind as he stood at a urinal and deftly plunged an ice pick upward into the base of his skull. A customer in one of the toilet stalls heard a loud thump as Rodney hit the floor. Emerging from the stall, he found a body sprawled face down. No one else was present.

The assassins quickly walked through the kitchen, barely noticed by the two cooks, out the back door and into a waiting SUV. The ice pick was wrapped in newspaper and placed into a black plastic garbage bag. They also stuffed their wigs, outer shirts, and caps into the bag and discarded it in an almost-full dumpster two miles away. Their research indicated it would be serviced on schedule by a waste management truck early the next morning.

Deirdre retrieved her cell phone and entered Lee's number. He answered after the third ring. "The package was delivered," she reported and immediately ended the call. The Morettis found a large envelope with ten thousand dollars in Deidre's Jaguar two days later. She called to acknowledge receipt of the money and to offer their services again in the future, but heard a message —*"the subscriber you have dialed is not in service."*

The Perez brothers' grandmother was informed of their deaths by a phone call from the hospital. The hospital representative making the call later remarked that Grandma didn't seem too upset with the news. Interviewed by police investigators, she appeared almost relieved they were gone. Investigators made no effort to tie her to the crimes.

30

"Double Homicide at Etta's Place"

T *he Arizona Examiner*
    Last night, two bar patrons were killed in what appeared to be a double homicide according to police. The killings took place almost simultaneously at 11:20 p.m. at Etta's Place, a bar located on Indian School Road in Phoenix. Reporters on the scene were unable to learn any details of the crimes other than the fact that both men died at the same time. Detectives said the causes of death would be determined by autopsy.

    One unidentified witness said, "He just collapsed on the floor and started foaming at the mouth. It was awful. There was a woman bending over him and seemed to be very distraught. That's all I know." A customer discovered another body in the men's room and immediately reported it to the bartender who called 9-1-1. The bartender offered an opinion that "These deaths could not have been coincidental. They were obviously well planned and coordinated." The bar was declared a crime scene and closed until the investigation is complete.

(The story continued with descriptions of unpleasant details and interviews with onlookers.)

Television coverage was rife with footage of the bar and on-camera interviews with employees and customers. Police detectives were not forthcoming with commentary in the early stages of the investigations.

IN THE BASEMENT, talk turned to the value of publicity or its downside.

"This is a huge story with legs to carry it for days, if not weeks," said Derek. "My cop buddies are quietly relieved that the Perez crimes are off the books, but homicide detectives are now under big political pressure to solve their murders. They have little to go on and with skimpy evidence, we can hope the case will go cold in good time."

"Will this publicity have a chilling effect on similar crimes in the future?" asked Dave. "Crooks will know they have a force to fear outside of police investigations," said Derek. "Even if they escape arrest, they are not in the clear."

"The deterrent value will be minimal," said Phil. "Thugs who commit these kinds of crimes don't follow the news. They don't read newspapers or watch TV news. They will not be deterred from the urge to knock over a convenience store for a few bucks."

"You're probably right," said Dave. "At least, we have satisfaction in knowing the Perez brothers are off the streets and no longer a threat."

During the nine months following the operation at Etta's Place, assailants attacked and severely roughed up eight suspected or convicted abusers of women. Two others were permanently eliminated and three were threatened with great bodily harm if they did not reform their ways. Of these thirteen subjects, only two made the mistake of repeating their offenses and assailants promptly eliminated them. As usual, MOs were similar in all cases, no witnesses were present, and no usable evidence was discovered.

31

Press Curiosity

"The price of justice is eternal publicity."

– Enoch A. Bennett

Walter Burkett was a reporter with the *Valley Viewer,* a local weekly with free distribution, struggling to stay alive. The newspaper started as a "shopper," found readership among young professionals and suburbanites after adding local news stories, and for the first five years, enjoyed increasing popularity. But after apartment complexes barred the paper and advertising diminished, it had fallen on hard times with tepid reporting and lack of the edginess that characterized its early times. Walter's role also included selling advertising which occupied most of his time.

In addition to a few wire stories and reportage focused on human interest topics, Walter and his editor scrambled for story ideas, mostly store openings, restaurant reviews, and minor local political scandals leading to exposés which they felt would boost readership. Once in a while they succeeded in finding a story in a local school district or municipal government involving inept management or a financial problem. This piqued the interest of readers, but only temporarily. Such stories had "legs," sometimes for two or three weeks, after which they could no longer advance the story.

ON A TUESDAY morning in a Starbucks coffee shop, Walter overheard the conversation of two cops seated nearby. He thought he heard one of them mentioning something about individuals conducting acts of vengeance against wrongdoers, referring to them as vigilantes. After several minutes of eavesdropping and catching only snippets of the conversation, Walter arose from his chair and approached the cops' table.

"Hi guys, I hope you don't mind but I couldn't help overhearing a little of what you've been talking about. I'm a reporter with the *Viewer* and I'm wondering if you could share with me more about these vigilantes. I'm curious to find out what's going on and if it develops into a story, you will remain anonymous and you will never be named as sources."

The policemen looked at each other, surprised they had been overheard.

Walter did not make a good first impression. Short, about five foot six, pot belly, droopy mustache, and long frazzled hair, he was not the picture of one who inspires confidence or trust. But there was something in his demeanor and the way he spoke that intrigued the officers.

"Sure, have a seat," one of them said.

The reporter showed them his press credentials and proceeded to talk about his background and the *Viewer* newspaper, emphasizing its interest in publishing stories with details about issues affecting the community. Attempting to earn their trust, Walter pitched them with his great admiration for law enforcement and the importance of bringing criminals to justice. The officers listened with polite indifference and then announced that their break time was over and they needed to return to work.

"Could I buy you guys a cup of coffee tomorrow or another time? I'm really interested in learning more about what you were talking about, strictly on deep background for another story I'm working on." He hoped he hadn't been too aggressive in his approach.

After a moment's hesitation, the cops exchanged glances. "I guess we could do that if you can absolutely guarantee that our names will not be used in any story you do."

"Certainly. No problem," replied Walter.

Two days later at the same Starbucks, the two cops, Marvin and Nick, after initial small talk, offered to open up with what they had heard among the ranks.

"We'll tell you what we know, which is not much, but again, we want a commitment from you that our names will not be mentioned," insisted Nick.

"That goes without saying, but I'm telling you now that I will quote only 'reliable sources' and your names will be held in strict confidence," said Walter.

"Okay, look, we don't know if this is true," Marvin began, "but there's a story around the department that there are people who have been taking the law into their own hands with vigilante action. There are several unsolved cases with similar MOs. They look like professional hits and our detectives have been unable to do much with 'em."

"Can you tell me what cases, specifically?" inquired Walter.

"There was the Ochoa hit in Paradise Valley, not in our jurisdiction, but well publicized. May have been the work of rival cartels but it was done with a long-range rifle shot. Then there was the Bernitz homicide, a guy who had assaulted his own mother and was shot dead on his front porch by a sniper from across the street," said Marvin.

"And don't forget the two drug dealers... what were their names?" said Nick.

"They were both taken out with rifles from a distance. Oh, actually it was just one of them who was shot with a rifle. His partner was whacked with a handgun from short range by a shooter who pulled alongside of his vehicle and opened fire. All four of those homicides had a similar MO—a rifle was used by a skilled marksman who was obviously familiar with the habits of his victims," said Marvin. "And there have been several cases of severe assaults on perps of domestic violence. There seems to be a pattern to that also."

"So far as I know, the obvious similarities in these cases have not been reported in any news stories," said Walter. "Who could I speak with in the PD who could provide more information about this?"

"The public information officer is Sergeant Maria Galen. You could start with her and see where it leads," answered Nick, "and remember, you didn't hear this from us."

"Don't worry," replied Walter. "I appreciate your help and this meeting never happened."

WALTER SENSED A scoop with what he had learned from the two officers. "This could be a big story and I'd like to follow up on it," he told Ed Morris, his editor. Morris was initially skeptical and wanted to know exactly how Walter would develop the story. Walter reassured him that he would not pursue the story after a week if he was unable to find enough information to justify it.

"I can't spare you to spend too much time on it," replied Morris. "But go ahead and see if you can interview Sergeant Galen. Find out what you can and let's talk again to decide if it's a solid story."

"You got it," said a pleased Walter.

Walter sat down at his desk and dialed the Phoenix police department switchboard.

"Police department, how may I direct your call?" inquired a woman's pleasant voice.

"Yes, I'd like to speak with Sergeant Galen, your PIO."

"And who may I say is calling?'

"This is Walter Burkett. I'm a reporter with the *Valley Viewer*, a weekly publication here in Phoenix."

"One moment... I'll connect you."

You've reached the office of Sergeant Maria Galen. I'm unavailable at the moment Please leave a message and I'll get back to you as soon as possible, droned her voice message greeting.

Walter left his name and number, along with the fact that he was a reporter and hoped she would return the call before the end of the day.

His cell phone buzzed just before 5:00 p.m. "This is Sergeant Galen, I'm returning your call."

"I'd like to make an appointment to come in and talk with you for a few minutes about several cases the department is working on. I don't expect you to tell me anything confidential but I'm working on a story about a rumor I've heard about citizen action to punish suspects outside of the criminal justice system," said Walter.

"I don't have any information about that and I don't know how I could help you," answered Maria suspiciously.

"You're the spokesperson for the PD and if you could just help me with a little background on the Ochoa and Bernitz cases, I'd be grateful."

That seemed to mollify her concern. She said, "I can see you at nine in the morning.'

"I'll be there, you're in the main PD headquarters, right?"

"Right, the receptionist will provide an escort for you. You'll be asked for your picture ID at the front desk and you'll be scanned for weapons, standard procedure."

Walter arrived at 8:50 the next morning, was cleared through security and ushered into the PIO's conference room.

"You should know up front that I can't share any information about an ongoing investigation," Maria said while directing Walter to a chair.

"I understand that. I just need some information about the victims of the Ochoa and Bernitz hits."

"Why do you use the term *hits?*" asked Maria.

"They were both shot with rifles from remote locations. The MOs appear to be similar. Could they have been done by the same party?"

"Maybe," said Maria. "But they are two different investigations conducted by separate detectives. The Ochoa case occurred in Paradise Valley, out of our jurisdiction. You'll need to speak with them about that."

"I've learned that the sniper distances in the Ochoa, Bernitz, and Barcroft cases were about seventy five to ninety yards. Doesn't the similarity seem suspicious?"

Hearing the Barcroft name in in her conversation with Burkett, she was mildly surprised at the question and answered with, "I don't have that information and we know of no relationship between the two cases."

"But you will admit that the similar distances would indicate some kind of suspicious connection," pressed Walter.

"I suppose that's possible, but no other similarities were discovered; for instance, ammo calibers were different in each case. They were not executed with the same gun."

Walter continued. "I've been monitoring police blotter reports. Let's talk about the assaults and disappearance of suspects in domestic violence cases. There was the case involving a mouth washing assault of a college instructor. These are cases involving what appears to be well-planned acts of punishment or outright vengeance against suspected wrongdoers with the objective of altering or stopping their behavior."

"Those cases were thoroughly investigated. Evidence was insufficient to make any arrests."

"What about the Perez boys at Etta's Place? That was obviously a clean professional hit on both victims at the same time."

"Yes, those cases are being investigated as homicides done by professionals but so far there is no connection between those crimes and the others you mentioned. The MOs are entirely different."

"Have arrests been made?" asked Walter.

"Not yet, but detectives are pursuing other leads."

This was not true because there were no other leads, but Maria sought to give the impression the case might be closed soon.

"Anything else you can tell me about suspected vigilante activity?"

"You might contact one of our retired detectives. I understand he has been in casual contact with his former colleagues here in the department with requests for information on current cases. His name is Derek Overton. But you didn't hear that from me."

With that juicy tip, the interview ended.

TWO DAYS LATER, a spokesman with of the Paradise Valley PD took Walter's phone call but was not forthcoming. "What can you tell me about the murder of Tomas Guerrero-Ochoa?" asked Walter.

"The case is still under investigation, the FBI is now involved and I can't comment much beyond that," replied Sergeant Rodriquez. "He was a drug cartel leader living in our town who had been tried twice previously and escaped conviction both times."

"Yeah, that's all public information. I'm asking about the circumstances of his murder. For instance, from what distance did the gunman fire the shot?'

"It was about ninety yards from a vantage point overlooking the estate where a party was underway. Officers never found the exact spot. The shooter took pains to eliminate evidence of his presence."

"Would you say that it was executed by a professional marksman?"

"Obviously so. There was only one shot and it was fatal."

"Were the party guests interviewed?"

"Most of them including the band had disappeared by the time police arrived. Only the household staff remained and they were unable to provide much information. Not one claimed to have seen the actual shooting. Forensically, we are at a stalemate."

"But you said the investigation is ongoing," said Walter.

"It is, but frankly, we are at a dead end. The FBI is involved in the investigation with no positive result so far. There is a line of thinking that the hit was done by a rival drug gang from Mexico. If true, the case will probably never be solved."

32

Deep Background

"Unwelcome intrusion."

Derek and Marjorie Overton did not have a published phone number, but a web search revealed their home address. A letter arrived, addressed to Detective Derek Overton from the *Valley Viewer*.

Detective Overton:

I was unable to find your phone number or email, so am using this means of contacting you. I am working on a story about certain unsolved vigilante-style crimes in Maricopa County. With your experience as a police detective, I'm certain you can provide valuable background information that would enhance the accuracy of my story.

Would you be open to meeting with me for a cup of coffee in the next few days? I would greatly appreciate your time.

My cell number appears below. I look forward to hearing from you.

Sincerely,

Walter Burkett, Staff Reporter

DEREK READ AND re-read the letter with apprehension. *What the hell does he want? Why is he contacting me? This can't be good.*

Derek hastily convened a basement meeting of the *Committee.* He read the letter aloud.

"This comes as a shock! He doesn't say how he knows my name or the fact that I was with the PD. What should I do? To ignore him might leave the impression I'm hiding something. On the other hand, if I meet with him and he starts asking probing questions about the operations we've been involved with, my answers would necessarily be evasive. This isn't good."

"You've been in touch with your former colleagues in the department," said Phil. "They probably gave him your name and suggested he contact you."

"Yeah, but they would have given me a heads-up that he might be calling."

"I think it would be best if you met with him," said Dave. "It'd give you an opportunity to plant enough information to put him off the vigilante narrative."

Derek waited two days before calling Walter's cell number. "This is Overton. I got your letter asking about a meeting. I've been retired quite a while now and doubt I'll be able to shed much light on the cases you mentioned. I don't have any first-hand knowledge on any of them."

"I understand," replied Walter. "I just want to get some background on investigative procedures and any opinions you might have on the MOs of these crimes. If you prefer, I'll use what you tell me on deep background without using your name."

"Your letter mentioned 'unsolved crimes.' Which ones specifically are you referring to?"

"I'm interested mainly in the sniper-related hits, Levone Barcroft, James Arneson, Reuben Bernitz, and Tomas Ochoa."

Derek felt slightly dizzy. "Like I told you, I'm not familiar with any of those situations so I can't really be of any help."

"I'm just interested in your professional take on…"

"Okay, I'll meet with you," blurted Derek abruptly. "But it'll have to be off the record and brief because like I said, I don't have any firsthand knowledge of those cases. How about ten tomorrow morning at the Starbuck's on North First up near McDowell?"

"I'll be there," replied Walter.

"THIS GUY WAS very nervous and reluctant to meet with me," said Walter to his editor. "I got the feeling that he just wants to brush me off with a quick meeting where nothing of any value will be gained."

"You'll have to earn his trust with some flattering remarks about his service with the PD. Everyone likes to be praised, but don't overdo it."

Both men showed up at Starbuck's as agreed and ordered caramel lattes paid for by Walter. Seated at a remote table, Walter thanked Derek for his time and expressed his admiration for the work he had done while on the force. Derek nodded slightly at the compliment. "So how can I help you?" he asked in a none-too polite way.

"Lt. Overton, I would like this conversation to be on deep background, rather than off the record. That just means that I can use what you tell me without naming you as the source. If it were off the record, I couldn't use any of it. Is that okay?"

"Sure," replied Derek with a sigh.

"As I told you on the phone, I'm working on a story about the murders of at least three victims with long rifles, another at short range with a handgun. All four were consummate bad guys and deserved what they got, but the police are investigating these cases as vigilante actions, undertaken by professional killers."

"I wouldn't know, said Derek defensively. "What do you know about them?"

"Pretty much what's been in the news," replied Walter without disclosing his meeting the PD spokesperson.

"How then would you know the police think these are vigilante actions?" Derek immediately regretted asking the question.

The question caught Walter off guard and he said something about it being his personal opinion. This was a tipoff to Derek that Walter had spoken with someone at the PD.

"I was wondering if you think these killings could have been done by the same person."

"I suppose it's possible, but why would anyone want to take a risk like that?"

"Maybe because they felt that the police investigations were not effective and that some independent actions were necessary to put things right."

Derek struggled to avoid squirming and appearing nervous. "That would require carefully planned, well-financed efforts by someone who had the means and motive to carry out very complicated operations. Probably involving more than one person in a criminal conspiracy. They would have done careful research to gather information about their targets; in other words, to understand the everyday habits and even the lifestyles of the people they planned to take out. I seriously doubt anyone could be that dedicated to a cause. I mean, why would they turn themselves into criminals to eliminate other criminals? It doesn't make sense." Derek was attempting to cast doubt on Walter's vigilante conspiracy theory.

"You're probably right, but the MOs were very similar, you know, the use of rifles from elevated positions. And the shots were accurate, obviously fired by an expert marksman."

"You're assuming it was one guy responsible for all of them?" inquired Derek.

"Not necessarily. If it's a conspiracy involving more than one person, it could have been three separate shooters. The Arneson and Barcroft executions were carried out by two gunmen— one who shot Barcroft from a perch across the street and Arneson who was wasted from a vehicle that pulled alongside his car after Barcroft was shot. It was very clean and perfectly executed. If anyone is looking for evidence of a professional hit, there it is. The shooters had scoped out the location and knew exactly what was going down. Rival gangs don't employ this level of sophistication in their hits. They prefer the drive-by method."

Derek did not have a reply to this and sought to change the subject. "I heard those two were deeply involved in the illegal drug trade so maybe it was a rip-off attempt that went south."

"Where did you hear that?" asked Walter.

"I kept up my contacts on the street after I retired because I didn't want my sources to be lost to the PD. Anything of value I learn, I pass on to the investigators."

Walter pricked up his ears at this and asked, "Who is your contact in the PD? I'd like to talk with him."

"That will remain confidential. I don't want that person to know I've been leaking to reporters."

"Is that what you're doing now? Leaking?"

"Not really, just trying to help you out. You know, some information on deep background. Remember, this conversation is confidential."

"Okay, are you familiar with the Perez brothers thing? You know, they were both taken out at Etta's Place at the same time. I understand they were suspects in several convenience store robberies and the K-Market case as well. Again, it was a smooth, error-free action that enabled the hitmen to do the deeds and depart cleanly. Not your garden variety homicides. It was done by professionals who knew what they were doing probably under contract by a third party."

"I read about it in the papers but don't know anything else," said Derek with increasing apprehension, not readily apparent to his coffee companion. He wanted to end this conversation as quickly as possible.

"In your experience, did you ever deal with a similar situation? You know, a double murder in a public place."

"Never did."

"How would the hitmen enter the establishment unnoticed and carry out a thing like that, then slip away so cleanly?" probed Walter.

"You're asking the wrong person." Derek plunged on, hoping to satisfy his inquisitor. "They were probably well disguised so as to avoid being identified. Did the bar have surveillance cameras in operation? If so, that might provide something of use to the cops."

"There were cameras outside covering the parking area, but not at the rear where the killers apparently made their getaway. The whole thing was well planned."

"Here's an angle that you might consider. Maybe it's policemen who are doing these hits. Remember the Clint Eastwood movie *Magnum Force*? It portrayed a small group of young motorcycle cops and a senior lieutenant who took matters into their own hands. Bad guys were dying. It ended badly for the officers. Look, I have another commitment. I haven't been very helpful but I look forward to reading your story."

"Thanks for your time today. Maybe we can get together again," suggested Walter.

Without replying, Derek rose from his chair, offered his hand to Walter in a firm shake, and quickly departed the shop.

OVERTON CONVENED A meeting of the *Committee* in his basement.

"This guy has got nothing. He's fishing. I think I gave him enough to satisfy him for now, but he believes he's onto something and he's not going away."

"Maybe it's time to eliminate this problem," said J.W.

"I'm thinking the same thing, but let's see how this plays out first," said Derek. "If he writes the story, it will contain clues as to how much he and the police really know. I'm sure he's interviewed people in the PD.

"This *Valley Viewer* is a small weekly throwaway paper with circulation pretty much limited to the central and north precincts of Phoenix," said Phil. "Readership is tiny. But if the big daily picks up on the story, it becomes an entirely different matter."

"Shouldn't we have anticipated media scrutiny of the actions we've carried out?" asked Dave. "This guy is connecting the dots and seeing a pattern. This makes me very nervous. How much longer can we continue to do this and remain undetected? Almost certainly, the heat will increase and the smallest mistake could result in disaster for us."

33

Unwanted Publicity

*"No one is so brave that he is not disturbed
by something unexpected."*

– William Shakespeare, *Julius Caesar*

"Vigilante Justice"
By Walter Burkett

For the past several weeks, the *Valley Viewer* has been investigating several cases of suspected citizen action against criminal suspects. Information was gathered from police blotter reports and sources within two valley police departments.

The *Viewer* has learned that a pattern of similarity exists among several homicides during the past year. Victims of these crimes were themselves criminal suspects or gang members all killed by sniper shots from remote locations. In other cases, perpetrators of domestic violence were severely injured, requiring medical treatment. Investigators believe there is an element of vigilantism at work here. "It appears that these killings involve some sort of coordinated planning and execution by highly skilled professionals," according to police sources.

Tomas Guerrero-Ochoa was assassinated last August 11 while hosting a poolside party at his estate in Paradise Valley. Ochoa was a well-known cartel kingpin who conducted narcotics operations on this side of the border. Twice indicted and tried on drug trafficking charges, he beat the rap both times. On one occasion, legal technicalities forced the judge to dismiss charges, and he was found not guilty on the second. Justice was finally delivered when he was felled by a single rifle shot from a distance of about ninety yards. Police investigators were unable to pinpoint the exact location of the sniper's nest nor the path used by the shooter through undisturbed desert behind Ochoa's estate. No physical evidence was left behind. Police theorize the hit was carried out by a rival drug cartel and the shooter most likely fled back into Mexico. In an interview, a Paradise Valley police spokesperson affirmed that the investigation is ongoing, but also seemed to suggest that it was not a high priority.

A similar shooting happened a month later. Reuben Bernitz was murdered on his front porch in the early morning as he was retrieving his morning newspaper. The rifle shot came from the second floor window of an empty house across the street a couple of doors down, at a distance of less than three hundred feet. Bernitz was free on bail and awaiting trial, charged with assaulting his mother in a dispute over the contents of her will. The beating resulted in her death a few days later but prosecutors could not directly tie her death to the assault and a grand jury declined to upgrade the charge to manslaughter. The shooting was carefully executed and no evidence was found. The upstairs window used by the shooter was left open but no fingerprints or shell casings were found. A small amount of gunpowder residue was found on the back of a chair apparently used by the sniper to steady his weapon but other than that, the place was clean.

On September 14th, Levone Barcroft, a gang banger and dope dealer, was executed by a rifle shot at Ballinger Park in south Phoenix. Again, the shot came from a second floor window of an empty house across the street. His companion, James Arneson, was shot dead at the same time while he waited for Barcroft in a coupe parked at the curb. A second shooter apparently drove alongside the coupe seconds after Barcroft was shot and fired several times with a handgun into the driver's side window, killing Arneson. To investigating detectives, it looked like a drug deal going down and was interrupted by gunfire from rival gang members. Barcroft was unarmed. Arneson was found with a handgun in his belt, of no use in his sudden demise. These homicides all had an eerie similarity—expertly executed by snipers, clean getaways, no usable evidence, and the elimination of bad actors suspected of criminal activity.

Another case involved two males suspected of murdering a convenience store clerk and committing several store robberies in the weeks following the murder. Brothers Alex and Rodney Perez were low-level career criminals with lengthy rap sheets. Police were unable to accumulate enough evidence to collar them for the murder or robberies. They were executed within seconds of each other in a bar on Indian School Road. Alex was swilling a beer laced with cyanide and Rodney went down with a sharp object in the back of his scull while standing at a urinal in the men's room.

"Someone was out of patience with the pace of investigations and decided to dispense justice when the official system seemed hamstrung," according to Maria Galen, police spokesperson. "These hits were obviously coordinated and carried out by professional killers. We are urging anyone with information about any of this to contact us immediately. Instant justice may provide a certain sense of comfort to certain individuals since it eliminates wrongdoers from society, but vigilantism cannot be tolerated in a democracy where the rule of law prevails." [6]

Our sources say there is a rumor afloat that these actions could be the work of angry, frustrated policemen. The skill with which the hits are conducted lead one to believe this is not the work of street thugs. One of our sources mentioned the movie *Magnum Force*—a story about police officers who take the law into their own hands.

---

[6] Walter had obtained permission from Sergeant Galen to use this quote in his piece.

This story will be advanced as we come into possession of additional facts.

The suggestion that police officers could be involved in felonies described in the news story brought a stern rebuke from the chief of police. In a strongly worded letter to *Viewer* editor, the chief denounced the "reckless implication that our officers are involved in these vile crimes." The letter was published in the next edition together with a tepid apology to the Phoenix PD.

34

The Hookup

"Oh, what a tangled web we weave,
when we first practice to deceive."

– Sir Walter Scott

"Hello, may I help you?" purred Deirdre's voice on Lee's throwaway cell phone.

"Hi, it's Jack. How are you?" It had been three weeks since the operation at Etta's Place. Lee was happily married to Janet but hadn't been able to get Deirdre off his mind since she drove away in her Jag. He nursed a vision of the cleavage between her marvelous breasts and conjured up images of how they would look unfettered. He caught a whiff of her perfume, or thought he did, when thinking about her.

"It's great to hear from you," she breathily cooed in her best Marilyn Monroe vamp. "I tried calling you to say we appreciate the package in our car and tell you that we are available for any future need you might have. So, what's up?"

"Just called to say hello and thank you guys for a job well done."

"Nice to know our work is appreciated. Anything else cooking right now?"

"Nothing at the moment, but maybe we could get together for a drink and talk about the operation at Etta's Place." There was a hint of familiarity in Lee's voice as if he was asking for a date.

"Sure, how about Ralph's?"

"I was thinking more of the Regency downtown. Do you know it?"

"Sure."

Lee suggested day after tomorrow at three, coincidentally the hotel's check in time. "Meet me in the bar?"

"I'll be there unless something comes up."

"Oh, I think you can count on something coming up."

Deirdre giggled and ended the call.

A WORDLESS MEETING in the lobby led to the elevator and then to the room Lee had booked on the tenth floor. Entering the room, Lee grabbed her arm, spun her around and pulled her into a tight embrace. She eagerly returned his open mouth kiss. The taste of her lips was slightly sweet with lingering overtones of cinnamon. This spurred his libido to previously unknown levels of raw desire. She locked one leg around his and he sought her posterior with both hands. Clothes were quickly stripped off.

His body was hard with well-defined muscles. She was firm with flawless female curves. Her skin was soft as the finest velvet. She forcefully pushed him back on the bed and leaped on top.

Love making was swift and aggressive. He explored every inch of her body. She returned the favor, hungrily caressing his chest and attending to his rock-hard boner. One vociferous climax led to another and then another twenty minutes later.

Exhausted and perspiring, they lay naked under the sheets for several minutes before Deirdre said: "This is the first time I've fucked a guy without knowing his name. What's yours?"

"I told you, it's Jack.'

"Bullshit, I want to know your real name."

In a cloud of post-orgasmic euphoria, he rashly blurted, "Okay, it's Lee, but don't tell anyone."

"Don't worry, your secret is safe with me. Just curious."

Lee enjoyed the view of her perfect backside and narrow waist as she headed to the bathroom.

They continued pillow talking for an hour about various topics. She loved his silky touch on her inner thighs as they lay together. This led to another vigorous coupling after which Lee suggested dinner.

"No can do, lover. Marcus is expecting me home for an early evening and I don't want him to be disappointed. Maybe another time."

"Does he know about what you're up to today?"

"No way, he thinks I'm attending a fashion show at the Merchandise Mart."

"Janet thinks I'm in some sort of meeting." After a pause, "Is this a one and out sort of thing, or will we do this again?"

"I'm not into one-night stands or in this case, one-time afternoon delights. How about same time next week?" she shyly whispered in his ear.

She got dressed, gave him a long, open mouth kiss, winked, and left the room. He took a long shower with plenty of hot water and soap to ensure no trace of her perfume lingered on his person. Returning to the hotel at 9:00 a.m. the following morning to settle the bill, he had no illusion the clerk was unaware of his agenda. He used a fake driver's license and a prepaid credit card under the name Louis Gladstone to hide the expense from his household accounts and from Janet's eyes. *Gladstone* was a recollection from his favorite movie *The Graduate*.

The tangled web of deception had begun.

35

The Persuaders

"Let us employ whatever methods are effective."

Business partners Russ Milam and Ben Moskowitz met for lunch at Scottsdale's Cactus Hills Club, their favorite place to have relaxed conversations in relative privacy. M & M Properties was a thriving land development enterprise. They took great satisfaction in their relationship with Marjorie Overton, the channel through which they provided funding to accomplish justice when it was needed, but not provided by conventional means. They remained unaware of the *Committee's* existence as stipulated by Marjorie Overton in her initial conversation with Russ that resulted in his daughter's attackers suffering much needed justice. Ben had never met Marjorie and didn't really need to, since all arrangements were made through Russ.

Midway through the meal, Ben was sipping his second martini. "Russ, you know Arlie Fremont don't you?" he asked.

"Yeah, he's that black guy on the city planning staff, isn't he? I don't know him well. I've talked with him maybe a couple of times about our projects. Why do you ask?"

"I had a strange conversation with him the other day. After a meeting to review our Rocky Ridge project, we were just chatting and he asked if we could have an off-the-record talk. I had no idea what he was about to say. He told me he admired our success in business and said he was sure I knew quite a few influential people around the area. I acknowledged I did and he wondered if I knew anyone who could help him with a personal problem."

"Weren't you a little suspicious with that request?" asked Russ.

"I was, but what the hell, it might be a chance to curry some favor, so I asked what problem he was having. He launched into a detailed story about his twenty-year-old daughter, Nicole, who is in a romantic relationship with a guy who is thirty-two years old and divorced. He said he and his wife both despise the guy and have urged their daughter to stop seeing him. She refuses to listen, saying they are in love and plan to be married. At that point, I asked why he was telling me all this. It was obviously a personal matter. He said he was desperate to reason with Nicole or find someone who could deal with her boyfriend. I took that to mean he wanted to find a means of persuading the guy to break off the relationship.

"I asked why he disliked the guy and he grew emotional as he gave me a list of complaints. He said the guy disrespects him and his wife, calling them "bureaucrats," is frequently late for dates with Nicole, and has no job. He also suspects that he is physically abusive with her because she arrived home several times after seeing him and retreated to her room crying. He said she let it slip that she usually pays the restaurant and bar tab for their outings. And, he thinks the guy is a drug dealer. He wants the relationship to end.

"I asked him again why he approached me with this problem and what, exactly, did he want to happen. He asked if I could recommend someone who could help. He seemed pretty desperate."

"What did you tell him?"

"I told him I might be able to help and asked him to furnish information about his daughter's boyfriend. I was shocked when he pulled a piece of paper from his pocket. He had it written down ... name, address, cell number, all the details. Here it is."

"I don't know if this is something we need to be involved in," Russ said. "How would he know to contact you to solve a problem like that?"

"He admitted that he remembered the incident with your Carlie and what happened to the 'young thugs,' as he put it, who beat her up. I left him with a weak commitment to look into it."

Russ phoned Marjorie and asked for a meeting.

THIS IS AN unusual request," Marjorie told Derek. "I didn't know what to make of it. I told him I wasn't sure we could help. Russ wanted to know how much we needed to solve the problem if we chose to accept it."

Derek contacted his PD colleague Wilkie and asked him to run a rap sheet on one J'Mayne Washington, Nicole Fremont's intended. What he found was shocking.

IN THE BASEMENT, Derek presented the complaint to the *Committee* together with what Wilkie had found. "This guy has been married twice. His sheet shows three arrests for domestic violence and one for a home burglary. He has two raps for selling marijuana. Norm tells me he's a suspect in a cocaine ring. It's a mystery what a nice young woman from a good family sees in a loser like this.'"

"I think it's time for one of our 'conversations' with him," J.W. proposed. "You know, something very persuasive about breaking up with Nicole." The group was in agreement except for Phil who once again questioned the necessity of an operation and was worried about risk. The vote was four to one in favor of gathering more information about the lifestyle and habits of J'Mayne.

Lee called Deirdre and asked her to meet him at Ralph's to discuss an operation. "We need to learn what he does, where he goes, who his friends are, you know... the usual stuff to plan an operation on him."

"It'll cost you three grand for a detailed report. More, if you want us involved any further."

"Go for it and let me know ASAP what you find."

A week later, Deidre reported to Lee. "He has no job and isn't trying to find one. He has no obvious means of income but looks like he's dealing drugs from his apartment. People go in and out mostly in late afternoon. We found him to be pretty active at night. He parties with his friends in one of their apartments or at a place called Night Hawk Lounge. It's a seedy bar in west Phoenix. He also visits upscale bars in Scottsdale and hits on attractive women, sometimes with success. He seems to have a certain charm women like. I think the best opportunity to contact him would be his apartment. He lives alone, goes out around nine each evening and returns between two and three in the morning. He fits

Nicole into his schedule a couple of times a week. They go out for drinks and dinner, then return to his place for sex. In my opinion, he has no idea of marrying her, but if he does, it will be to get his hands on her family's assets."

"This is great info. Just what we need," said Lee. "Here's you fee and I'll see you next week... can't wait."

THE *COMMITTEE* PUT their plan into place to separate J'Mayne Washington from Nicole Fremont. It was scheduled for the following Sunday morning at 3:00 a.m., a time he was certain to be at home.

J'Mayne's cell phone started ringing at 3:02 a.m. It went to voice mail but the caller did not leave a message. Instead the phone kept ringing. On the third set of rings, a groggy J'Mayne picked up. "Yeah, what is it?"

"Hey man, this is Ricky. I need a fix real bad and I'm willing to pay a premium for it. I'll be there in ten minutes."

"Hold on dude, it's the fuckin' middle of the night. Call me tomorrow."

"Your buddy Gordy told me to call you. Said you were a good source. I need an 8-ball of coke and I'm willing pay five bills for it right now. Come on man."

Five hundred dollars was about twice the going street rate for that quantity of the drug.

"You said Gordy referred you? When did you see him?"

"Yesterday, man. He's a tall dude with bleached hair."

It did not occur to J'Mayne to confirm that meeting with Gordy. Instead, his greed prevailed. "Okay, come on over and have the fuckin' cash ready. I'll need to see both your hands when I open the door and I'll pat you down when you step in. Get it?"

"Yeah man, no problem. I'll be there in ten."

"HE'LL BE HOLDING a gun on you when he opens the door, so be sure to hold both arms up high. He'll be on the lookout for treachery since he doesn't know you," cautioned Lee.

J.W., dressed in shabby clothing, unmarked baseball cap, and wearing a fake straggly beard, knocked on the door. It opened slowly to reveal J'Mayne with a handgun pointed at J.W.'s head. "Come in, close the door and turn around."

"J'Mayne inserted the pistol in his belt, did a thorough pat down of J.W. from head to foot after which he said, "Okay, you got the bread?"

As J.W. was pulling a roll of currency from his front pocket, Lee burst through the door with a 9mm Ruger leveled at J'Mayne. Before he could retrieve his weapon, the two intruders roughly forced him into a chair and disarmed him.

"What the hell? Who are you guys," shouted J'Mayne.

"Be cool dude, we're not here to rip you off. We're here to discuss your relationship with Nicole Fremont. Remember her?" With that, J.W. delivered a stinging blow to J'Mayne's face that split his lip followed by a gut punch that knocked the wind out of him. After a minute of struggling to regain his breath, he asked weakly, "What do you want?"

"Listen carefully, asshole" said Lee. "Nicole's family thinks your relationship with their daughter is bad news and needs to end. So, you will tell her it's over and you will not attempt to contact her again or create any form of trouble for her. She probably won't take it well, so be nice. Understand something clearly... if you don't get this done, we will visit you again when you least expect it and you will go to the hospital for a very long period of time. Think of us as fixers. We fix problems for our clients and if we hear that you are still a problem, you will pay a price, a very heavy price. Get it?" No response from J'Mayne.

"Answer me, asshole. Get it?"

"Yeah, yeah, I get it."

"You don't want to see us again, so call Nicole today with the news. By the way, where do you keep your stash?"

"What the fuck, you said this wasn't a ripoff."

"We lied."

While Lee was pointing his weapon on J'Mayne's head, J.W. turned the apartment upside down and found the drug stash in zip lock bags taped to the bottom side of a dresser drawer. Three ounces of cocaine and four ounces of heroin were flushed down the toilet while J'Mayne watched in horror.

ARLIE FREMONT CALLED Ben Moskowitz to thank him. Ben feigned ignorance. "What are you talking about?"

"Nicole broke up with her boyfriend and we couldn't be happier. Whatever you did was effective. Let me know if I can ever do something for you."

"I'm not sure what we did, but I'm glad it worked out for you," Ben said. "We look forward to working with you on our future projects." The meaning of this statement was not lost on Arlie.

36

Crack in the Facade

"All façades fall sometimes, then the mask comes off..."

– Lisa Unger, *A Memoir of Mercy*

Only two outsiders were aware of the existence of the *Committee* and its mission. Marjorie Overton, Derek's wife, and Janet Simmons, Lee's wife, were briefed by their husbands early on and persuaded to accept the concept of dispensing justice to those who deserved it and delivering it to those who suffered in its absence.

Marjorie was fully aware of the *Committee's* activities and Derek's leadership role. He never allowed her to attend any of the basement meetings, explaining that her presence might cause unnecessary awkwardness in members' conversations and decision-making. The only other person who knew about the *Committee* was Lee's wife, Janet. Even then, she was not fully aware of Lee's involvement as the central figure in several of the operations. Upon returning home after an operation, he was typically silent and morose for a day or two and reluctant to talk about where he had been or what happened. She knew in her gut that he was deeply involved in something serious. This was a source of worry that somehow their marriage was about to be disrupted by a mysterious force she did not understand and could not control.

Marjorie was generally familiar with the specific operations carried out against criminals and other wrongdoers. She never told Derek that she approved of these actions nor did she say they were wrong. She willingly acted as the funding facilitator between the *Committee* and its benefactors.

Phil Maguire chose to keep his wife Dana blissfully ignorant of his involvement in the *Committee's* criminal activities. Since he was so often absent from home on hunting trips, he allowed her to believe that he was attending gatherings of hunting buddies when he met with the *Committee* in Derek's basement. The five members, three of whom were married, no longer socialized at the Elks Club; therefore, there was no danger of awkward conversations that could be overheard. The only socializing among the principals took place between the Overtons and Simmonses who were next door neighbors.

THE FIRST CRACKS in the *Committee's* solidarity started to appear. Phil was the only member who did not actively participate in any of the *Committee's* operations despite his experience with firearms used in hunting. His role was to scout locations, obtain equipment (principally firearms), and plan logistics. Derek and J.W. repeatedly urged him to come along when they were on *Committee* assignment to observe the operation, but he always declined, except to drive vehicles occasionally. And sometimes he was the lone dissenter when the group decided to take action.

At a meeting of the *Committee* during a review of potential operations involving domestic violence, Phil became emotional and railed, "Isn't it foolish to continue what we're doing? There will come a time when one of us or maybe all of us will end up facing arrest. We can justify to ourselves what we do on the basis of delivering justice where it's absent, but at the end of the day, aren't we committing crimes that make us just as bad as the guys we are dealing with? When we first started, I was convinced what we were doing was useful and good. Now, I realize it's an enormous personal risk to all of us. Hell, let the cops do their job. Why should we place ourselves at risk over unpunished criminal behavior? We have taken satisfaction in the outcome of our operations, but so far it's just a small fraction of the total universe of wrongdoing. Think of the downside to all this."

The others allowed him to go on like this for several minutes until finally he seemed to calm down after getting these thoughts off his chest. The meeting ended with tension in the air. Phil didn't stay around for drinks.

THIS WAS A source of great concern to Derek who worried that Phil was not fully on board. He shared his concern privately with the others who agreed this could be a problem. Derek decided to discuss the matter with Lee and J.W. at McDonald's the next morning.

At a corner table with no customers nearby, the three sat down over coffee and No. 1 breakfasts. "I'll be honest," Derek said with a troubled look on his face. "That newspaper story and being interviewed by detectives scared the hell out of me. It means that someone including that reporter is sniffing around trying to find something, and I'm thinking the worst about Phil. Is he leaking stuff on us or just being a contrarian? A couple of the reporter's questions left no doubt in my mind that he has talked with someone at the PD or one of us. He wouldn't get that information from any other source unless…" His voice trailed off.

"Phil states his opinion frankly each time we're considering an operation," said J.W. "And his comments are generally supportive, but he doesn't always see things as we do. I'm having trouble understanding his role with us. In the beginning, he seemed to be absolutely committed to the cause, but lately not so much."

"He participates in the planning details and it's usually constructive," said Lee. "I recall a few times when he raised a valid question about the escape route and it saved us a lot of time in the getaway and may have saved us from getting pinched. And he's driven the van a few times."

Derek continued, "Still, I'm worried about him. He seems aloof at times during our sessions. I remember telling him he wasn't obliged to participate directly in the operations if he didn't want to, but I'm beginning to regret that now. All of us need to get in the game to ensure our loyalty to the mission."

"Dave hasn't been as active in the field as we three," said Lee. "But he's fed us valuable information from his office. And, he's helped you guys on a couple of operations."

After a pause in the conversation and several sips of coffee, Lee said: "Look, I'm going to suggest taking another breather. Unless something drastic comes to our attention, I think we should take a few weeks off until we're comfortable the heat's off."

"I've been thinking the same. I'll call a meeting to discuss the idea," Derek said to Lee. "Just don't let on you've already brought it up. We don't want Phil and Dave knowing we've met behind their backs."

Derek and Lee had come to MacDonald's together in Derek's SUV. On the way home, Derek said, "I'm thinking of planting a piece of phony information with Phil to see if it finds its way to that reporter, or worse, to the PD. We need to know if we have a mole in our midst."

"Are you that worried?" asked an incredulous Lee. "Surely Phil wouldn't betray us like that."

"We'll see," said Derek.

37
The Plant

"Deceit made necessary."

Phil arrived early for the next *Committee* meeting. Derek had deliberately asked the others to arrive fifteen minutes later. While mixing drinks, Derek casually spoke of the Perez operation. "I think the Whistlers did a great job. They apparently left no trace of evidence and made a clean getaway. There was so much confusion over two dead bodies, no one noticed them as they exited the place. It was very smooth."

Derek's mention of the name "Whistler" was a deliberate and false information plant delivered smoothly in casual conversation.

Phil recalled that Lee had previously declined to provide names of the contractors. He made a mental note of the "Whistler" reference but didn't ask Derek about it. The other three arrived and the meeting began.

"The Perez operation went down very well," Derek told the *Committee*. "We couldn't have asked for a better outcome. It was done cleanly with great precision. We owe

Lee our thanks and gratitude for finding the contractors and coordinating the operation so successfully."

"A double homicide definitely gets the attention of the authorities," said Lee. "The investigation will take days and if the contractors were as skillful as we believe, nothing will come of it. The news media will eventually lose interest and so will the police. After all, we just cleared the books on two suspects and multiple crimes. The police are quietly grateful, believe me."

"If this case finally escapes from police scrutiny as we think it will, I'm in favor of hiring these people again. They appear to be dependable and efficient," said Derek. "It will go to cold case status after about six months if no usable evidence is found. But even as a cold case, it will never be completely off the books. Felony murder cases never go away."

More discussion followed and drinks were poured. When the alcohol had done its work in relaxing the members, Lee opened a new topic of conversation. "Phil, you proposed taking a break from our activities some time back. I think the time is right to do just that. Derek and I discussed it briefly the other day. I don't like the publicity that's been coming down and even though the Perez operation was a success, we didn't foresee the flood of publicity that resulted."

"I agree," said Dave. "We've had a lot of success so far and I would like to take some time to digest it and figure out where we go from here, if anywhere."

"You sound like we might terminate this thing," said J.W.

"We're not making that decision now, let's just take a rest and think about what the future holds. That's all I'm saying," said Dave.

"I detect a consensus that we take a pause, am I right?" inquired Derek. "What do you think about six months?" Nodding from all four indicated agreement.

"So that's it, let's convene again in six weeks and share some assessments of our operations. Maybe a pause will allow us to see ourselves in a different light."

38

"Vigilante Justice"

Valley Viewer
By Walter Burkett

Police detectives are investigating a double murder recently at a bar in north Phoenix. The victims were identified as Alex and Rodney Perez, two brothers who were frequent customers at the bar and were playing pool at the time of their deaths. Several people were in the establishment at the time but none actually witnessed the killings as they happened. The bartender and two customers who were playing pool remember an attractive woman playing pool with Alex. They recall her kneeling over the body of Alex and frantically asking someone to call 9-1-1. In the confusion, no one remembers when she left the scene or which door she used. Her identify is unknown and police believe her to be a person of interest. Alex collapsed after drinking a glass of beer laced with cyanide. Alex's brother Rodney died at almost the same time from a stab wound to the base of his skull by an unknown person while standing at a urinal in the restroom.

The investigation so far has not turned up substantial evidence, at least none the police are revealing to reporters.

In a news conference, Police spokesperson Maria Galen said these crimes were almost certainly planned and coordinated to occur simultaneously. "The victims were not in the drug trade and were not gang members as far as we know, so there is no suspicion of rival gang reprisal. Anyone with information about these crimes is urged to contact the crime information number you see on the board behind me. Your identity will be protected. Further, if you know anything about the Whistler gang, we need to talk with you."

Pressed for more information about 'Whistler,' Galen explained that this was a group of street killers who were active several years ago. Drive-by shootings were their specialty. They were known to have engaged in armed robberies of convenience stores as well. Known as the Whistlers, they used athletic official's whistles as means of warning innocent bystanders when a shooting was about to occur. Why they would reveal their presence in this fashion was a mystery.

Over coffee at Starbuck's, a deeply troubled Derek had a copy of the current edition of the *Valley Viewer.*

Derek showed the story to Lee. "Have you seen this?"

"Yeah, but so what? There's nothing that would lead back to us," said Lee.

"I fed Phil a bogus piece of information the other day and here it is, in this story."

"What are you talking about?"

"It's the reference to 'Whistlers.' I deliberately used that term when Phil and I were alone before you guys arrived at our last meeting. He has obviously leaked it to the press. We may be in deep trouble."

"Oh Jesus, this can't be happening. Could he be that stupid? Maybe it's just a coincidence. If he reads this news story, he will know it came from him."

"Let's just sit on this for the time being and see what happens," said Derek. "I'm going to call a meeting of the group and try to work it into the conversation to gauge Phil's reaction. We can't over react to this."

Lee agreed and they left the coffee shop.

IN THE BASEMENT, twenty minutes of casual conversation turned to the Perez brothers operation.

"This is hilarious," said Derek. "The police think this is somehow related to that gang, the 'Whistlers,' that committed several drive-by shootings years ago. As long as they think that, we're okay."

"It could be a bait to get someone to come forward and provide evidence about the crimes," said Lee. "I'll ask our contractors if they know anything about it."

Phil remained silent during this conversation.

39
The Elk Hunt

*"There is a passion for hunting,
something deeply implanted in the human breast."*

– Charles Dickens

On an elk hunting trip to the White Mountains of eastern Arizona, Philip Maguire went missing. He was scheduled to meet Joe Dennison, a hunting companion, in the picturesque hamlet of Greer, Arizona, on a Saturday morning in October. They planned to meet at Midge's Café on Main Street at 10:00 a.m., have coffee and proceed to the hunting camp about two miles from town.

Elk hunting is tightly regulated in all states where the animals occur, especially in Arizona. Serious hunters understand the need to employ professional guides. And it's expensive. For a "one-on-one" guide, (one guide per hunter) both men had forked over $5,500 for a seven-day bull elk hunt plus a tag fee of $160. They had successfully applied for tags and were drawn in the process used by the Arizona Fish and Game Department to allocate the limited number of animals to be harvested each season.

When Phil didn't show up after a half hour, Joe called his cell number several times thinking there had been a misunderstanding as to where they were to meet. But the calls went to voice mail and a call to the hunting guide provided nothing about Phil. By noon, with no sign of Phil, Joe called Dana, who told him her husband had departed Phoenix early that morning in his pickup. Phil had spent the previous Friday evening packing his hunting gear and loading his truck. She understood he was leaving for Greer the next morning though he had not informed her who he was meeting. Each hunter had provided the other with contact information on next of kin, "just in case."

Alarmed, she called his cell phone, got no answer and began calling friends and employees at his plumbing company. None of them knew anything other than the fact that he was going hunting for a week in the White Mountains. Unaware of his activities with the *Committee* and without knowledge of its members, she didn't call them. Repeated calls to his cell phone went to voice mail.

Now thoroughly alarmed, she called 9-1-1 and frantically reported her husband missing on the way to Greer for an elk hunt. The indifferent 9-1-1 operator connected her with a person in the police department who dutifully took some basic information and counseled patience. "It's only been a few hours he's been out of contact, ma'am. Don't panic. Maybe he had car trouble or ran out of gas and is out of cell phone range somewhere."

Annoyed with this attitude, Dana called sheriff's offices in four counties through which he would have driven: Maricopa, Gila, Navajo, and Apache. None of them knew of any highway accidents in the last twenty four hours involving a pickup truck, but promised to let her know if any such reports came in.

Joe drove to the hunting guide's camp but decided not to pursue the hunt until Phil's whereabouts were known. By 6:00 p.m., eight hours after their appointment to meet, no one had heard from Phil. The guide was mystified and concerned that his prepaid client was missing. Joe decided to spend the night at the camp. Something was terribly wrong. The topic of the nonrefundable guide's fee proved awkward. It amounted to $11,000 for two hunters. Both men had purchased cancellation insurance but it wasn't clear that it would cover last minute abandonment of the hunt without cause.

"Before you make a claim to collect the insurance, let's wait until we know what happened with Phil," suggested the guide. "You may want to reschedule the hunt at a later time. Our fee to reschedule is $500, but I'll waive it in this case." Somehow, the generosity of this offer was lost on Joe.

Next morning, a trout fisherman noticed an abandoned pickup truck at the end of East Fork Road before it reached a small creek known as the Little Colorado River, just south of Greer. Lettering and a logo on both doors said "Sonoran Plumbing & Heating" with a phone number. It was locked and still loaded with hunting gear. Seeing no one around, he reported it to 9-1-1. Philip Maguire of Phoenix was quickly identified as the vehicle's owner after the deputy furnished the plate number to his dispatcher. The sheriff notified Dana of the discovery.

At 11:00 a.m., Joe again called a distraught Dana who had just learned of the pickup discovery. "I know something dreadful has happened," she said. "He wouldn't just disappear without a trace. The sheriff and police departments between here and there haven't turned up anything. There haven't been any road accidents. I'm calling all the hospitals in the region now. Please, please call me even if it's in the middle of the night if he turns up or you learn something else."

"Of course I will."

THE COMMITTEE LEARNED of Phil's disappearance the next day. Dana had called the Elk's Club to inquire if someone there had heard from him. No one had.

Derek was nursing a beer at the bar when the club secretary approached to ask if he had heard about Phil.

"No, what's up?"

"His wife called yesterday afternoon to ask if we had seen him. Apparently he went missing on a hunting trip to Greer and wasn't heard from all day. She was understandably very upset. She called again this morning."

"I didn't know him that well," lied Derek, absently replying in past tense. "We had a few drinks together here and I remember he was a serious hunter. Let me know if you hear anything else about him."

A week passed with intense efforts to find Phil. Search parties were formed to scour the roadsides and forested areas around Greer. His pickup was devoid of evidence, only his fingerprints were found. Dana placed "Missing Person" notices with Phil's headshot on utility poles, newspaper boxes, and in windows of Greer merchants who would allow it. The notice offered a $10,000 reward for information leading to the whereabouts of Philip Maguire. A couple of would-be reward seekers came forward with suggestions including the city dump and fresh graves in a nearby cemetery. These "leads" went nowhere. The reward remained unclaimed.

It's not a crime when an adult goes missing unless evidence of kidnapping or murder turns up. However in this case, the pickup found where it was located indicated the possibility of foul play.

A missing person report was filed with the Apache County Sheriff's office and then forwarded to the FBI. Missing persons investigations are not a high priority with law enforcement agencies unless foul play is obvious, or the subject is a child. Days passed, then weeks, until it became obvious that Phil's disappearance would not be solved quickly. The National Center for Missing Persons in Phoenix was advised of Phil's status as a missing person. Their inquiries turned up nothing.

IN DEREK'S BASEMENT, four *Committee* members discussed Phil's disappearance.

"He seemed to be having second thoughts about what we do," mused Dave. "Several times, he questioned the justification of an operation and appeared to be worried about the risk involved."

"I always wondered if he was truly committed to our mission," said J.W. "He never participated in any operation despite being invited to join us on several occasions. And he was a great shot with a rifle. I saw that at the practice range a couple of times. He could have put that skill to good use for us when we needed sniper support. His research and planning were useful but not that important in the overall sense. We could have done without it."

The topic of Phil's possible betrayal of the *Committee* arose.

"If he ratted us out to the police, we would have heard about it by now," said Dave. "He might have confided information to someone other than the police."

"Right now he's just missing. If he's found dead, it will relieve everyone's mind."

Derek and Lee remained silent during most of this conversation. They exchanged slight smiles and did not mention the "Whistler" leak.

FOUR YEARS LATER, a wilderness hiker found what appeared to be human bones with an intact human skull. Badly decomposed clothing was strewn around a shallow gravesite. The remains were found about ninety yards from a hiking trail two miles from Greer, and might never have been discovered if not for the unusual outdoor habits of the hiker who preferred to avoid established trails and instead trudged through undisturbed vegetation and rough terrain. The remains were partially buried and had been ravaged by animals. An autopsy failed to identify the cause of death, though investigators were certain it was a homicide. Dental records identified the remains as those of one Philip Maguire, owner of Sonoran Plumbing and Heating of Phoenix. Maguire had gone missing four years previously while preparing to participate in an elk hunt. Dana finally was able to conduct a proper funeral and burial, well attended by friends, plumbing company employees, and family. No member of the *Committee* attended.

A homicide investigation was opened by the sheriff of Apache County without immediate result.

40
Grief

"Was ever grief like mine?"

– George Herbert

Dana Maguire suffered emotionally in the aftermath of Phil's disappearance. Frustrated with lack of progress by the authorities, she alternated between fits of weeping and spending two or three hours a day on the phone talking with friends and relatives, and calling Greer police, Apache County Sheriff's Office, FBI, and the National Center for Missing Persons, all to no avail. Online missing-persons services turned up nothing. She did not contact any members of the *Committee*, about which she had no knowledge.

No evidence was found that he had withdrawn funds from his personal or business bank account, his credit cards had not been charged, no calls to or from his cell phone had been recorded. Realization set in that Phil would not be found alive. He was officially listed as a missing person by investigating agencies.

She hired a private investigator in the hope of turning up something, anything, related to Phil's disappearance. After three weeks of activity with no result, she fired him. An invoice arrived in the amount of $5,457 less the $2,500 retainer fee he had demanded.

Dana appointed Robert Hazelton, vice president of Sonoran Plumbing & Heating, to lead the company in Phil's place. He was a close personal friend of the family who was respected by employees and had Dana's trust. Free of the worry of running the company, she devoted all her time and energy to finding her husband.

Phil's finances were in good order. Dana's signature was sufficient to withdraw funds and write checks against their personal bank accounts. Phil had authorized Rob Hazelton to sign company checks. He continued paying Phil's salary. The company continued to operate smoothly. Money was not a problem for Dana. Phil had two life insurance policies in effect, one for a half million dollars and the other for one million. She was the sole beneficiary on both policies. No claim for insurance proceeds could be made for seven years or until Phil could be declared legally dead. However, dealing with life insurance was the last thing on Dana's mind. .

Phil kept an office in a separate room on the second floor of their home. Three weeks after his disappearance, in the hope of finding something useful that might explain his disappearance, she went through everything on top of the desk and found only old hunting and outdoor magazines, a few newspaper clippings, miscellaneous papers, several "to-do" notes, and his laptop computer. A calendar noted the dates of his hunting trip to Greer. Opening the computer, she inserted the power cord to recharge the battery. Ten minutes later, the screen flickered to life, but a password was needed to gain access. She found a small notebook in the top middle drawer with numerous user names and passwords Phil used for various websites and found one entitled "Laptop." It succeeded in unlocking the device with access to files, but it was clean of anything remotely related to his disappearance.

Opening drawers, she found nothing of interest until she attempted to pull out the bottom drawer on the left side. It was locked.

A search for the key in other drawers turned up nothing. Then she remembered that the Greer police, after impounding his pickup, had returned his key ring to her. Retrieving it from the kitchen counter, she found what looked like the key she sought and returned to his desk. It worked and she pulled the drawer open. In it, she found a manila file folder with several ruled sheets in Phil's handwriting entitled "MY PERSONAL CONFESSION".

Halfway through the second page, tears were streaming down her cheeks.

"ROB, I DON'T know what to do," wailed Dana tearfully. She had driven herself to the business location of Sonoran Plumbing & Heating and was sitting in the office of Robert Hazelton, now in charge of the company. He sat reading the document Dana had just handed him.

"You understand this explains his disappearance, don't you? He got involved with this crowd and now they've eliminated him. I hate to discourage you, Dana, but we must face the fact that he's not coming home." This sent her into an additional flood of tears.

"Yes, I know. But what if I take this to the police and they follow up on it. Then my girls will be in danger. I can't risk that."

"We need to find a way to put this group out of business without jeopardizing you. Give me some time to think about this. But don't do anything rash like calling the cops or attempting to contact this Derek Overton. We don't want him knowing anything about this document... at least not yet."

41

The Contractors

"An Unconventional Relationship"

Deirdre had been married to Marcus Moretti six years, having met him at a golf event after he completed a two-year prison sentence. It was a second marriage for both. They resided in a large Scottsdale home in an upscale neighborhood and were generally aloof from neighbors. He was forty-three years old and handsome in a tough-guy sort of way. She was ten years his junior with striking good looks—long brunette hair, dark brown eyes, perfectly proportioned hourglass figure, always impeccably dressed with flawlessly applied, understated makeup.

Their lifestyle was lavish. He drove a Mercedes Benz S 550 Lunar Blue coupe and she enjoyed a black Jaguar XJ sedan, both leased new in the last year. Neighbors saw other luxury cars entering and leaving the Moretti driveway at various times.

In the limited face time he had with neighbors, Marcus represented his business as "investor" working from home. Observant housewives saw Deirdre leaving home two or three times a week and staying gone several hours. The Morettis employed weekly uniformed housekeeping and pool services.

Marcus couldn't help noticing men staring at his wife in restaurants and their club. She turned heads in every room she entered. She leveraged her looks with an outgoing personality, winning smile, and mild flirtation with members of the opposite sex. Other wives were suspicious of her demeanor, and most disliked her for that reason. She related more strongly to men than to women. She was invited to participate in a new reality production for television, "Real Housewives of Scottsdale," but declined to do so.

Marcus's real work was as a highly confidential hit man, hired to do contract murder for large fees. His employers were typically wealthy businessmen and drug lords who wished to settle scores, eliminate enemies, and otherwise remove from society those whom they disliked for one reason or another. One of his recent clients was an important Hollywood movie producer who hired him to eliminate a rival with whom he was having a financial dispute. Marcus was away on "assignment" at least once monthly, earning a fee that varied from $25 to $50K, sometimes more depending on the difficulty and risk associated with the assignment. Clients contacted him through an underground network he had carefully cultivated, so that there were several layers of separation between him and his clients. Payment for services was made by electronic transmission to offshore banks. When fees were paid in cash, it was laundered through a string of car wash facilities[7] located throughout Arizona. Taxes were filed and paid.

---

[7] Self-service car wash facilities are all-cash businesses. Money laundering happens when extra cash is reported together with legitimate receipts, but not in sufficient quantities to attract suspicion.

Deidre sometime accompanied him on his professional trips, but usually not. He preferred to work alone. When Deirdre was along on an assignment, her role was to provide a needed distraction to the central task at hand. She was good at it. Her role in the operation at Etta's Place was a rarity, made necessary by two targets at the same location.

When traveling on assignment, he was gone from home three days to a week at a time. It was during these times that Deirdre was free to pursue her own interests—meeting friends for lunch at high-end restaurants, going on shopping sprees, and meeting Lee Simmons for trysts at the Regency and other hotels. Their affair was passionate. Their "hookups" were carefully planned. They had dinner together on two occasions but decided being seen together in public was too risky. They never arrived or departed from the hotel at the same time. Lee would check in, inform the room clerk that his wife would be arriving a bit late, and slip the clerk a hundred dollar bill. "Just between us, right?" he would say. Deirdre never invited him into her Scottsdale home.

Employed at the pet supply company, Lee was unable to get away during the day and so followed a pattern of leaving work around 4:00 p.m. two or three times a month on various days to meet Deirdre for a couple hours of fun between the sheets. This allowed him to arrive home about 6:30 as usual and therefore not appear to be suspicious to Janet.

As the affair progressed, they became less careful each time in their rush to jump into bed. As Deidre was leaving a Holiday Inn one chilly February evening after a date with Lee, a friend of Marcus who was there for a business meeting recognized her as she walked through the lobby. He followed her outside as she got into an elegant Jaguar sedan and drove off. A few minutes later, Marcus' cell phone buzzed.

MARCUS HIRED A private investigator who specialized in domestic matters to monitor Deirdre's activities for the next month. His report to Marcus contained dates and times, together with photos of her entering and leaving the Regency on one occasion and a Comfort Inn on two others. He also had photos of every man leaving those hotels within an hour after Deirdre's departure. Several of the images showed overweight, older men. Others were obviously tourist types. A process of logical elimination identified a physically fit guy in his forties with an upright posture and short haircut as her likely lover. Inquiries at the front desk accompanied by a couple of hundred dollar bills revealed the identity of the man as Louis Gladstone, the alias Lee used when registering at the hotel. The investigator suspected this was a false identity. He recorded the plate number of Lee's car as he drove away and later, through contacts with the Arizona Department of Transportation, identified the car's owner as Stephen Lee Simmons of Phoenix. He duly reported this fact to Marcus Moretti.

"WE'RE PARTNERS RIGHT?" Marcus confronted Deirdre at breakfast the following morning.

"Sure, why?"

"I think you've been fraternizing with some guy and it's been going on a long time."

This was not the first time either of them had conducted extra-marital affairs and there was an understanding between them it would be tolerated as long as it didn't affect their core business. This time was different.

"Your excuses for being gone, including shopping or going to movies are bullshit. I've suspected what was going on and now I want it stopped. Do you love this guy?"

"No way. Look, the guy is our client. He hired us for the bar and elk hunter hits. More business may be coming. He has hinted at the existence of a well-funded organization that undertakes to deal with people they don't like. He has all but promised there will be additional assignments down the road. Think of my time him as business development."

"So why the hell didn't you tell me about him in the first place? I mean if it means more business, I would have gone along with it, although I have trouble imagining you in this guy's arms. Or any guy for that matter."

"I guess I was scared of your reaction. And by the way, you and I have had our little dalliances in the past without any disruption to our relationship. Haven't we always thought of ourselves as a team? You know, kind of like Bill and Hillary." Deirdre paused momentarily and then said, "I admit I was attracted to him."

"Was? As in past tense? What about now?"

"Don't worry, it's just a quick roll in the goose down. Like I say, I think it's good for business. If I stop seeing him, it may hurt our chances for more assignments."

"Well, I guess that's a convenient reason to keep fucking him. I'm okay with it for now."

In Marcus' order of priorities, their business activity and the money it produced trumped any moral considerations. "As long as you're not seeing him more than once a month. And find out what you can about him and his organization. I'd like to know who we're doing business with. Order champagne to the room and keep filling his glass. Getting his rocks off with a little alcohol in his veins together with your feminine wiles may get him talking. Make him feel that he is expressing his masculinity by opening up to you."

42

The Parolee

"Convict's Release Surprises Local Law Enforcement"

A rizona Examiner, October 12
Maricopa County authorities were caught off guard Tuesday when informed a convicted double murderer might be residing near an elementary school in a west Phoenix neighborhood. In a shocking development, Raymond C. Gates, 73, was granted parole Monday by a vote of 9-2 of the Arizona Board of Pardons and Paroles. Gates had not been eligible for parole until 2030 for the 1980 shooting deaths of Gabriel and Teresa Pearce in their Tempe, Arizona, home. The parole board imposed several conditions—no contact with victims' families, must register with authorities, and report to his parole officer weekly. The board issued a statement that read, "In consideration of Mr. Gates' record of good behavior in prison and his efforts at rehabilitation, the Board has concluded he is an acceptable risk for parole."

The Phoenix PD, county attorney's office, and sheriff were notified late Tuesday by email message that Gates would be released Friday and would live with relatives at a specified address in Phoenix. By press deadline, the Department of Corrections had not issued a time for Gates' release.

"This office was not notified of Gates' parole hearing, nor were the victims' families, so no one was present to oppose the release. We cannot understand why he's being freed after killing two people," assistant county attorney William Graves said in a phone interview.

Gates was charged with first degree murder after forcing his way into the Pearce home with a handgun early February 20, 1970. He killed thirty-year-old Gabriel with a single shot to the head. He then entered a bedroom where twenty-four-year-old Teresa was hiding and shot her twice in the chest. Investigators learned he had been having an affair with Teresa which she had recently ended. He didn't take it well and told friends, "If I can't have her, no one can."

Gates was soon arrested and after his guilty plea, escaped from the county jail by cutting through bars with a file stolen from the prison workshop and tying sheets together to lower himself down to the street. He spent more than three years on the run in California before being nabbed in Oakland and returned to prison in 1974. He was charged and pled guilty to additional felonies. Sentencing for all his crimes totaled 230 years.

"I can't believe this guy is about to be paroled," shouted Derek to the *Committee* while reading the story in the *Arizona Examiner* newspaper. "Listen to this, 'Raymond Charles Gates, who was sentenced to 230 years in prison, is scheduled for release from state prison in Florence, today informed the Arizona Department of Corrections that he planned to live in Phoenix.'

"I remember the case. Our officers made the arrest after he'd fled the crime scene in Tempe. How is he getting out after killing two people?" Derek demanded.

"We were blindsided by this," said Dave. "We were not advised of Gates' hearing and consequently, none of our people appeared to oppose his release. The victims' families are devastated. They've been calling our office nonstop to ask what can be done to reverse this, but we have to tell them it's out of our hands."

J.W. was equally incredulous. "This is another example of how the criminal justice system is failing the public. How does the parole board believe he is not a danger?"

"That board has become more and more lenient over the past ten years," Dave said, "and our office is worried that politically correct horse manure is creeping into their decisions. Several of their members have been outspoken about the prison population growing too rapidly, and too many nonviolent offenders spending more time in prison than their offenses warrant. They've been very generous with paroles for nonviolent criminals, but this is the first time a violent criminal with a sentence that long has been released."

"If we deem this an affront to justice, what can we do to put it right?" asked Lee.

"Let's talk about that," Dave said. "This guy committed cold blooded murder and should have received the death penalty. He avoided it by confessing and pleading guilty. Now he's on the street and several of the callers to our office have promised to deal with him in their own way."

"There must be conditions attached to his parole," said Lee. "Can he just do as he pleases?"

"Absolutely not," Dave said. "Parole imposes severe restrictions on parolees for protection of the public. In Gates' case, he must report to his parole supervisor weekly, have no contact with his victim's families, live in one place known to his supervisor, possess no guns, not break the law, even traffic violations, agree to random searches of his home by law enforcement, and avoid the use of alcohol and drugs."

"I recall he was a heavy drinker at the time of his arrest," said Derek. "This may give us an opportunity. If we could somehow lure him into a bar and get him drunk, he would land back in prison pretty quick."

Marjorie stuck her head in the room and motioned for Derek to join her. In a low tone of voice she said, "Russ called me today and said he is outraged at the parole of a killer from Florence State Prison and asked if anything can be done. I told him I would get back to him."

"We're talking about that now. Thanks for letting me know."

"Gentlemen, I've just learned we will have resources from our benefactors to support an operation against Gates if we elect to take it on," Derek told the group. "Let me talk with our contractors to see if they have an interest in this project. Dave, in the meantime, find out what you can about

Gates, where he lives and how his parole officer supervises his time, okay?"

THE *COMMITTEE* CAME together two weeks later to consider the Gates matter.

"We have his address," Dave reported. "He lives quietly with his sister and her husband in a northwest Phoenix neighborhood, almost never goes out. He meets with his parole officer weekly."

"Our contractors have researched his habits and developed a plan to take him out," Derek said. "The plan is to whack him in the house where he lives since he's rarely out in public. His hosts would be at risk if they got in the way and could be also eliminated. That's an outcome we don't need. It's going to cost fifteen grand, and I'm not sure it's worth that."

Further deliberation led to grave doubt about the need for the elimination of Gates. Plan B was discussed and adopted.

DEIRDRE MORETTI WAS pressed into service. Her assignment was to visit Gates in his home and introduce herself as a representative of a nonexistent local organization providing social services to parolees. She rang the doorbell at 10:00 a.m. two days later and was greeted by Gates who had just gotten up. She was dressed conservatively without flashy makeup but still carried the scent of a subtle perfume. She was very attractive and presented a professional persona.

"Good morning, Mr. Gates, my name is Evelyn Moore. I'm with the Houseman Foundation. We contact people who have been recently released from prison to assist them in transitioning into the community. May I come in?" she asked, showing a false ID card.

Gates was immediately spellbound by Deirdre's appearance and asked her come in. Engaging him in conversation was easy. She was skilled at making him feel comfortable and overcoming his initial suspicion of her motives. Twenty minutes of small talk followed. Then she said, "There is a public library nearby and I would like to help you set up a library card so that you can check out books that might interest you. Then I can check back with you from time to time to see how you're doing." This was an offer Gates could not refuse. It did not occur to him to confirm the existence of the Houseman Foundation.

IT WAS A hot day, not unusual in Southern Arizona. Deirdre and her companion emerged from the library and got into her car. It was stiflingly hot there before she turned on the air conditioner.

"Hey, let's drop by Mortimer's for a cool one on the way home," suggested Deidre. "I'm buyin.'"

"Okay, but I'm not allowed to drink any alcohol," said Gates.

Deirdre drove Gates to the library on two successive occasions. By this time, he was thoroughly captivated and looked forward to his time with her. During their third time out at Mortimer's, she said, "Oh, it's all right. Go ahead and have a beer. I promise you won't get into any trouble with your parole supervisor." Two beers and a shot of tequila later, she slipped a small quantity of white powder into his drink while he was in the men's room. After draining his glass, he passed out, slumped over the table, intoxicated with alcohol and cocaine.

She quickly exited the bar and using a burner cell phone, placed a call to his parole supervisor and advised him where he could find his client.

Raymond Gates was returned to prison and was kept there to complete his original sentence. He died of a sudden heart attack two years later and was interred in the prison cemetery.

43

Another Assignation

"Pleasure's a sin, and sometimes sin's a pleasure."

– Lord Byron, *Don Juan: Dedication*

Lee and Deirdre met at the Regency for their monthly tussle on Saturday, his day off. Again, the sex was vigorous and raw. Lee had learned what aroused her to wonderful slipperiness and she was an expert at orally pleasuring him. Together, they were the perfect embodiment of amatory passion. After thirty minutes of erogenous exertions, they collapsed exhausted. Ten minutes of silence and heavy breathing followed. Then Deirdre said "Could it get any better?"

"If it were any better, I would melt," said Lee.

"Let's listen to some music and order room service." Deirdre tuned the TV to a classical music channel and picked up the phone. Punching up room service, she ordered a bottle of Veuve Clicquot Brut.

"What's that?" asked Lee.

"French champagne, lover. Police Chief Louis Renault in *Casablanca* said: 'It's a very good wine.' Let's do some sipping and then order food if you're hungry."

"Okay by me."

"How are things with your organization these days?" Deirdre asked innocently.

"What organization? I'm not a part of any organization."

"Oh come on, we've done some very successful assignments for you. I was just wondering if anything else is on the horizon."

"Not at the moment, but I'll let you know if a need arises for your services." Lee was mildly annoyed at the question.

Five minutes later, they heard a light knock on the door. Lee disappeared into the bathroom. Deirdre quickly wrapped herself in a terrycloth bathrobe and fished a couple of bills from her wallet before admitting the server.

A liveried attendant entered the room pushing a small serving table carrying a bucket of ice with champagne and two crystal flutes. "Shall I open it for you, ma'am?"

"Yes, please."

With minimum effort, the cork was removed with a pleasant pop.

"I'll do the pouring... that will be all," said Deirdre as she accompanied him to the door. Slipping a twenty to him after initialing the tab, she whispered, "Thank you, and bring up another bottle in thirty minutes, okay?"

"Gladly, ma'am."

"You can come out now, lover. Here is something nice we can enjoy." She filled two glasses with fizzy liquid. Lee emerged from the bathroom wearing only his shorts.

"God, that's good," he said, rapidly draining half the glass. She immediately topped it off.

"Fill it to the rim, I like the bubbles tickling my nose."

They retreated to the sofa and soaked up a Chopin etude, not knowing or caring about its title or name of the pianist.

Three refills of Lee's glass almost emptied the bottle. Deirdre was careful to nurse her one serving. Alcohol lubricated the conversation. At first, talk centered on the Arizona Cardinals. Deirdre was a fan of the team with knowledge of players, their positions, and statistics. The team had just completed a disappointing season, but she predicted a brighter future with a promising draft of young, talented players, and a new head coach who had recently coached a Big 12 college team. When she was certain that Lee was well relaxed, she broached the topic of the operation at Etta's Place and how skillfully it had been carried out.

"It went down without a hitch. Timing was perfect and we managed to exit the place before anyone knew what happened. You said they had it coming, but why exactly?"

A knock at the door brought Deirdre to her feet. "That's another bottle I had sent up just in case." The server popped the cork and departed again with another twenty. She filled his glass three fourths full with the ice cold beverage. It was his fourth glass. She was still working on her first.

"Where were we? Oh yeah, you were going to tell me why those two at Etta's Place deserved what they got."

By now, Lee was thoroughly relaxed, light headed, and much more talkative. "We had strong evidence that they were responsible for the K-Market murders awhile back. Remember that? A young girl at the cash register and a customer who got in the way were gunned down in cold blood during a robbery attempt. The two thugs got away with a few bucks and a six pack. One witness in the store at the time wasn't helpful, and there was no surveillance tape, so the cops had little to go on. Then we learned they were involved in at least two other convenience store robberies. It was only a matter of time before someone else got killed, so we felt they had to be taken out."

More champagne was poured.

"Interesting. So you guys are in the business of dispensing instant justice where you think it's needed?" Deirdre let the front of her robe fall open, partially revealing one of her breasts.

"Damn right. And that wasn't the first time." Lee was feeling the champagne and was losing his normal guarded attitude.

"Sounds like you guys mean business."

"We hired you when we needed a fresh set of eyes and a new approach in that particular case." Lee's words were slightly slurred. "Remember the Ochoa hit a couple of years ago? That was us, or more accurately, me." He instantly regretted that statement and sought to walk it back. "I mean, we knew who did the hit and it wasn't a rival drug cartel."

"Nothing ever came of that as I recall," said Deirdre. "No arrests were made."

"That's right, and none will ever be."

"More bubbly?" Not waiting for an answer, she filled his glass again. "Are you hungry? I'll order a couple of BLTs if you like."

"Sure." Lee was inebriated at this point, feeling no pain, and chattering continuously about anything that popped into his head. Deirdre rang room service and ordered two BLTs and another bottle of champagne. When it arrived, the server accepted another twenty with profuse thanks. Lee was unaware that Veuve Clicquot was being billed to his account at $132 per bottle.

She settled once again on the couch and topped off his glass. "Marcus and I get the feeling that you guys are into a lot of extra-legal stuff. So we're able to offer a reduced rate for local assignments. For instance, we could do the thing at Etta's Place for about twenty percent off from what we charged if we can do at least two a month for you. We want to cut back on out-of-state assignments because they're very complicated and costly to boot. It's hard to justify our fee to clients when travel and other expenses are factored in, not to mention the greatly increased risk. Tell me about other actions you could use some help with," she cooed while rubbing the back of his neck.

Lee was almost asleep at this point but managed to make a half-hearted response: "We don't like creeps who abuse women. We put things right when cases came to our attention if we're able to confirm the facts and develop a plan of action."

"That's fascinating. Tell me about something you did to put things right."

Lee tried to arrange his thoughts but was too bombed to provide a coherent story. "Look, I don't want to talk about this anymore. Let's hop back in the sack. I need to get home pretty soon." Deirdre had learned all she could at this point and let the robe slip completely off before climbing into bed for a final cavorting on this occasion. This coupling was nowhere near as satisfying as the former.

She made coffee in the brewer provided in the room and made him down a cold BLT sandwich. "Lee, you can't go home in this condition." Following a second cup of black coffee, he stumbled into the bathroom and took a long, hot shower.

He regretted his relationship with Deirdre, but was beginning to envision spending the rest of his life with her.

LEE HAD LEFT home at one that afternoon with the excuse that he had a meeting with J.W. He told Janet they would be out all afternoon planning a future operation. She grew concerned by 7:00 p.m. when he wasn't home. He told her he could not be reached by cell phone because he would be contacting certain individuals who demanded his undivided attention.

But when he arrived home at 8:35, she demanded to know where he had been and what he was doing. "My calls to your cell phone went to voice mail and your hair is damp. Have you been swimming somewhere?"

"Look you know what we do. We're planning a very complicated operation, so we need time and space to scope it out," he lied. "I stopped by the club for a quick workout and took a shower there. I should have called, I'm sorry." She could easily disprove this claim by a phone call to the club and he was terrified she would do just that. Her suspicion was alarming. He realized she knew he was up to something.

He left a message on Deirdre's phone the next day: "We have to take a break. I can't see you again for a while." He didn't return her repeated calls to him over the next week, nor did he return her text messages.

Lee felt remorse and guilt about his affair with Deirdre. When looking into Janet's eyes, he saw an innocence that wasn't there before. She was always loving and faithful. He felt worse than a prick for lying and betraying her for the sake of physical pleasure in the arms of Deirdre. Why had he submitted to her flirtation? She was a beautiful and seductive woman with a great body, passionate and aggressive in love making. He indulged in all this willingly. The affair was thrilling and provided fulfillment of base desires he had not experienced before, and was a mortal sin the in eyes of his Catholic faith.

44

Unforeseen Tragedy

"An American Tragedy."

– Theodore Dreiser, *Novel*

Marcus was on the verge of panic. "He won't return your calls or texts? What the hell is going on?"

"I don't know. The last time I saw him, he seemed fine. I got him to drink a lot of champagne but he never gave any indication that he was about to terminate our relationship," replied Deirdre. "I even offered the volume discount we agreed to."

"This is not good, in fact this is a threat to everything we're doing. If this guy is turning on us, it could be disastrous. Keep trying to reach him and keep me posted."

TWO DAYS LATER, Deirdre's cell phone buzzed from an "unknown caller." It was Lee. "Meet me at Ralph's tomorrow afternoon at three o'clock. I have some news for you."

"Okay but why haven't you been returning my calls?"

"I'll tell you tomorrow. Just be there." The line went dead.

LEE ARRIVED AT ralph's at two thirty. Seated at a remote table, he ordered Jack Daniel's on the rocks, then another fifteen minutes later. Deirdre appeared at ten minutes past three, looking great as usual and sat down. She reached across the table and gently took one of his hands in both of hers.

"Drink?" he asked lifting her hands to his lips.

"I'll have what you're having. Now tell me what's up. You won't return my calls. Marcus and I have been worried there is a security breach somewhere."

"No, nothing like that. I think Janet suspects I'm seeing someone, and I just needed to take a breather and think about our relationship, that's all."

This did not satisfy Deirdre's question. "You could have returned my calls and said that. I would have understood. But ignoring me raised alarm bells."

"Look, I'm sorry. Janet scared the crap out me when I got home after our last time together and I needed some time to think about how you and I can continue. I think I'm in love with you and I don't want it to end," he blurted. Two whiskies arrived.

Deirdre sat shocked and still for several seconds and slowly said, "This changes things, Lee. I'm not sure what to say. I've never thought we were more than casual lovers... you know... I care for you very much.... sex with you is great and all, but it can't be more than that."

Lee was feeling the effects of three shots of Jack Daniel's. "We're so great together. I've never had it so good with a woman. You can't know how much I look forward to being with you. Even when you're sometimes in that difficult time of the month, I love being with you. We enjoy talking about everything, and the music you select is always perfect. I think about you all the time. My boss at work has reprimanded me a couple of times for daydreaming. Derek notices when my attention wanders during our meetings." This was his first mention of anyone associated with the *Committee.* "I haven't told them about our affair. They think it's all about your professional services."

"Who is Derek, I don't remember hearing that name before."

"He's our chairman and basically decides which projects we take on," Lee said carelessly in a wavering voice.

Deirdre sensed he was divulging something he didn't intend and began to gently press him with conversational questions in the hope of extracting as much useful information as possible. After his third drink and a wobbly trip to the men's room, he said: "I should go. I'll give you a call tomorrow. No wait... I want to know your feelings for me now. Do you think we have a future together? It's really important to my peace of mind. This whole thing is eating at me. I'm not sleeping or eating. I'm drinking too much and…" His voice trailed off as he started to sob. She had never seen him like this. He was always so strong and self-confident. She felt the need to say something that would indicate the possibility of a relationship but not anything resembling a commitment.

"I didn't realize you felt this way and I'm really overwhelmed with emotion right now. Are you suggesting you might leave Janet for me?"

"I never thought I could say this, but yes. Your attraction is so strong, I can't think of anything else. I need another drink."

"No, you've had enough. Look, I promise to think very carefully about what you said. We're both married to someone else. I'm not sure if you're suggesting we live together or if you're proposing marriage."

"I don't know, my mind is so confused," he mumbled.

"Come on, I need to go now. I'll call a cab for you. You're in no condition to drive. I'll pick up the check."

"No, no, you go ahead. I'll have a cup of coffee to clear my head. I'll be all right."

"Promise me you won't leave until you've sobered up. Drink coffee and relax for at least an hour," she said walking away.

Instead of coffee, he finished Deirdre's drink and called for another Jack Daniel's, this time a double with a beer chaser. Twenty minutes later, having drained both glasses, he found his car and got in. At a high rate of speed six blocks on, he ran a red light and was T-boned on the driver's side in the middle of an intersection by a Ford F-250 pickup traveling at forty miles per hour. The force of the collision spun his vehicle onto the sidewalk on the opposite side of the street facing the opposite direction. Two pedestrians were alert enough to jump out of the way just in time. Rescue workers had to use Jaws of Life to free his body from the wreckage. His blood alcohol concentration (BAC) was later found to be .18, far above the level at which he could have been charged with DUI. He was blind drunk. The F-250 driver was slightly bruised but saved from serious injury by the air bag. He was found sitting on the curb with his head in his hands. A uniformed officer delivered word of the accident and Lee's fate to Janet at their home. She collapsed in the arms of Derek who rushed over from next door when he saw the police car parked out front.

Lee's cell phone, a burner, was retrieved from his body at the ER and given to investigating officers, together with his wallet, pocket knife, a ball point pen, and a small quantity of loose change. In attempting to identify the victim, Patrol Officer Pirtle found two driver's licenses – one in the name of Stephen Lee Simmons and another in the name of Louis Gladstone. There were also two credit cards with those names. These items and the phone were turned over to the patrol division commander who recognized the suspicious nature of two forms of identification. Lee's personal effects, minus his driver's license, phone, and credit cards, were delivered to Janet in due course. Detectives who assumed control of the investigation were able to trace Lee's route back to Ralph's where the bartender confirmed his presence with a beautiful woman earlier that day. She left the bar ahead of him and paid the tab with a credit card bearing the name of Deirdre Moretti. The detectives didn't disclose this to Janet. A small slip of paper was also found in his wallet with a phone number and a note that read—"Call Derek." A call to the number yielded an answering message: "The number you have called is not in service." Forensic examination of the cell phone, a burner, yielded nothing other than a couple of calls, one to a burner no longer in service and the other to Deirdre.

Detectives found the names of Marcus and Deirdre Moretti at an address in Scottsdale.

45

Post-Accident Inquiry

"Do not block the way of inquiry."

– Charles Sanders Peirce

The Morettis heard a loud knock on their front door early in the evening at their home in Scottsdale. Deirdre opened the door and was confronted by two well-dressed men who flashed their badges and identified themselves as Detectives Browning and McAvoy with the Phoenix PD.

"Good evening ma'am, are you Ms. Deirdre Moretti?"

"Yes, why? What's up?"

"Just a few questions. Do you know a Stephen Lee Simmons?"

Deirdre felt faint, gasped, hesitated, and said "I know Lee Simmons, what is this about?"

"He was killed in an auto crash earlier today and we have reason to believe you were with him in a bar before the accident. We need you to come downtown with us for a conversation."

"I don't understand. What do you want from me?" She began to weep from the shock of hearing about her friend's death.

"It's routine, ma'am. Please come with us." Not allowed to change clothes, apply makeup, or make a phone call to Marcus who was not at home at the time, she was placed in their car and driven to the nearest police substation in the eastern district of Phoenix.

Arriving at the substation, she was patted down by a female officer and relieved of her cell phone and wallet. Escorted to an interview room, she waited alone for thirty minutes—a police tactic to produce apprehension in the person under investigation. She was then led to another room where Browning and McAvoy were waiting.

With a weak voice she asked, "Am I under arrest?"

"No ma'am, but we have some questions. Let's talk about Stephen Simmons. How long have you known him?" asked Browning.

Thoroughly shaken she said "About a year I guess, but I knew him as Lee."

"Do you deny you were drinking with him at Ralph's this afternoon?" asked McAvoy.

"No, we were there. We're friends having a drink together. Is that against the law?" she angrily demanded.

"How well did you know him, were you in a romantic relationship with him?"

Now past her initial shock and alert to her culpability, she said: "I don't have to answer that question and I certainly didn't have anything to do with the accident."

"How much did he have to drink when you were with him at Ralph's?"

"Just a couple of whiskies, I don't know how much he had before I arrived or after I left."

"What was the topic of conversation?" asked McAvoy.

"I want to know what this is all about before I answer any more questions."

"Stephen Simmons was under investigation in connection with a sniper-related homicide and for his part in a conspiracy to punish certain criminal suspects with extra-legal methods. We know all about your affair with him," McAvoy said.

"Let's talk about your conversations when you were with him. Did he ever discuss his use or ownership of firearms, specifically hunting or military-style rifles?" asked Browning.

"Not that I recall," Deirdre answered evasively.

"Anything about target shooting or game hunting?"

"No."

"Did he ever express an opinion about the criminal justice system, as when suspects are not adequately punished for their crimes?"

"Never. Why does any of this matter now that he's dead?"

"Because we believe he was involved in something much larger than one or two shootings and if you know something, now's the time to help us out. If you do not cooperate, you will become a focus of our investigation," said Browning menacingly.

"I don't have anything else to say and I don't like being threatened."

"Did he ever mention someone named Derek?" asked McAvoy.

"I don't know what you're talking about and I'm not answering any more questions. So take me back home now or let me call my lawyer." Her request for a lawyer ended the interview.

"She knows something," Browning whispered to McAvoy in the hallway.

She was told they would be in touch and was driven home in a marked police cruiser. Nosy neighbors observed this with great interest.

MARCUS WAS IN a highly agitated state when Deirdre walked through the front door. She had called him on the way home and told him she had just been questioned by the police.

"What the hell did they want?"

"Lee was killed in a car wreck earlier today," she shrieked. "And they told me he is a suspect in a criminal investigation. Oh my God! Oh my God! They know about my relationship with him." She started to cry.

"Okay, okay, we need to stay cool and not panic right now. I'll call Jimmy and let him know what happened. Now try to calm down and tell me what you told them," said Marcus, handing her a glass of brandy.

"They wanted to know about Lee's knowledge of guns and hunting. And they asked about his attitude towards the criminal justice system. I didn't answer any of those questions. And they asked if I knew someone named Derek. I said I wouldn't answer that question and told them to either take me home or allow me to call our lawyer. That ended the interview and they drove me home, not in their unmarked car but in a police cruiser. I'm sure our neighbors enjoyed that."

Marcus called the cell phone of James O'Rourke, attorney at law. As a well-known criminal defense attorney, he had represented Marcus in his previous criminal indictments and trials. "So what's up this time?" he asked.

"We have a problem, Jimmy. Deirdre was hauled in for questioning by the Phoenix PD today. It came out of the blue and she is very upset. They're interested in her lover and told her he is under investigation for some kind of criminal matter. I should say *was* under investigation. He was killed in a car wreck after the two of them met in a bar. The first she heard of it was when they knocked on our door. We don't know…"

"Wait a minute," interrupted Jimmy. "Are you telling me she had a lover on the side?"

"It was a business thing. You know we have an understanding in our marriage that allows for certain, uh, shall we say, choices, as long as the other party consents. This was a guy we've done business with before."

"Okay, just sit tight and relax. I'll do some digging and see if I can find out what's going on. In the meantime, tell her not to answer any more questions from police. Call me immediately if they contact you again."

McAVOY AND BROWNING dug deeply into the backgrounds of Marcus and Deirdre Moretti and learned that Marcus was convicted felon, had spent time in prison, and was not currently visible in any legitimate enterprise. On the other hand, Deirdre had a clean record. She was not identified as a suspect in any crime, nor could she be linked to Lee Simmons in any way except for their personal relationship. They dropped their suspicion of her as a "person of interest."

FORTY-FIVE YEAR OLD James O'Rourke knew his way around the criminal justice system. Marcus Moretti was one of numerous clients. Practicing criminal law for twenty-one years in Arizona, he had represented numerous defendants accused of serious felonies, many who did the crime and a few who did not. At least a third of his clients were found not guilty at trial, another third plea bargained down to lesser charges with reduced prison time, and a third had their cases dismissed entirely. He enjoyed a record of six consecutive not-guilty verdicts. Prosecutors in the county attorney's office hated him. His law office was staffed with four lawyers (one woman and three men) in addition to himself, two male investigators, two paralegals, and four office assistants who were all women. He sought to avoid personal entanglements in the firm; consequently, his female hires were generally married, middle-aged, overweight, and unattractive.

He always served as lead counsel at trial—clad in tailored, thousand-dollar suits, hundred-dollar silk ties, gold Rolex watch, diamond pinky ring, and shoes polished to a high shine. He wore expensive cologne, the essence of which lingered after him. Six feet tall and physically fit from frequent gym visits, he sported a well-trimmed mustache and dark wavy hair carefully styled each week by Will, his personal barber. His persona was off-putting to opposing lawyers but attractive to a certain class of women who found him fascinating, even charming. Married and divorced twice, he was known as a womanizer, having indulged in numerous liaisons involving lovely married and unmarried women, all younger than himself.

Two days after the call from Marcus, he summoned the Morettis to his office for a 9:00 a.m. meeting. After coffee and pastries were offered and declined, he reported his findings.

"Police are focusing on several unsolved homicides including sniper shootings and two simultaneous hits at a bar in North Phoenix. All the victims were criminal suspects so cops are not that grieved over their loss, but that leaves them with subsequent crimes to solve. Deirdre, they think your former boyfriend was involved with a guy named Derek and possibly others in an organized action. We need to learn who this Derek is and have a talk with him."

"Lee referred to him just once and didn't mention his last name," said Deirdre. "I plied him with champagne and he admitted he was part of an organization that takes action to punish wrongdoers when the justice system doesn't do its job. They concentrate on guys who abuse their women. You know, domestic violence cases. He told me about several operations where they confronted abusers and reformed their behavior by beating the hell out of them and threatening to whack them if they continued to mistreat their women. He said their methods were effective. And, he mentioned the Ochoa hit in Paradise Valley, remember that? He implied that was their doing."

"Interesting. How did you meet Lee?" asked Jimmy.

"He found our ad in *Adventure Today* magazine and called. We met on several occasions and he ended up hiring us for an operation. I drew him into a personal relationship as a business development effort. I sensed that he might be good for other jobs. Oh, and he said something about the Elks club... that he was a member somewhere. And he mentioned a guy named Derek during our last time together."

"Did he say anything else about Derek, where he could be contacted, anything at all?" inquired Jimmy.

"No, nothing."

"Okay, I'll put my investigators on it," said Jimmy. "They should be able to find him quickly. I'll keep you posted. In the meantime, don't talk to the police unless I'm with you."

DETECTIVE NORMAN WILKIE called Derek at home. Marjorie answered and recognized the voice. "Hey Norm, how are you?

"Busy, we're covered up with cases. The wife and kids don't know me, but the overtime pay is pretty nice. Anyway, is the old man around?"

"Derek's not here just now. Can I have him call you?"

"Sure, no hurry."

An hour later, Derek rang Norm's cell phone. "Hey, what's up?"

"We need to talk buddy. Can you meet me at the Sunburst on Camelback?"

The Sunburst Bar and Grille, with loyal clientele, was a popular sports bar located on a major thoroughfare named for a well-known rock butte resembling a camel's hump.

"This sounds ominous," said Derek. "Should I be worried?"

Without answering, Norm said "How about six o'clock this evening?"

"I'll be there."

SEATED AT A remote table, both ordered draft beers.

"Well, what's going on?" inquired Derek.

"Do you know a lawyer by the name of James O'Rourke?" asked Norm.

The name caused Derek to freeze for a brief moment.

"I know the name, never met him personally, but I know he's successful in getting favorable treatment for his clients from the courts. We've put things straight several times when the justice system didn't perform adequately."

"Well, his investigators have been poking around trying to identify a person whose first name is Derek. Our detectives interviewed a woman named Deirdre Moretti recently. They traced her movements from Ralph's bar after Lee Simmons was killed. They were together drinking for about two hours prior to the accident. They had been having a rollicking affair for the past several months and our people believe she may be tied to an organized group involved in several hits on criminal suspects."

Derek's stomach was suddenly in turmoil and he had to grab the table edges to steady himself. Nausea swept over him and he almost threw up. The news that Lee was involved romantically with this woman came as a shock. After a couple of sips of beer, he felt better.

"Was my name given to the O'Rourke people?" asked Derek.

"I don't know but it might have been. Look buddy, you've confided in me what you guys have been up to and I've been as supportive as possible. But you should know that Lee was already under investigation."

"I know that his home was searched several weeks back, but nothing ever came of it. What do you think I should do? I mean, do these people pose a threat?"

"I'm just giving you a heads-up.

46

Suspicion

"If you kill, I WILL find you."

– Lt. Joe Kenda,
(Ret.) Colorado Springs Homicide Detective

A few days after the vehicle collision that claimed the life of Stephen Lee Simmons, Detective Browning was routinely reviewing the report of patrol officer Pirtle, who with his partner had investigated the accident. It contained typical information about the accident scene—vehicle descriptions, time, weather conditions, road conditions, and statements from eye witnesses. Then near the end, he read that the officer had been directed to deliver the victim's personal effects to his widow, Janet Simmons at an address in north Phoenix. *That address looks familiar,* he thought.

Searching notes from his interviews with retired detectives several weeks earlier, he found the home address of Derek Overton. *My God, that's next door to Simmons.*

"Hey McAvoy, look at this," he yelled. "This can't be a coincidence. Lee Simmons was a next-door neighbor of Derek Overton. He must be the Derek we're looking for."

"Retired Detective Derek Overton? The one we interviewed several weeks ago?"

"The same."

"We searched the Simmons home without finding anything. I think we should interview the widow to find out what she knows about her neighbor."

DETECTIVE McAVOY INVITED Janet to the precinct station on pretext of closing their investigation of the vehicle accident that took Lee's life. "Just a few details." Janet appeared at the front desk and asked to see Detective McAvoy with whom she had an appointment. Ushered into an interview room, she was immediately apprehensive. *This is where they interview criminal suspects.*

McAvoy and Browning entered the room, extended their hands and thanked her for coming. "You said this was about the accident, is that true?" she asked angrily.

"We need to ask you a few questions about your husband's activities and his relationship with Derek Overton, your next door neighbor," McAvoy said.

"You didn't find anything when you ransacked our home, so what is this about?"

"Were you aware that your husband was having an affair at the time he was killed?" asked Browning. "In fact, it had been going on a long time." The question was intended to create shock in Janet's mind over her husband's betrayal of her with another woman. "Hell hath no fury, and all that," Browning commented to McAvoy before the session began.

"He was with the woman before the accident."

Janet sat silent for several seconds and started to weep. "I suspected it. His behavior was strange. He was very late getting home several times and he didn't have very good reasons when I questioned him about it. But what does that have to do with our neighbor?"

Browning offered a box of tissues. "We have reason to believe that Lee and Derek Overton either committed or were complicit in several homicides involving criminal suspects and we would like you to tell us what you know about that."

"I have no idea what you're talking about," Janet said with conviction. "We're friendly with the Overtons. They live next door. Are you suggesting that Lee and Derek were involved in some form of criminality? That's absurd. Derek is a retired police detective and would never be associated with anything like that."

"Your husband betrayed you with another woman. This person may have been a part of a conspiracy. Did he ever mention anything about meeting anyone after work for any purpose that didn't fit his usual routine?" asked Browning.

"I want to know who his lover was," Janet demanded assertively.

"That's not necessary for you to know, Mrs. Simmons. You need to understand—this is a criminal investigation of a very serious nature. We're sorry for your loss, but now is the time for you to cooperate. If you were involved in Lee's activities or have knowledge of them, you could be exposed to criminal suspicion. You can help yourself now. If you are forthcoming, we can speak with the prosecutor to arrange immunity for you." This comment produced an effect on Janet that was electric. She remained silent for a full minute while the detectives silently stared at her.

"Lee never shared any details about what they were up to, but it was something about 'putting things right' as he called it. They met in Derek's basement pretty often, sometimes for several hours. I never attended these meetings."

"They?" asked Browning. "Who was involved?"

"Lee didn't mention names but I think it was at least four individuals. I sometimes saw them arrive and park in the back alley. One of them drove a pickup with the company name on the side. I didn't get the name."

"Can you describe the individuals?"

"All men, white I think—I didn't pay that much attention."

"Did the meetings happen on a regular schedule, like a specific day of the week?" asked McAvoy.

"They were usually on Friday evenings, but sometimes on other days. Lee just announced that he was meeting with Derek and disappeared."

"How close are you to Marjorie Overton?"

"She's my next door neighbor and we've been friends almost from the time we bought our house."

"How often do you speak with her?"

"Several times a week. We have coffee a couple of times a week."

"Here's what we need you to do," McAvoy said. "Continue your relationship with Marjorie and without being obvious, observe comings and goings to the Overton residence. Keep a log of meetings, number of visitors, times, and length of stay. Write down make of vehicles, color, and plate numbers. Do this beginning now. We'll drop by in two weeks to collect the information you've gathered."

"You're asking me to spy on my neighbor?"

"We're asking you to assist in an important investigation to your own benefit," replied Browning.

AFTER INTERVIEWING JANET, McAvoy and Browning canvassed neighbors across the alley behind Overton's house asking if they noticed vehicles parked there occasionally. Two homeowners who did not know the Overtons or Simmonses personally told the detectives of times when sometimes three vehicles were parked there about once a week in the evening for several hours. Men emerged from the vehicles and entered the house from the rear. The neighbors had drawn the assumption that they were there for some type of meeting. No women were ever involved, it was strictly a stag thing. Marjorie was never seen greeting the visitors or bidding them goodbye.

"Three vehicles at a time was happening several months ago, but recently only two at a time were there," said Keith White, the homeowner directly behind Overtons. "It hasn't been there in a long time, but I recall a pickup with the name of Sonoran Plumbing & Heating on the side."

"Did you happen to get a plate number for that vehicle?" asked Browning.

"I didn't pay that much attention."

Back at the office, McAvoy googled "Sonoran Plumbing & Heating, Phoenix" and found the owner's name—Philip Maguire, a missing person.

JANET SIMMONS HAD no intention of doing as the detectives asked and fearing wire taps on both their phones, she wanted to talk with Marjorie Overton face to face. She spotted Marjorie in her back yard the next afternoon and summoned her over to the fence.

"Marj, you need to know they're investigating Derek," said Janet in a panicky voice. "The cops have asked me to spy on you for the next two weeks. They want to know all about people who come and go and the vehicles they drive. Lee didn't tell me everything he and Derek were up to but he told me enough for me to understand that it was probably illegal."

"I can't discuss it with you, but know that Derek's group is doing necessary work. Look, I'll relay what you've just told me to Derek," Marjorie said. "Thanks so much and don't worry, Janet. We'll take care of this."

When Marjorie told him of Janet's warning, Derek immediately called his colleagues on the *Committee* and informed them that no meetings would be held in the near future. Contacted by detectives two weeks later, Janet had nothing to report. There had been no meetings at the Overton home during that time.

"She obviously tipped off the Overtons," McAvoy remarked to Browning. "I think we're at a dead end with her. We should be concentrating on Overton."

47

Conspiracy Continued

"To further the cause of justice."

S am Dexter, one of Jimmy's investigators, was assigned to find and identify a guy named Derek who was an associate of Stephen Lee Simmons. It didn't take long.

Entering the B.P.O.E. lodge in North Phoenix, Sam presented his picture ID to the lodge manager. It falsely indicated his status as an officer of the benign sounding and non-existent "Family Research Association of Arizona."

"I'm here on behalf of the family of Lee Simmons," he lied. "They're preparing a biography of his life. He was a war hero you know, and knowledge of his contribution to the Elks would be a valuable addition to their research. They would like to know more about his friends and associates so they can form a more complete understanding of his life's story."

"We were deeply shocked and saddened at the news of the accident." the manager said, and without thinking to ask for authorization from the family, offered to help any way he could.

Sam asked several generic questions and took notes about Lee's membership history, projects with which he was associated, and events he organized. "Could you give me names of some of his fellow members for follow up contact? They would be a valuable source of additional background information."

Impressed with Sam's description of the project and flattered that the Elk's Lodge would be asked to participate, the manager offered the names of James Peterson, Wade Adams, David Baumann, and Derek Overton. Bingo!

"It would be very helpful if you can provide the contact information for these individuals," said Sam. Armed with the information he sought, he thanked the manager and quickly ended the interview.

"THE GUY'S NAME Is Derek Overton and he lives next door to Lee Simmons," Sam reported to James O'Rourke. "He's a retired police detective and a known critic of the criminal justice system. He's a regular at Toby's Tavern and one of the bartenders told me he normally comes in on Thursday evenings, sometimes Fridays. He sits at the bar. We could contact him there."

"Okay, do it," said Jimmy. "Today is Wednesday, be there tomorrow evening and see what you can learn."

ARRIVING AT TOBY'S, Sam slid a twenty to the bartender with a request to point out Derek Overton when he came in. "Sure, no problem," was the response.

A half hour later, Derek walked in and sat at the bar, four stools away from Sam. The bartender nodded slightly in his direction and smiled at Sam who got up and went to the men's room. Returning, he perched on the stool next to Derek. After a few minutes of small talk, Sam extended his hand and introduced himself. "My name is Sam and I think yours is Derek. Am I right?"

"How the hell would you know my name and why am I talking to you?" asked a shocked Derek.

"I'm with a law firm that represents people who had a friendship with your late neighbor, Lee Simmons, and we are interested in continuing that relationship if possible. Does the name 'Laura' or 'Deirdre' mean anything to you?"

"You are going to have to come to the point and tell me what this is all about."

"Deirdre was the person contacted by Lee in connection with certain extra-legal activities under contract by your group. Does that ring a bell?"

"Oh my God," breathed Derek. "We better talk, but not here. Meet me at the northeast corner of Ballinger Park in half an hour on foot. And I'll have to be sure you're not wearing a wire."

THEY MET AT the park. When both were seated at a picnic table, Sam began the conversation. ""She is Deirdre Moretti, wife of Marcus Moretti. They operate a problem-solving service of which you are well aware."

"Lee never revealed who he was dealing with for security reasons," Derek fibbed. "So why are we talking?"

"Deirdre was interviewed by the police after Lee's fatal accident. They suspect she is involved in a conspiracy to punish certain miscreants when the criminal justice system fails to do so. She and Lee became lovers and he divulged some information to her under the influence of alcohol. So this is where we are. We have no wish to cast suspicion on you or your group, only to ensure that both parties understand there is a mutual interest in protecting the other's interests."

Confirmation that Lee and Deirdre were involved in a romantic relationship caused Derek to gasp. *My God, how could he have been so thoughtless? What could he have told her about the Committee?*

Sam continued. "My clients are interested in continuing the business relationship they have with you. I'm also authorized to offer our legal services to you. Our principal attorney is James O'Rourke. Perhaps you have heard of him? His representation is available to you at any point if you so desire."

Derek made a quick decision not to disclose what little he knew about Deirdre. "I'll consider your offer if and when the time comes. I'll need to contact this Deirdre. We'll need to talk about any future arrangements."

Producing his phone, Sam said: "Give me your cell number. Someone will give you a call very soon to set up a meeting." Punching the number into his phone, Sam offered his hand to Derek and walked away.

Two days later, Derek's cell phone buzzed. A woman's voice said: "Hi Derek, this is Deirdre. I believe we should meet to discuss a few things."

"When and where?"

"Lee and I used to meet at Ralph's on North Central. How about three tomorrow afternoon?"

"That works. See you then."

MID-AFTERNOON FOUND ONLY five other customers in the establishment, two young men at the bar and three middle-aged women seated at a table near the entrance. Their conversation was frequently punctuated by laughter oiled by a third round of drinks. Derek arrived at three o'clock sharp and sat at a table away from the bar. Deirdre arrived five minutes later, introduced herself, and sat down opposite him. Wearing little makeup, she was dressed conservatively and did not exude the sexy female persona Lee was accustomed to. Derek ordered two iced teas.

"I'm wondering why you seduced your client and my friend?" asked Derek assertively. "He drank too much in this bar the last time you two were together and now he's dead."

"The seduction was mutual, I assure you. Look, that's beside the point and in the past. I grieve for his loss as you do. What's important now is to define our business relationship going forward. That's why I called you. Lee retained us for a specialized operation and we are looking to work for you again if the need arises."

"Do your services always include sleeping with your clients?"

"Absolutely not. Our affair was very unprofessional and I regret it. But what's past is past. Now can we get down to business?"

"We may have something for you in about two weeks. Ever hear of Dr. Wilbur Owensby, the abortion doctor?"

Deirdre had a quizzical look on her face for a few seconds. "Oh yeah, we had a contract to deal with him about a year ago but our client backed out at the last minute. We kept the initial payment because we'd already planned the operation."

"Who was your client?" inquired Derek, knowing the answer would not be forthcoming.

"Can't tell you... confidential."

Derek nodded and went on: "He's still in business and he operates in the shadows because abortions in Arizona are legal only up to twenty four weeks of pregnancy. His clients come to him through dark referrals from legitimate abortion providers and from a few primary care physicians. You probably know that his specialty is late-term abortions in the third trimester of pregnancy, otherwise known as infanticide. We've learned from a source inside his clinic that he botched at least four procedures in the past month. Two of his patients almost died from severe complications, the other two disappeared. Their conditions are unlearned. All four were poor Hispanic women. He's been in the business of murdering unborn babies for five years and has become very wealthy. We figure he has killed at least two hundred unborn infants. Now it's time to put him out of business permanently. Is that a project you would be interested in accepting?"

"Marcus and I are strongly pro-choice, but if he's doing awful stuff, then he needs to go. What do you have in mind?"

"Our first impulse is to whack him at his clinic. But that would be too messy and would attract too much publicity. We need to find a more subtle method. Think about an approach you might use and I'll call you in a few days when we have a decision."

"We might have a quiet solution, one that wouldn't be too splashy." Deirdre got to her feet and smiled slightly, then departed. Derek remained behind and ordered a draft beer.

48

Infanticide

"Any nation that accepts abortion, is not teaching people to love, but to use any violence to get what it wants."

– St. Teresa of Calcutta

Derek summoned J.W. and Dave to the basement two evenings later.

"We've discussed the abortion industry before," Derek said. "Lee was firmly opposed to abortion in all cases and became upset when talking about it. He was Catholic and his priest constantly inveighed against it from the pulpit. On one occasion, I recall him saying his fondest wish was to live long enough to see Roe v. Wade overturned by the Supreme Court.

"Today, abortions up until the day of full-term delivery of a healthy infant are legal in several jurisdictions including the nation's capital," said Dave.

"I really don't have strong feelings one way or the other when the procedure is done early in a woman's pregnancy," J.W. said, "but late term is another matter when the infant can clearly survive. This guy Owensby is killing babies."

Derek continued. "Human life is the key. That 'thing' growing in a woman's womb isn't a rabbit or a pigeon. It's a little human for God's sake. Every abortion destroys a distinct and unique human life. I'm convinced that if people really understood what happens in an abortion, they would be overwhelmingly opposed to it. First trimester abortions up to sixteen weeks are done by an instrument called an aspirator. It literally sucks the fetus out of the uterus. Second trimester operations are more gruesome. From thirteen to twenty four weeks the body of the fetus is too large to be broken up by suction and removed through the suction tubes. So the opening to the uterus is enlarged allowing the doctor to dismember the body and crush the skull to facilitate removal. The baby, of course, dies immediately. After twenty four weeks of pregnancy, the procedure is unspeakably atrocious. And the horror of partial birth abortions? No civilized society can tolerate this sickening procedure. I say this guy should be eliminated."

"You mean Owensby is doing partial birth procedures?" asked Dave.

"I don't know, but it wouldn't surprise me," Derek said. "Remember that guy Gosnell in Pennsylvania? He owned and operated a hideous abortion mill and was convicted of murdering babies that were born alive after attempted abortions. Like Owensby, his clients were poor minority women who paid up to $5,000 for an abortion. Seven newborns were found to have been murdered when their spinal cords were severed with scissors after being born alive. He was convicted on three counts of murder and of involuntary manslaughter in the death of a woman who died after an abortion procedure. Investigators found filthy conditions and baby parts stored in various containers in his clinic. He was said to be American's worst serial killer and is now in prison for life without parole.

"And to extend the horror, New York State has now enacted legislation signed by the governor, who is Catholic for God's sake, that allows third trimester abortions where the fetus is nonviable or to protect the mother's life or health. This determination must be made by a licensed, certified, or authorized health care professional, thereby removing the need for a doctor to perform the abortion. Therefore, one person "authorized" by the state, such as a charge nurse or midwife without supervision from an MD, can abort a healthy infant up until the moment of birth. This is just pure evil. Why the governor's bishop doesn't excommunicate him is beyond me. This law removes abortion from the penal code and makes it a public health issue—a sly way to obscure the horror of it.

"And the governor of Virginia, who is a pediatrician, said an infant surviving a botched abortion should be kept "comfortable" while the mother and doctor have a "conversation" about the baby's future. Never mind giving the infant medical care or feeding it. Just have a "conversation" about the option of letting it die. Unbelievable.

"Some pro-choice politicians are now admitting that late-term abortion is murder. That must be small comfort to the procedure's victims." He railed on, "Exceptions can be made for rape, incest, and when the life and health of the mother are threatened. But what they call 'woman's reproductive health care' is actually the killing of a human life by means of abortion."

"Look, the public is over fifty percent pro-choice," said J.W. "If we whack this guy, it's going to be national news and a shitload of publicity will create enormous pressure for the cops to act. Every pro-choice organization and politician in the country will be breathing down their necks."

"Not when it becomes known that he specializes in ghastly abortions like Gosnell," Derek said. "I met with our contractor the other day. I told her the good doctor might be in our crosshairs and asked if they would be interested in taking on the project. She said they would plan a 'quiet solution' as she termed it and get back to me. If it's a go, I'll tell Marjorie to contact our benefactors for the funds."

"Go for it," said Dave. J.W. agreed.

MARCUS MORETTI HIRED a private investigator to monitor the life habits of Dr. Owensby, but did not inform him of the reason. It was a business relationship that stretched back several years and yielded vital information about the targets Marcus had been hired to eliminate. To execute assignments successfully, the hit man must operate in total stealth, neither creating nor leaving behind clues to his existence.

During the following two weeks, the investigator found the home and clinic address of his mark, followed him everywhere he went, noted all of his trips including destinations, time of arrival and departure, identities of the few persons with whom he met outside of his clinic. Owensby had moved his clinic to new locations twice in the previous eighteen months, both in low-rent strip malls. No name or sign identifying the facility was obvious. No exterior surveillance cameras were in sight.

To ensure his anonymity and avoid suspicion, the investigator used three different vehicles for his movements, all ordinary, older model sedans. He observed that the mark frequently used a ride sharing transportation service to and from his clinic, sometimes leaving his home on foot and walking to a convenience store three blocks away to await his ride. When using his own vehicle, he parked at a dollar store two blocks away and walked to his clinic in the alleyway, never entering through the front door. He and his wife had no friends and no visitors to their home. He obviously maintained a low profile to avoid unwanted attention to his illegal activity. His daily movements were never quite the same, except for one. He made a weekly stop at a coffee shop, Wednesday mornings about 9:00 a.m. Seated alone, he always had a frothy latte concoction and bagel while he read the morning newspaper. These findings were duly reported to Marcus who paid the investigator in cash and cautioned him to destroy all notes, camera images, computer data, and other evidence of his investigation. "And remember," said Marcus, "this investigation never happened."

"Got it," said the gumshoe. "Let me know when you need my services again."

HEAVILY DISGUISED, DEIRDRE entered the coffee shop at 8:45 on two successive Wednesday mornings and identified the doctor from images of him captured by the investigator. He always ordered his coffee and bagel, sat at the same table facing the aisle, and talked with no one. She noticed that he usually held the newspaper in an upright position close to his eyes, occasionally putting it aside to take a sip of coffee. *He must be very nearsighted.* This presented an opportunity. The coffee mug was not in his view while he was lost in the story he was reading. Deirdre carefully observed other customers at that time, was satisfied they minded their own business and paid no attention to the coffee drinker sitting alone. She reported her observations to Marcus.

"Does he drink all the coffee or leave some of it in the cup?" asked Marcus.

"He never goes for a second cup and he usually stays at least twenty minutes. I think he drinks it all, but slowly."

"In that case, we'll have to use the concentrated form of powder. We don't want him to be sickened with a nonlethal dose of juice and survive the episode. So take your usual position at the shop next Wednesday. You know what to do."

"WHAT OPERATION AM I funding this time?" inquired Russ Milam.

"It's an abortion provider who is breaking the law by doing late term abortions," said Marjorie. "And his screw-ups are injuring his patients. To avoid attention, he operates secretly and accepts clients only by referrals. The state medical board or local law enforcement authorities seem to have no interest in pursuing him. He needs to be stopped."

Russ had a troubled look on his face. "I don't know. I think an abortion decision should be between a woman and her doctor. There have been several well publicized murders of abortion doctors across the country and I don't think we need to be involved in that."

"This is not just any abortion doctor, Russ. This guy performs the most appalling procedures including killing unborn infants very late in gestation at a time when the baby could clearly survive a natural birth or C-section. That's not something that bothers you?"

"Does he perform abortions early during pregnancies or just the late-term ones?'

"No early ones that we know of. His specialty is late-term procedures and he has become very wealthy at it. Most of his clients are low-income minority women who have to scrape up his fee however they can. Russ, I can show you some horrifying pictures of dismembered infants who have been victims of this procedure that will turn you stomach. Do you want to see them?"

"No, I get it. How much do you need?"

WEARING NO MAKEUP and dressed in baggy pants, sweat shirt, unmarked baseball cap, and sunglasses, Deirdre arrived at the coffee shop just after 8:45 the following Wednesday morning and ordered a regular coffee. Owensby hadn't arrived ten minutes past nine and she feared he wasn't coming that day. Five minutes later, he walked in and ordered the usual. Several customers were present and were walking back and forth in the aisle where he sat.

After he was settled reading his paper in front of his face, she got up, walked by his table unnoticed, and deftly emptied the contents of a small tube of white powder into his coffee. Exiting the shop, she sat in her car nearby and waited. Twelve minutes later, an ambulance, fire truck, and two police cruisers roared up with sirens blaring and emergency lights flashing. The chaotic scene was quickly secured by officers. A half hour passed. She observed EMTs rolling a gurney with a body bag out of the shop and loading it into the ambulance. She punched a number into her phone and said "The package was delivered."

She had used the precaution of taking her paper coffee cup with her as she exited the store. She carefully wiped it down to remove any fingerprints or DNA that might have been present and tossed it in a waste container located in front of a store several doors away. Surveillance cameras were not used in the shop.

EMTs on the scene found Owensby slumped over the table, unresponsive and pale. Cardiac failure was the initial diagnosis. Chest compressions were ineffective. Six weeks later, the coroner confirmed the cause of death as an overdose of Rohypnol, known as the "date-rape" drug, combined with cyanide poisoning. By this time, news media had published the appalling activities occurring in Dr. Owensby's "clinic." The story grew cold. National and local pro-choice organizations did not pursue the matter. The combination of date-rape drug and cyanide was a mystery not addressed by the coroner. Dr. Owensby's clinic did not reopen.

PERIOD FOUR

49

School Shootings

"Violence and injury enclose in their net all that do such things, and generally return upon him who began."

– Lucretius

The *Committee* frequently discussed the appalling incidence of school shootings across the U.S. during the past two decades. Public attention to these crimes crystallized in 1966 following the shooting rampage of Charles Whitman atop the tower on the University of Texas campus in Austin. He had knifed to death his wife carrying her unborn child and his mother the day before, and used multiple weapons to kill fifteen people and injure thirty-two others before being gunned down by an Austin police officer ninety-five minutes after the shooting began. An autopsy revealed a brain tumor that was likely the factor in Whitman's dementia. Since then, other shootings causing mass casualties occurred on school properties.

One of the most notorious incidents occurred in April, 1999, at Columbine High School in Littleton, Colorado, near Denver. Eric Harris and Dylan Klebold, both students at the school, entered the building and shot dead twelve students and one teacher before turning their weapons on themselves. Both boys were known as misfits who had been bullied by jocks at school. In recent years, the school has been increasingly frequented by trespassers (curiosity-seekers) seeking to visit the site of the atrocity twenty years previously. To prevent these constant interruptions, school officials considered demolishing the entire building and rebuilding it.

In April, 2007, at Virginia Tech University in Blacksburg, Virginia, Seung-Hui Cho, a student, shot and killed thirty two students and faculty members. This was the deadliest school shooting in U.S. history at the time.

All school shootings causing deaths were horrendously tragic, but perhaps the most heart crushing was the incident at Sandy Hook Elementary School in Newtown, Connecticut, in December, 2012. Adam Lanza, using a semi-automatic rifle stolen from his mother, killed twenty first graders and six teachers, then turned the weapon on himself.

Six years later in February, 2018, a nineteen-year-old former student of Marjory Stoneman Douglas High School in Parkland, Florida, killed seventeen students and injured another seventeen before being taken into custody by law enforcement officers. This and all other schools where shootings occurred were "gun-free zones." Not one teacher, administrator, or custodian possessed a weapon to confront the shooter with the real possibility to save lives. The school's resource officer, a sheriff's deputy on duty at the time, was denounced for not entering the building during the shooting. Signs on front entrances saying "No Guns Allowed" were an announcement to bad guys and psychos that they will be unopposed by a good guy with a gun. "Come on in and do your worst."

In the aftermath of both the Columbine and Douglas High School incidents, law enforcement was heavily criticized for failure to act more aggressively to control the situation and stop the carnage.

In May, 2018, a shooter armed with a shotgun and a .38 caliber handgun killed ten and injured twelve more at Santa Fe High School in Texas. Prior to these incidents and intermittently, dozens of school shootings occurred—each causing injuries or one or two deaths but not attracting massive press attention of those resulting in multiple casualties.

COUNTY ATTORNEY LUKE THORNTON assigned a case to prosecutor David Baumann involving a teacher allegedly attacked by Gerald Boynton, an eighteen-year-old junior at Desert Spring High School in west Phoenix. Gerald was a year older than most of his classmates because he had been held back a year in middle school. The school principal attempted to handle the matter internally using established disciplinary procedures, but the assault caused facial lacerations and bruising on the female teacher's face resulting in calls to 9-1-1. She was transported to the ER, treated, and released.

Gerald was arrested and released to the custody of his parents the same day. Placed on indefinite school suspension, he was forbidden to enter the campus on assurance of arrest and additional detention. Police referred the matter to the county attorney for evaluation of possible criminal charges.

SCHOOL OFFICIALS INITIALLY refused to release Gerald's disciplinary records, but when promised a subpoena, they relented and turned over his student files. Dave's investigation resulted in a shocking pattern of bad behavior. He was out of control most of the time since the age of thirteen. In middle school, he set fires in waste baskets, frequently cursed teachers, and was caught "tagging" an exterior wall with swastikas. In high school, he hurled racial epithets at minority students, started fights, shoved and cursed female students. He vandalized a restroom causing over $1,200 in damages. On several occasions, he threw objects across classrooms, causing minor injuries to other students. He threatened his teachers, and several times promised to shoot up the school. He had been temporarily suspended on multiple occasions. Police were called to the Boynton home numerous of times during his middle and high school years. On one occasion, he hit his mother in the face, knocking out several teeth.

At school, he constantly talked about guns and how his father collected them. He was caught with a large fixed blade knife and a box of .22 caliber ammunition in his backpack. That got him suspended for three days. A scribbling was found in his notebook saying "THEY WILL DIE." Teachers and classmates were afraid of him, but their complaints to the principal produced no meaningful action to correct his behavior. His parents refused to seek psychiatric evaluation, telling the principal he would "grow out of it."

One day after school, a group of four boys, all brawny football players, confronted Gerald in an alley near his home and roughed him up with warnings to cease his "shitty behavior" at school or suffer the consequences. A frightened but unhurt Gerald arrived home, locked himself in his room, and vowed to seek vengeance on the four who had threatened him.

The school district had a policy called "MS&E" – Mentor, Support, and Educate, modeled on a similar program adopted by Broward County Schools in Parkland, Florida, in effect at the time of the tragic shooting at Marjory Stoneman Douglas High School in that city.

This was the policy at Desert Spring High School, under which students who commit crimes and misdemeanors in school would not be reported to police but evaluated and handled by the school's various student counseling programs. The school district's superintendent and his supporters referred to the policy as "discipline restraint." Disruptive students, even those who issued threats and committed violent acts, were required to attend "recovery sessions" where students sat in a circle and shared comments about their life experiences. These were intended to produce internal, non-judicial remedies. Instead, mentally disturbed students were allowed to occupy and disrupt classrooms with normal students and teachers who couldn't control them since they couldn't call the cops.

This policy was an obvious failure in Gerald Boynton's case.

Political correctness is running amok and this kid is a clear and immediate menace to the school, thought Dave. To the charge of assault and battery, Gerald pled guilty, was sentenced to a two-year probationary period and suspended from school for the duration of the school year. The injured teacher filed a lawsuit to recover medical expenses together with punitive damages in the amount of $50,000. The Boyntons' insurance carrier settled for $12,000.

"I'M TERRIFIED this will become another Parkland High School tragedy," Dave told the *Committee* with rising emotion. "The Boynton kid displays all the characteristics of the Parkland shooter—a strong pattern of psychopathic behavior from an early age, disruptive acts, vandalism, violence, threats to teachers and students, and now an attack on his English teacher that got him a tap on the wrist from the judge. He's been suspended from school but that may not deter him from doing something violent. This kid is a walking time bomb. He might as well have had a sign around his neck his entire life yelling "I will become a mass murderer if I you ignore me."

"What do you recommend?" asked J.W.

"School officials have treated him with kid gloves for years and his behavior has only become worse," Dave said. "The school's crazy MS&E policy prevents calling police even when felonies are committed including sexual assaults, weapons in school, and drug dealing. Where there is no record, there is no crime. So when a kid graduates and goes to buy a gun, background checks are pointless. This is politically correct horse shit and it'll lead to another Parkland, mark my words. Gerald entered the criminal justice system only because another teacher called 9-1-1 to report the crime." Dave went on, "He's too young to purchase a firearm legally, but his father has a gun collection. We don't know how secure that is. Are weapons kept in a gun safe or in an open cabinet where Gerald could get at them? That thought is scary."

"How should this *Committee* become involved?" asked Derek. "I don't want to hire our contractors for an operation to take out a kid."

"Given his record of offenses and his suspension from school, he may be an imminent threat. If we're going to take action, it should be soon. Very soon," said Dave.

"We need to develop a plan," said J.W. "Remember Alton Ferguson the wife beater? He just disappeared, never heard from again."

"My friend Norm Wilkie tells me his case isn't closed but is no longer under investigation," said Derek. "They will pursue it only if new evidence arises."

"Without Lee, we no longer have a long-rifle marksman and the idea of killing a teenager isn't appealing even when it's a potential monster like this Boynton kid," said J.W.

"Let me talk to Deirdre to see if they would be interested in finding what the kid is up to. You know, follow his movements, where he goes, who he talks to, all that," Derek offered.

DEIDRE MET WITH Derek four days later to report her findings. Gerald stayed at home most of the time, seemed to have no friends, and left home late each afternoon for a short walk to a small neighborhood park where he sat on a bench and smoked cigarettes for about an hour, sometimes longer. This was usually about dusk each evening. Deirdre noticed few park visitors at this hour. No one paid any attention to Gerald. She concluded these park visits were the only opportunity to contact him alone outside the Boynton home.

"Is he always alone?" asked Derek.

"He seemed to be. I monitored him three evenings from across the park and he never interacted with anyone."

"We have no interest in eliminating him. After all, he's still just a kid. We're not in the business of whacking children."

"Get this. I put binoculars on him and I'm sure he's packing heat. He pulled out a semi-automatic handgun and gazed at it for several minutes, cocked it and pulled the trigger a couple of times, then put it back into his pocket."

"So he must have pilfered his dad's gun collection. My God, this is our worst fear. If he has access to a weapon, he might go to the school anytime and shoot up the place."

"What if I were to casually drive by the park when he's there, and stop along the curb," Deirdre suggested. "The park bench is about thirty feet away. I would get out and lure him into the van using certain skills I have. You guys could take it from there."

Derek considered that for a moment. "Interesting, I'll let you know."

Deirdre's phone buzzed the next morning. "We need to go with this today. Are you available?" Derek asked.

AT 6:00 P.M., a dark windowless cargo van pulled up and stopped in front of Gerald who was slouched on his usual park bench smoking. Deirdre emerged, wearing short shorts, halter top, spangled sandals, and elegant makeup with intense lipstick and heavy perfume.

"Hi there," she said seductively as she approached him. "I was wondering if you could spare a cigarette. I ran out of them just now and saw you here enjoying a smoke so I thought you might help me out."

Gerald gawked at her cleavage. "Sure," he mumbled, pulling the pack and lighter from his shirt pocket. He shook one out and lighted it for her. They sat smoking for a few minutes while Deirdre made small talk. He had never had a date with a girl in his life and now he couldn't believe his good fortune. He was entranced with this beautiful woman who was giving him all her attention.

"Say, I have an idea," she purred. "It's getting a little chilly. Why don't we get in the van and have another smoke. We'll be more comfortable there."

Gerald obediently followed her back to the van and climbed into the passenger seat. Before Deirdre could get in, strong hands jerked his head back and plunged a needle into his neck causing instant paralysis. He was dragged into the rear of the vehicle and laid out on the floor. A 9mm semi-automatic pistol was found in his jeans. Deirdre started the engine and hurriedly drove away.

WHEN GERALD HAD not returned home by 9:00 p.m., his parents became concerned. He had not stayed out that late before. He usually returned from the park about seven, ate a few bites of dinner, and retreated to his room for the rest of the evening playing video games. Since he had no friends, they didn't know anyone to call. They drove to the park, didn't find him there, returned home and scoured the neighborhood on foot and then in their car, searching the streets for many blocks in all directions. A call to 9-1-1 produced no response from the police. "Teenagers frequently leave home for several hours. He's probably visiting friends and lost track of time," said the 9-1-1-operator. This did not satisfy the Boyntons.

The call came at 12:20 a.m. "Sir, this is Dr. Adair at Northwest Community Hospital. Are you the parent of Gerald Boynton?" he asked with a British accent.

"Why yes I am, he's been missing all evening, what's up?" Mr. Boynton asked with dread.

"I'm afraid I have bad news, sir. Your son was found injured this evening in a park amongst some tall grass. He was transported to the ER in critical condition. He's not expected to live. You should come in straight away."

The Boyntons rushed to the hospital and were greeted by Dr. Adair who introduced them to Police Detective Robert Ramirez in the ER waiting room. He ushered them into an adjoining office and closed the door. "I'm very sorry to tell you that Gerald is deceased."

The Boyntons were oddly calm and did not seem to be overly grieved, a reaction Ramirez found highly unusual. "What happened, how did he die?" asked Mr. Boynton.

"Our preliminary investigation points to suicide. A 9mm semi-automatic handgun was found nearby. Do you know how he came to have that weapon in his possession?"

"I have a collection of guns—all types. I own two guns in that caliber. My God, he must have taken one of them."

"Do you mean your collection was not secured?"

"Not well enough, obviously."

"Did he appear to be upset about anything recently? Did something happen that may have brought this on?"

"Our son has a troubled history since his early teens. Constant trouble at home and at school. He slugged one of his teachers and was arrested on a charge of assault and battery. He was sentenced to probation and suspended from school.

He didn't take it well. Kept threatening to get even with some 'jocks' as he called them."

"Did he ever mention the possibility of taking his own life?" asked Ramirez.

"No, he didn't, but he was always angry. We found that he was going to the park every afternoon to smoke. That's where we thought he was today. He didn't come home and we had no idea where he was until the hospital called."

"I'm very sorry for your loss. We'll be in touch when we complete the investigation. Is there anything I can do for you?"

"Can we see him now?"

"He's in one of the ER examining rooms. I can take you there if you like."

Mrs. Boynton, who hadn't said anything, spoke up. "No, that won't be necessary. We should go home." The Boyntons arose, walked out to their car, and drove away. Detective Ramirez could only wonder about the uncaring attitude of parents who had just lost a child.

Four days later, he phoned them with an update. "We've confirmed the bullet that killed your son came from the weapon he was holding. His death has been ruled a suicide."

The Boynton's claimed Gerald's body from the county coroner and had it immediately cremated. His ashes were scattered at the park he visited each evening.

IN THE BASEMENT, Derek addressed the remaining two members of the *Committee*. "Did we do the right thing? Unlike our previous operations, I have this dark feeling of guilt. He was only a kid."

"Get over it, Derek," J.W. said. "He was a walking stick of dynamite with the fuse lit. We saved a lot of lives this week."

"This kid was mentally ill and had a pistol in his possession. It was only a matter of time until he used it on his former classmates. End of story," said Dave with conviction.

J.W. summed up the *Committee's* attitude: "Every school in this country should be protected by armed, uniformed, trained security personnel in numbers proportional to the schools' enrollment. Instead of signs prohibiting guns, they should say, 'This Facility is Protected by Armed Security Officers at All Times.' And if metal detectors can be used at airports and government facilities, why not at all schools as well?"

50

Justice Delayed

"Justice delayed is justice denied."

– William Gladstone

Superior Court Judge Leland Vaughter had been on the bench for twelve years and thought he had seen everything. The case before him involved the death of a young man who had been shot to death in his own car by a deranged woman he had previously met in a bar. They drank together and played pool.

He offered her a ride home. She accepted.

Arriving in front of her upscale apartment, he sensed the evening was not over, reached over and took her hand. Her previously pleasant attitude changed in a flash. She angrily jerked away, pulled a small .38 caliber revolver from her purse and pumped three shots into his chest at short range. She then exited the car, wiped down the weapon and heaved it into a nearby pond on the grounds of the apartment complex, entered her apartment, locked the door, showered, and went to bed.

Two hours later, a knock came at the door, she was arrested, handcuffed, and taken to police headquarters. Her name was Sylvia Padilla. A witness who resided in the apartments identified her as the shooter. He was walking through the parking lot about forty feet away when he heard a popping noise and saw flashes in the car. He had a perfect view of Sylvia as she opened the car door and walked toward her apartment. She did not notice him as he crouched behind a bush fearing he might be next in the line of fire.

When detectives arrived at her door, she claimed to have been asleep and was unaware of anything happening outside. But the statement of the eyewitness was strong enough to make her the only suspect in this homicide. Motivation, however, could not be determined.

Sylvia was the daughter of Guillermo Padilla, the wealthy owner of an import/export business with interests throughout Central and South America. Her parents were aware that she had a mental disturbance but approved of her wish to live independently, thinking a change in living environment might be beneficial. She found a job in sales, performed well and seemed to be living a normal life.

After processing at the police station, Sylvia called her father who immediately called criminal defense lawyer James O'Rourke. A half hour later, O'Rourke arrived at the station, demanded to see his client, and ordered all questioning to cease. Detectives had no choice but to place Sylvia in a holding cell without a statement. O'Rourke cautioned her not to say anything to anyone.

Detectives pieced together the evening's events beginning with the pair's meetup in the bar. An unmistakable timeline was drawn. The eyewitness had hidden and saw her tossing the pistol into the pond where it was quickly recovered. Ballistic analysis left no doubt this was the weapon used in the fatal shooting. At trial, the PD's forensic expert faltered in his testimony, at first stating the weapon used was a .380 ACP semi-automatic pistol, then correcting himself by identifying the weapon as a .38 caliber revolver. It was his first experience testifying in a criminal trial and his nervousness was obvious.

County attorney assistant Matias Carrasco prosecuted the case for the people and sensed his case had been weakened. He tried to repair the damage with several questions regarding the witness's knowledge of firearms only to further confuse the witness and the jury. O'Rourke destroyed the expert's testimony on cross examination. The eyewitness, on direct examination, was in no doubt when he firmly identified Sylvia Padilla as the shooter. But again, he wavered on cross when O'Rourke was able to raise skepticism about his testimony owing to his distance from the shooter, darkness, and the absence of his glasses normally used to correct near-sightedness. Detectives who investigated the case were not well prepared to give testimony. They did not present a convincing story to the jury.

O'Rourke did not raise the insanity defense but put a psychiatrist on the stand who testified that Sylvia suffered from bipolar disorder that caused her to exhibit violent behavior sometimes without any obvious stimuli. Objections to this testimony from Carrasco were overruled.

Sylvia was found not guilty. Carrasco was stunned. James O'Rourke collected a large fee from Guillermo Padilla.

The case came to the *Committee's* attention through Dave. "This was an act of second degree murder and Sylvia was not held accountable. She's a walking stick of dynamite and something like this will probably happen again, given her unstable mental condition. Once again, the system is placing the community at risk."

A month later, she was found dead, drowned in the pond on the grounds of her apartment complex. Her death was ruled accidental after the coroner's autopsy found toxic levels of cocaine in her system. Over two hundred mourners attended her funeral Mass. The case was closed.

"It went down well," J.W. told the *Committee* when they were assembled in the basement.

51
The Gambler

"Learning is not attained by chance..."

– Abigail Adams

Matias Carrasco was the fifth of seven children in a struggling Hispanic family in Floresville, Texas, and was the first in his family to attend college. His father worked as a handyman on cattle ranches in south Texas and barely earned enough to provide for his ever increasing brood. Matias was a standout student in high school—academically and athletically. He was offered football scholarships at the University of Texas, El Paso, and Texas A&M University, Kingsville. Standing just over six feet tall at 195 pounds and highly talented as a linebacker, he accepted A&M's offer to join that school's successful football program. As an NCAA Division II school, the program had won numerous Lone Star Conference championships and had sent several players to the NFL. Matias was also attracted to the engineering program when he learned that it graduated more Hispanic engineers than any college in the country.

Following graduation with honors, he worked as a civil engineer for the City of El Paso, Texas, for two years. During this time, he became disenchanted with his chosen profession mainly for its meager remuneration provided by the city and lack of opportunity for advancement within the city's civil service system. Still unmarried, he spent time in local bars after work where he met young men and women his own age, some of whom were attorneys. Over beers and wings, they related fascinating stories about clients and cases they worked on, and joked about the "majesty of the law."

One story in particular about a criminal case one of his drinking friends defended aroused his interest. The defendant appeared to be obviously guilty, had confessed to the crime, but eventually through the skill of his lawyer, was found not guilty by the jury. Matias was greatly impressed with this story and its outcome. That night, he made a decision to leave municipal employment and apply to law school.

Scoring in the top ten percent on the Law School Admission Test (LSAT), and presenting a stellar academic record, he was readily accepted by St. Mary's University School of Law in San Antonio. He was also accepted by law schools at Texas Tech University, Baylor University, and Southern Methodist University, but chose St. Mary's owing to its close proximity to his family in Floresville.

He earned a J.D. degree, finishing third in his class of 158 graduates. He passed the bar exam on his first try and was promptly employed by Barnes, Gallagher, and Day LLC, a large law firm in Dallas where he spent three years working sixty to eighty hours a week in billable time. Seeing no pathway to a partnership and exhausted from long hours at a private law firm, he resigned and joined the Dallas County District Attorney's Office, made famous by DA Henry Wade, of Roe vs. Wade notoriety. His first position was Attorney I (associate prosecutor) at a salary considerably less than he had been making with Barnes Gallagher, but the stress level was tolerable and he was able to have a life outside of the law. He met Linda, his future wife, through a mutual friend and after dating for six months, they married. A year later, he was promoted to Attorney II at a salary allowing him and Linda to purchase a home in nearby Richardson.

Since his early twenties, he suffered increasingly from respiratory disorders, first with pollen allergies then with severe problems including coughing, sneezing, and labored breathing. The allergies began triggering asthma attacks. After three brief hospital stays and continuing outpatient treatment not covered by his employer's health insurance, his doctors recommended a change of living conditions. Arizona's drier climate was his first choice so he resigned from his position and moved to Phoenix along with Linda. His résumé demonstrated advanced abilities as a prosecutor. That fact combined with his superior academic record and minority status persuaded the Maricopa county attorney to hire him as an assistant.

A careful review of his personal finances might have prevented his employment by the county. His credit score was sub 650, identifying him as a "subprime borrower"—not good. Not only did his record show frequent late payments to his creditors, he carried close to $25,000 in credit card debt resulting from his uninsured medical treatment and Linda's spending habits. She was fond of shopping sprees with her friends. Clothes and shoes were her primary purchases.

Possessing dozens of pairs of shoes caused Matias to call her the "Imelda Marcus"[8] of Dallas.

Matias' health improved after the move to Phoenix and he easily adjusted to his new job. His personal debts continued to climb from his frequent weekend visits to Las Vegas, now only a six-hour drive away, forty-five minutes by air. Credit card limits were maxed out. This put an end to Linda's shopping habits but not to the couple's heavy debt load.

To say that Matias had a gambling addiction was to greatly understate the severity of his problem. Now desperate, he borrowed large sums from loan sharks at usurious rates of interest and began placing wagers on sporting events with local bookmakers[9] who operated illegally in the shadows. These services filled a void in the Arizona gaming industry since Indian-owned casinos typically did not offer sports books. Soon, Matias' gambling debts topped $100,000. He had no prospect of paying it off.

Initially assigned by the county attorney to less serious misdemeanors, he graduated to handling Class 4, 5 and 6 felony cases, then to more serious Class 2 and 3 felonies. One of his cases involved a wealthy defendant charged with

---

[8] Former first lady of The Philippines, famed for having closets full of shoes

[9] Bookmaking is a gambling practice to determine point spreads and odds, and to accept or pay bets on sporting events and horse races. Bookmakers operate legally only in established casinos in Nevada and New Jersey. Underground "bookies" operate on morning line information printed in the sports sections of most major newspapers. His bookie knew Matias was a lawyer with the county.

voluntary manslaughter. He allegedly killed a business associate while on a hunting trip claiming it was an accident, but the facts were murky. His attorney, one William Randolph, Esq. of shady reputation, had learned of Matias' financial difficulty through the grapevine of contacts he had with the Phoenix underworld. Matias was approached in the parking garage one afternoon after work by lawyer Randolph who offered to buy him a drink. A few minutes later at a nearby bar, the lawyer disclosed his intent.

"You realize getting a conviction of my client is going to be difficult, right?" said Randolph. "The facts are not on your side, so why embarrass yourself by risking a lengthy trial, the outcome of which will be very much in doubt? You can use some help with the huge pile of debt you owe, right?" Without waiting for an answer, he went on. "We can make it worth your while to move for dismissal of the charge. A large portion of your debt to Beto will go away. ("Beto" was the loan shark's professional brand.)

"Are you trying to bribe me? That could get you into a lot of trouble," Matias said with a slight smile on his face.

"True, but what the hell. We're both looking for solutions to our problems and this is a practical approach. I scratch your back, you scratch mine."

"Not interested." Matias abruptly got up and walked out of the bar.

The next day, Randolph's cell phone rang. It was Matias. "Meet me at the same bar, 6:00 p.m. this afternoon." Click.

Matias was waiting at the front door when the lawyer arrived.

"I need to know you're not wearing a wire," said Matias cautiously. "Let's go out to my car."

Seated in the car, Matias said "Open your shirt and pull it up from the back. I need to have a look at both sides."

The attorney did as he was told. Satisfied, Matias said "Okay, what do you have in mind?"

"Look, you can easily justify a dismissal. The judge and your boss will go along given the weakness of the case. You will find a sack containing $25,000 in cash in your car within five days of the ruling. Here's a good faith payment."

Matias counted out fifty hundred dollar bills. "How do I know the balance will be forthcoming? What if I get it done and you don't pay?"

"You're a lawyer. Do your goddam job. Just refile the charges based on new evidence that's come to your attention. Come on, we're not playing games here ... and by the way, this conversation never happened."

A full minute of silence ensued. Neither man said anything. Finally, Matias said: "I'll need at least fifty large to do this."

"This is not a negotiation, pal," said Randolph. "Our final offer is thirty-five, take it or leave it."

With a sigh Matias said "Okay, you've got a deal." On the way home that day, Matias felt unclean. He took a hot shower before dinner.

52

The Corrupt Prosecutor

"He is a man of splendid abilities, but utterly corrupt."

– John Randolph

Matias used fifteen thousand to reduce his credit card debt. He did this without Linda's knowledge to prevent further spending sprees. The remaining twenty went to Beto. The debt, partially satisfied, got Beto off his back and they were willing once again to advance him credit. Over a month's time, he found himself once again deeply in hock since most of his wagers were losers.

Word spread on the street that, under the right circumstances, one of the county attorneys could be bought. Matias was approached by defendants' family members, lawyers, and by defendants themselves with thinly veiled offers of "assistance" if he could help them with their legal troubles. Shocked at the brazenness of these offers and suspicious that he had been betrayed by lawyer Randolph, he refused them all for six months, during which time his gambling debts were climbing.

Carefully, gradually, one at a time, Matias accepted proffered "gratuities" in return for favorable recommendations for bail, reduced charges, or outright dismissals. The latter had to be plausible in the eyes of his superiors and the judge, but the prevailing culture of getting cases off the radar was effective in allowing his actions to go unnoticed.

Soon, he was raking in thousands each month, allowing him to gradually retire his debt. Linda enjoyed the new freedom and resumed her shopping habits. But an unanticipated problem arose—how to process and launder the money. Cash in small amounts was one thing. It could be used for groceries, restaurant meals, personal services and other minor expenses but when it reached several thousand dollars at a time, it would attract unwanted attention. Matias was aware that cash transactions over $10,000 must be reported to the IRS as required by law.

Matias' remedy for this was to set up a corporation owning five laundromats (cash businesses) that he had purchased at bargain basement prices in rundown condition. The incorporating documents listed one Linda Belen as the owner and president. The address was the street number of a postal box provider with "Suite 405" instead of a box number, suggesting a physical office location. Cash receipts were duly deposited into a business bank account. Accounting records were kept meticulously. Taxes were filed and paid when due on reported revenues, considerably more than actually collected. Matias and Linda alternated days in visiting the locations to collect cash from the machines and service change-making machines. A handyman was hired to provide service calls on short notice.

David Baumann (Dave), a member of the *Committee* and Matias' coworker, noticed that Matias was sporting a gold Rolex watch and apparently owned a new Mercedes-Benz

S450 sedan. Matias did not drive the Mercedes to work, but Dave saw him being dropped off and picked up in the car by his wife.

"Nice car, how long have you owned it?" asked Dave casually one day.

"What car?"

"The Mercedes your wife drives. It's a beauty. How do you like it?"

This conversation obviously put Matias on the defensive. His answer was awkward and not believable. "It was a gift to her from her grandmother who died and left a pretty large sum of money to Linda in her will. Actually, the money was a bequest that we used to buy the car."

Based on this response from Matias, Dave undertook some research into the department's files being handled by Matias. What he found was shocking.

Over the past eight months, eleven cases had been pleaded down to lesser charges, bail had been set at levels below what was asked by defense attorneys in another three, and four felony cases had charges dropped for lack of sufficient evidence. This was far out of line for the normal rate of cases handled by the office. Matias seemed to be especially accommodating with cases defended by James O'Rourke. Something was wrong with that picture and Dave thought he knew what it was—bribery.

The following Monday morning, Dave appeared in the office of county attorney Luke Thornton and presented the facts he had uncovered.

Thornton was mildly interested for a few minutes, then became distracted and indifferent. "What conclusion do you draw from your findings?" he asked.

"He has come into some unexplained wealth. Have you noticed his Rolex watch and new car? His salary doesn't exactly support those kinds of luxuries. I complemented the car and he offered the explanation that his wife had come into money from her grandmother's estate. It didn't sound plausible. Word around the office is that he has a gambling problem. He flies to Vegas on weekends at least twice a month. If he's on the take, he's using the proceeds to support his gambling and spending habits."

"What do you want me to do about it?"

"I think this deserves an investigation," said Dave. "More than I have time for."

"Let me think about what you've found. Come back tomorrow." Thornton's tone was oddly dismissive.

At their meeting the next morning, Thornton said he had reflected on what Dave had reported. "Okay, I'm appointing you to undertake some detective work. Start by finding out if the grandmother tale is true. I'll reduce your case load, but not enough to attract attention from your colleagues. Use the extra time to pursue this. I'll also authorize you to examine his personnel file and do a complete background check on him and the wife. Keep me posted."

Dave learned the maiden name of Matias' wife was Linda Jeri Belen, and began an online search of her background. She was a native of West Virginia and was the second of three children of Sarah and Jeremiah Belen of Wheeling, both deceased. Further exploration revealed the names of both grandmothers, Elizabeth Rothmeyer and Sarah Isabella Belen, also of Wheeling and widowed at the time of their deaths.

Sarah Belen's estate totaled less than $20,000, mostly in personal savings and her five -year old car. She willed it in equal amounts to her three children. Elizabeth Rothmeyer had a life insurance policy in the amount of $50,000 with her four grandchildren named as beneficiaries. They each received $10,000, and the remaining $10,000 went to the Jeffrey Chapman Faith Ministry of Wheeling. Dave could not find a record of any large bequest to Linda from her grandparents or parents. It was obvious that Matias was lying about his wife coming into some money.

"His claim of receiving money from his wife's grandmother is false," Dave reported to Thornton. "I believe he is accepting bribes from defendants or their families to go easy on them. "Also, I found several months ago, that his credit card debt was over 50K. Now it's about twelve thousand and his wife still loves to shop. He sometimes pays the minimum due and other months pays up to $2,000—very erratic.

"Owning a new watch and car can't be construed as evidence of unlawful behavior Dave," said Thornton. "Neither can paying his credit card debt. We'll need to get more if we want to build a case. Now, if you'll excuse me, I need to attend a meeting of my reelection committee. Raising money for a political campaign is a bitch."

DAVE ADDRESSED a meeting called by Derek for the purpose of hearing his story. "This guy is totally corrupt and he's putting criminal defendants' victims at risk. The county attorney is involved in a reelection campaign and appears to have little interest in doing anything so I'm raising this to the attention of the *Committee.* Can we do something?"

"Why not report this to the state attorney general's office?" asked J.W. "They would certainly have an interest in this corruption of one of their own officials."

"I've done that... anonymously, three months ago, and so far nothing has happened. As far as I know, they are not investigating it."

"So the guy had a lot of debts that he paid off and now he has big spending habits. Is this something we need to get involved with?" asked J.W.

"The criminal justice system is being abused and defendants are not being held accountable," said Dave. "I think that qualifies as a legitimate issue of concern. Unless he gets caught out, which right now seems unlikely, he'll just continue his criminal habits."

"What do you suggest?" asked J.W.

"Let's have a 'heart to heart' with him as we've done in other cases, give him a warning backed up with our usual persuasive threats, and make it clear that he has to clean up his act," Dave said. "He's a smart guy and a good lawyer. Right now, he needs direction for his life and career. We'll confront him at a time and place he least expects and put the fear of God into him."

"That's a good last resort, but I have a better idea, something we haven't tried before," said Derek. "Let's compose a letter to be delivered to him by courier at his home informing him that we know what he's up to and warning him to cease and desist. It will be signed by *Group for Prosecutorial Justice*, or something like that."

"I like that idea Derek, will you be the author?" inquired J.W.

"No, I think Dave should write the letter."

Derek called a meeting of the *Committee* two days later and distributed copies of the letter authored by Dave.

Dear Mr. Carrasco:

Pay close attention to the contents of this letter and don't think for a moment we are not serious.

We are fully aware of your corrupt and illegal behavior with the county attorney's office. Did you think that you would get away with it indefinitely?

You accepted a cash bribe from Bill Randolph on behalf of his client who was charged with manslaughter. Coincidentally, you moved for dismissal of all charges which was granted by the judge who asked you in open court why charges were brought in the first place. We have knowledge of other bribes paid to you for favors from the county attorney.

The corporation you set up in your wife's name has enjoyed laundromat revenues of $84,000 in the last six months. The corporation is obviously a money laundering operation. We could go on but you get the point. We know all about you. You have a gambling problem and your wife has a spending problem so here is what will happen:

First – You will give up all gambling. No more trips to Vegas or to local casinos, no more bets with local bookies, and not even any friendly Friday night poker games with your buddies. Yes, we know about those too.

Second – You and Linda will cut up your credit cards. From now on, until we determine you have reformed your monetary habits, all of your personal transactions will be by cash or personal check.

Third, and most important—no more bribes accepted from anyone having business with the county attorney's office. And in case you are tempted to extort funds from anyone, forget about it.

Fourth – You will sell your Rolex watch and Mercedes automobile and pay off all debts within one year.

Fifth – You will resign your position with the county attorney within thirty days for the stated reason that you are pursuing other opportunities in the legal profession. With your experience and academic record together with your minority status, it shouldn't be too difficult to find a job with a local firm.

Failure to comply with these requirements will result in these consequences:

All evidence we have developed will be furnished to the county attorney and to the state attorney general accompanied by sworn affidavits from numerous witnesses. Your family back in Texas will be informed of your perfidy. Your reputation will be ruined, your law license will be revoked permanently, and you will lose your career, your family and probably your marriage. You will be prosecuted and you will go to prison.

These requirements are in effect immediately. There is no way to avoid them.

Why are we doing this? Why are we giving you a deal that will allow you to escape prosecution and probably prison? The criminal justice system is dysfunctional in many ways and it doesn't need a major scandal to further degrade its reputation. Those who prosecute crime must maintain a scandal-free image. The public must regard the system as effective and free of corruption. You will be allowed to follow the above steps in cooperation with this objective and to save you own worthless hide.

We will soon be in touch to assess your progress.
Committee for a Corruption-Free Justice System

"You did a great job Dave. My high school English teacher couldn't have said it better," said J.W. "Let's go with it."

"I agree," said Dave. So did Derek.

The letter was delivered to Matias at his home by courier the next evening. Opening and reading it, he turned ghostly pale and poured himself a full tumbler of single-malt scotch whiskey (another of his luxuries). Then another.

"What was in the package?" asked Linda.

"Oh, just some stuff they sent from work. I'll take care of it tomorrow." He quickly placed the letter in his locked briefcase. Sleep did not come to him that night.

One week later, Matias Carrasco placed a letter of resignation on the desk of county attorney Luke Thornton who was relieved to avoid the possibility of an internal investigation and scandal involving one of his assistants.

Arriving home that evening, Matias informed Linda that he had resigned from his position with the county attorney's office. "Luke is on my ass all the time. He demands that I take on a workload that basically doubles the cases I handle. It's more than I can endure." This was not true, but it was the most plausible explanation Matias could think of.

"You never mentioned this before," a shocked Linda said. "But I've noticed you haven't been yourself lately."

"Look, I'll start looking for another job, but in the meantime, you need to stop spending and I need to fix my gambling habit."

Matias was still unable to find work as an attorney eight months after separating from the county attorney's office. Several law firms interviewed him but declined to make an offer of employment when background checks revealed his poor credit history. His Rolex, Mercedes, and some of Linda's more expensive jewelry were sold to raise cash. This produced sufficient proceeds to pay off credit card debt, but not enough to pay Beto, to whom he still owed slightly more than $45,000. Selling their home barely covered the mortgage balance and lien against it from a second mortgage loan taken a year earlier to pay debts.

Linda, no longer endowed with the lifestyle to which she had become accustomed and deprived of shopping, her favorite activity, told Matias the marriage was over and she was moving back to Dallas. Divorce proceedings were begun. Fortunately, no children were involved.

Still unable to control his gambling habit, Matias borrowed five thousand dollars from friends in El Paso and promptly blew it at local Indian casinos. Unable to pay Beto, he pleaded for more time and was granted several extensions, but the patience of an illegal bookie is limited. Matias was given ten days to pay at least half of what he owed or suffer the consequences.

Two weeks passed. Matias was found dead behind a convenience store on Bethany Home Road in North Phoenix, shot twice in the head with a .38 caliber weapon. Linda returned from Dallas and made arrangements to send his body home to Floresville, Texas, for burial. His family was devastated and demanded justice from Arizona authorities. The murder was never solved.

At a *Committee* meeting in Derek's basement, Dave sat glumly as the death of Matias was discussed.

"Greed killed him, pure and simple." said Derek. "He was unable to control his urges and fortunately, we didn't have to take any action of our own."

The *Committee* planned and executed three more operations during the six month period after the death of Matias Carrasco.

53

Child Molestation

"We are the world, we are the children."

– Michael Jackson

In certain domestic environments, children are tragically vulnerable to mistreatment. Detective Norman Wilkie brought several cases to Derek's attention. They involved levels of cruelty and death to children that were so distressing and monstrous that *Committee* members had difficulty discussing them. Children's abusers are usually parents or live-in partners of parents. How anyone could harm a child was an unanswerable question the *Committee* pondered at length.

RON AND CYNTHIA Ardele's four-year old son Matthew accompanied them to Midway Mall on a Saturday shopping trip. They bought a couple of DVDs at the book store then entered the large department store to shop for several articles of clothing for Ron. Matthew stayed close, holding his mother's hand most of the time. After several minutes of Ron's browsing through the racks of men's sport shirts, Matthew wondered off and disappeared. Ron and Cynthia were not worried at first, thinking he was nearby. Calling his name repeatedly for several minutes brought no response and both parents grew alarmed. Matthew could not be found. Ron rushed to the nearest checkout station to report a missing child while Cynthia frantically searched for her son.

A half hour passed, then an hour, with no sign of Matthew despite store-wide searches by every clerk on duty. By this time, both parents were desperate and terrified their son might have been abducted. Cynthia was hysterical and weeping. Mall security had been given a description of the missing child and a search was begun of the entire mall without result. Ron, terrified, called 9-1-1.

Police officers arrived and conducted interviews with the child's parents and store managers who were asked to produce the store's surveillance tapes. Numerous cameras were situated throughout the store providing a clear view of aisles and entrances. Officers pieced together segments of tape showing images of young Matthew accompanied by a tall male of undetermined race in baggy clothing, large sunglasses, and large hat pulled down to obscure his face. The tape showed the two, holding hands, departing the store through a side door into a parking lot. The footage followed them to a vehicle parked at least a hundred yards away. It was identified as a light colored, four door Kia SUV. As it drove away, the license plate could not be ascertained. Ron and Cynthia were devastated with the knowledge that their child had been kidnapped. Cynthia, screaming and weeping uncontrollably, collapsed on the floor. Officers summoned EMTs immediately. An all-points bulletin was issued to patrol units in jurisdictions throughout the region to search for a light colored Kia SUV driven by a male suspected of child abduction. The child would possibly be with him in the vehicle. EMTs arrived and patiently talked with Cynthia, calming her down. She did not require transport to the ER.

Thirty-five minutes later, state trooper Lewis Fulton was parked under an overpass on eastbound Interstate Highway 10 to Tucson, twenty miles south of the Baseline Road exit. He had been on duty seven hours that day, exhausted from dealing with heavy traffic and issuing numerous citations for speeding violations to unhappy motorists. He was looking forward to ending his shift and getting home to his wife and family.

His radar equipment clocked an oncoming vehicle doing 89 miles per hour in a 75 mph zone. It passed his position without slowing down. Fulton flipped on his flashers and gave chase. Troopers have discretion to allow drivers a cushion of five to ten mph, but ten mph or more over the limit usually resulted in a citation. Three minutes later, the speeding vehicle slowed and pulled over on the shoulder with the trooper's cruiser close behind. It was a tan colored Kia SUV driven by a male. No child was immediately visible. Fulton recognized the vehicle from the APB received minutes earlier and was on full alert. Cautiously approaching the driver's side with service weapon drawn, he ordered the driver to show his hands, exit the vehicle and place his hands on the roof. Moving closer to the vehicle, the trooper noticed a child without a seat belt apparently asleep in the rear seat. The driver was now a suspect in a crime and was cuffed behind his back. He did not resist arrest.

"What is your name, sir?" asked Fulton.

"Bill Tankersley," answered the suspect.

"Who is the child in your back seat?"

"He's my sister's kid. I'm taking him home."

"What is his name?"

"Jimmy," Tankersley lied.

"Where did you pick him up?"

Silence from Tankersley.

"Okay, come with me and stand behind your vehicle facing me."

After verifying his ID from Tankersley's driver's license, Fulton retreated to his cruiser and radioed the details of the arrest to his dispatcher. Several minutes passed and the trooper returned to the Kia and opened the back door. "Hey, partner, how are you doing? What's your name? Starting to cry, the child said "It's Matthew, where's my mommy?"

"She's waiting for you and we're gonna take you to her real soon. Now tell me, are you hurt? Did that man hurt you?"

"He slapped me and told me to keep quiet and stay down in the seat," Matthew said, still crying.

"You're safe now Matthew. Some nice people are on the way to take you home to your mom and dad."

Scarcely able to control his anger, Fulton placed Tankersley in the back seat of his cruiser and took Matthew in his arms, holding him until EMTs arrived along with backup state police. A female EMT gave Matthew a quick examination and determined he was not seriously injured. She gently took Matthew in her arms, spoke to him softly and told him they would take a ride in that "big red vehicle" over there and everything would be all right.

Ron and Cynthia were notified their son had been found alive and well and had been taken to St. Anthony's Hospital in the Phoenix suburb of Chandler. Cynthia fell into Ron's arms weeping, this time with joy. Ron's tears blended with hers. A half-hour later, they rushed into the hospital's ER for a joyful, tearful reunion with their son.

"CAN YOU IMAGINE the agony of those poor parents when they realized their four-year-old child had been taken?" Derek posed this question at a meeting of the *Committee* in his basement. "Not knowing who had taken him, where he was, how he was being treated. Thank God the kid's okay." Derek was seething.

Dave reported the details of William Tankersley's case file. "His rap sheet runs to two full pages. Everything from drunk and disorderly to burglary to domestic violence. Not only is he a wife beater, he's been arrested three times for child molestation. The last time was for suspicion of raping his eleven-year old stepson. His wife initially called police to report the crime, then later changed her mind and told cops it was all a mistake. At his arraignment on the current charge, the judge set Tankersley's bail at $200,000. This is less than the usual amount for child abduction, but since Matthew was not hurt or molested, the judge deemed the amount sufficient. Bail for such crimes can run as much as a half million. The bail bond company demanded and received title to the couple's home with an estimated equity of $150,000 and the remaining $50K was put up in cash by Tankersley's family members. Incredibly, he's out on bail as we speak."

"I would love to get my hands on him, just once," said J.W. "I would rip his balls out and stuff 'em down his throat."

"Is this a case we need to get involved in?" asked Dave. "He's gonna be tried and most likely convicted."

"Maybe so, but he's out now and given his predatory record, he could grab another kid and do God knows what,"

Derek said. "I think we need to move against him. He's out of jail which provides us an opportunity."

The conversation continued for a half hour without a decision. After further discussion, Derek recommended hiring the Morettis to undertake surveillance on Bill Tankersley to learn his daily habits and identify a possible opening for an operation.

"NICE TO HEAR from you. How can we help you?" asked Deirdre when Derek placed a call to her.

Derek related Tankersley's history and the details of his latest crime involving little Matthew Ardele.

"If the circumstances are right, are you interested in taking him out?" asked Deirdre.

"Quite possibly. Find out what you can about him and let me know ASAP, okay?"

"Okay, but our fee for the research will be two grand whether you decide to go forward or not. Is that acceptable?"

"Sure. Just be careful and get back to me quickly. This guy was bailed out of jail and we're worried he could be tempted to repeat another kid crime."

AT RALPH'S SIX days later, Deidre reported her findings to Derek over drinks. "He stays home most of the time but gets in his car about 8:00 p.m. and drives to the Palm Breeze Lounge on South Central. He drinks club sodas and strikes up conversations with other drinkers. He stays about three hours before heading home. He parks in a carport that opens on the alley behind his house. It's very dark back there and no one's around. There is a dense hedge alongside the carport where someone could wait without being seen. When he drives in, it would be pretty easy to take him out as he exists his car."

"Sounds like a piece of cake," said Derek, now fully understanding what attracted Lee to Deidre who was provocatively dressed and wearing an enticing perfume.

Derek reviewed Deirdre's report with the *Committee.* Discussion centered on risk, always a major concern, if not the only concern. The vote to proceed was unanimous.

DEREK AND J.W. observed the Tankersley home from seven to around 9:00 p.m. over the next four evenings and found that he did not go out at any time. On the fifth night, he was seen driving out of the alley. They followed him to the Palm Breeze where he settled into his usual seat and ordered a club soda. This was their signal to set up the hit. Returning to Tankersley's neighborhood, Derek dropped J.W. off at the alley's intersection with the cross street just three doors down from Bill's house. J.W. was dressed in dark clothing and carried a .380 caliber semi-automatic handgun equipped with a noise suppressor. Walking quickly down the alley, he stationed himself behind the hedge alongside the carport. Tankersley arrived ninety minutes later. J.W. was ready for him.

Fifteen minutes later, Derek picked him up at the drop off point.

"So how did it go? Any problems?" Silence from J.W. for several seconds.

"I couldn't do it, Derek. I was sitting there waiting for him to return and I began to think what I was about to do. Cold blooded murder. When the time came, I just couldn't do it. So I pumped a couple of slugs into his knees. He will be out of commission for a long time."

Derek was aghast, then it was his turn to remain silent. Two blocks later he quietly said "You should wipe the GSR off yourself and we need to ditch that gun."

Driving back to the basement, there was no more conversation. Dave was waiting for them. "What happened?"

"Cold feet, Dave," answered J.W. "It dawned on me that I was about to take a man's life. Maybe he had it coming, I don't know, but I sat there in the dark and decided I couldn't do it."

"I was shocked and angry at first, but on the way back, I realized what J.W. did was just right," Derek said. "That bastard will suffer appropriately. And we need to get a message to him so he understands that his predations on children will end regardless of the outcome of his trial."

"I can handle that," offered Dave.

"We've lost two of our group and we're not going to replace them," said Derek. "I'm tired of this, so let's suspend operations at least temporarily and review our mission."

William Tankersley was convicted of kidnaping and sentenced to thirty-five years in prison. He would most likely die in prison. Prison authorities had to make special accommodations for his disabled status.

Derek was blissfully unaware of what Detectives McAvoy and Browning had in store for him.

54

Search Warrant

"And out of good still to find means of evil."

– John Milton

McAvoy and Browning had scraped together snippets of information leading to their conclusion that a search warrant of the Overton home could be justified. They relied on statements from several contacts that one of the attackers had a southern drawl and was overweight, a description that fit Derek Overton as they remembered and noted from their interview with him. Their suspicion that his home was the repository of weapons used in numerous operations was specified in the warrant application. Also included was the term "explosives," a product of their imagination. This was Browning's idea. He had no evidence that explosives would be found, but falsified the application with a statement from a nonexistent witness claiming to have processed an order from Derek for C-4 plastic explosive at a hardware store. Further, he was a next door neighbor of Stephen Lee Simmons who had been under investigation prior to his death in an automobile accident.

STANLEY McPHAIL, COMMISSIONER of the Initial Appearance Court of Maricopa County, referred to as the IA Court, issued a search warrant for the home and property of Derek and Marjorie Overton. Search warrants are issued on a showing of probable cause that a crime has been committed and that items connected to the crime are likely to be found at the location specified in the warrant. Items listed in the application included weapons, weapon accessories, explosives, written and digitized documents, records, emails, and information found on computer hard drives and cell phones. McPhail was known for his accommodating attitude toward the police and prosecutors. He issued the warrant with minimal evidence of probable cause.

At 5:00 a.m. the following morning, McAvoy, Browning, and three SWAT team officers approached Overton's home. SWAT team members were in full uniform and equipped with semi-automatic weapons. Rather than ringing the doorbell and informing the Overtons why there were there, they commenced the search by forcing the front door open which proved to be unnecessary since Derek and Marjorie were asleep in their bedroom and were not aware of the assault until it began.

Loudly yelling "Police, get on the floor" several times, the team was ready for action in the event of resistance from the Overtons.

Derek jumped out of bed, retrieved a .45 semi-automatic Glock kept in his night stand and started for the bedroom door. Opening the door and seeing two officers in combat gear, he immediately threw down his weapon and raised his hands. In the noise and terror of the initial assault, he hadn't heard officers shouting "police." Marjorie and Derek were terrified and believed their home was being invaded by God-knows who. They were both thrown face down on the floor and handcuffed. Derek's right shoulder was dislocated and his face severely bruised. Marjorie was slightly bruised but otherwise unhurt.

Amid the noise and chaos, Myrtle," the Overton's Siamese cat, fled through an open door and disappeared.

Neighbors gathered in the street that had been barricaded at each end of the block and gaped with alarm at the flashing lights of emergency vehicles arriving and departing from the Overton's home. Television and print reporters soon arrived on the scene and presented a severe logistical problem for the police.

THE ENSUING INTERNAL police department investigation revealed a number of things wrong with the aggressive execution of a search warrant on the home of Derek and Marjorie Overton. Police spokesmen tried to justify the operation as essential, based on their suspicion that Derek was harboring numerous firearms and explosives.

Cops stayed in the home several hours seeking any possible evidence of criminal activity. Derek was informed his computers would be removed for forensic analysis. He offered to open both computers for immediate examination. Browning, who possessed advanced technical skills, thoroughly searched hard drives and found nothing incriminating. Nevertheless, the computers were confiscated. No storage devices or peripherals other than printers were found in the house. The Arbalest signal jammer had been stored in the garage, an area not specified in the search warrant. By noon, cops realized their search was going nowhere. Despite ransacking the house with thorough attention to the basement, no incriminating evidence was found. The SWAT team leader falsely told reporters that Derek resisted the warrant and failed to cooperate with the search by reacting violently.

When officers realized Derek had been injured, handcuffs were removed and he was transported to the nearest ER, treated by an orthopedist and discharged from the hospital the following day when police realized they had made a mistake.

Four days later, Myrtle the cat deemed it safe to return home. She spent the next two days sleeping and grooming herself.

Walter Burkett reported the incident extensively in two issues of the *Valley Viewer,* this time forgetting his commitment to "deep background" in his previous story, making full use of Derek's name, former career, and details of police search of his home.

55
Finality

"The evil that men do lives after them,
the good is oft interred with their bones."

— William Shakespeare, *Julius Caesar*

Derek sat in his basement with his arm in a sling reviewing his life and his decision to organize the *Committee*. Unwanted negative publicity, contacts by police detectives, and finally, the early morning invasion of his home by search warrant. Derek struggled to avoid panic. He summoned J.W. and Dave to a basement meeting four days after the police assault, cautioning them to travel by taxi or ride sharing service rather than their own vehicles. Several rounds of gin and tonic were poured.

"I never imagined matters would come to this or how it would end. I'm under suspicion and I'm not sure where we go from here," a dejected Derek told J.W. and Dave. "By the way, Marjorie and I are suing the city. Jimmy O'Rourke thinks we have a strong case."

"I think it's clear they don't have anything more than suspicion," Dave said.

Another hour of conversation followed with all three expressing doubt about the future of the *Committee*. At one point, Dave suggested that perhaps they had reached a conclusion. "We can take a lot of satisfaction in what we've done, but with the loss of two of our members under tragic circumstances... " His voice trailed off. Then abruptly, "Derek, would you like to tell us the truth about Phil?"

Derek sat silently for several seconds looking at the floor. "Okay, Lee and I had him whacked. We were sure he was betraying us and we couldn't take the chance that he might drop the final hammer. We hired the contractors to do the job and we didn't want you guys involved for your own protection."

"What led you to believe he was a mole?' asked Dave.

"I fed him a phony line about the "whistlers" gang that found its way into a news story. That tipped us off. I guess we should have consulted you guys. Looking back now, I'm not sure why we didn't. I'm not sure of anything anymore."

"I can't do this anymore, Derek," blurted J.W. "The episode with that child molester Tankersley almost finished me."

"That's totally understandable," Derek said. "We need to wrap this up." He went on with a pained expression. "I only wanted to do good, to put things right and provide justice where it was lacking, to bring closure to those who had been seriously wronged." The gin was talking. "I knew we were doing crimes and I knew it was highly risky despite our careful planning. I was placing myself, you guys, my wife and son in great jeopardy. I guess my drive to punish wrongdoers trumped all of that. It became very personal, you know? I began to imagine our targets' behavior was directed to me personally and it garbled my mind. My heart aches for Dana Maguire and her girls; and for Janet Simmons and Daryl. My God, what those families have been through."

"Let's take a breather and lie low for a while," Dave said. "We're all stressed out and need a long break. I say we go our separate ways for awhile."

DAYS TURNED INTO weeks. Derek thought long and hard about his life and what the future held. Alone in the basement, he drank gin and tonics. Thoughts flooded his mind. *Who am I? What am I doing? I thought I was a good man doing what was righteous. Where is all this going? Where does it end? It's taking a toll on my marriage not to mention the emotional stress it's causing. This is an emotional rollercoaster. There is no way I can win at this. I will probably die. How much longer can I expect to get away with this?*

Marjorie had begged him to disband the *Committee* and cease all their operations.

He had gained over fifty pounds since retirement and was diagnosed with high blood pressure and diabetes. He resolved to lose weight and get healthy again. His first idea was to walk. A lot of walking—around the neighborhood and then hiking in mountain parks nearby. It didn't work. He continued to pack on weight from habitual overeating. He couldn't restrain himself from snacking between meals and after dinner resulting in still more weight. This complicated management of his diabetes. His clothes no longer fit and he felt miserable most to the time. All this put him in a deep depression aggravated by stress caused by mentally dwelling on the *Committee's* activities.

THE PAIN IN HIS SHOULDER DID NOT SUBSIDE. Derek sought help from the orthopedist who had treated him in the ER. Additional x-rays were ordered but failed to indicate the cause of pain. The doctor prescribed physical therapy and opioid pain relievers in mild doses. When that proved ineffective, dosages were increased. Finally, Derek found relief and was able to get by on two tabs a day of Oxycodone, 15 mg each. This strength was three times that of the original prescribed dosage. He walked around in an opioid daze most of the time. Marjorie was worried that he was addicted and begged him to see a chiropractor she heard of who had a reputation for successfully treating chronic pain without medication. Derek refused to make an appointment.

A REGISTERED LETTER in a 9 x 11 envelope addressed to Lt. Derek Overton arrived. The return address was a box number in Tucson. Marjorie signed for it and gave it to Derek unopened. He took it to the basement where it lay for two days before he summoned the will to open it. It contained several sheets of paper in longhand script. It was obviously a machine copy of the original and was a little difficult to read. Placing it under a bright lamp, Derek felt faint after reading the title and first sentence.

MY PERSONAL CONFESSION

My name is Phillip J. Maguire. I am the founder and owner of Sonoran Plumbing & Heating Company of Phoenix, Arizona. I am the husband of Dana Maguire and father of Alice and Marie Maguire. I love my family and all my employees so much.

I have committed a huge error in my life. I have allowed myself to become involved with a group of vigilantes called the Committee. God help me! They take the law into their own hands and commit crimes to provide justice for those they believe have not received it from the criminal justice system.

It all began at the Elk's Club after my hunting trip to Wyoming. We were sitting around having a few beers discussing politics and how the criminal justice system frequently went awry. One guy suggested forming a group to undertake actions to "put things right." We met a few days later in his basement and formulated a plan to identify wrongdoers and punish them outside the scope of law enforcement. I just got swept up in the emotion of the movement. After hearing descriptions of some of the horrible crimes that had not been successfully prosecuted, I went along with the idea of putting things right. They knew of my love of big game hunting and assumed my knowledge of powerful firearms would be useful.

We were assured there was little risk involved and we would avoid suspicion. After all, Derek, as a retired detective, is familiar with criminal investigative procedures and knows how to avoid leaving evidence at any of the operations.

I never took part in any of the actual operations except to plan logistics and drive vehicles a few times. Derek, Lee, and J.W. inflicted punishments which varied from physical beatings to murder. The more I saw what was happening, the more I knew it was wrong. But I couldn't pull away from it. To have done so would have put me at risk from those guys. I am afraid of them. Several times, I suggested suspending operations to consider what we were doing and whether we should continue. That worked a couple of times, but they always went back to their routine. As time went by, I felt personal guilt piling up.

The leader of this group is Derek Overton, a retired homicide detective with the police department. We meet in his basement in north Phoenix. The others are J.W. and Dave. I don't know their last names and never tried to learn them. Dave is a lawyer. Another member is Lee. He was an expert marksman and eliminated several targets from sniper positions.

Lee hired people he called "contractors" to carry out an operation at a bar called "Etta's Place" on Indian School Road. They killed two thugs suspected of robbing convenience stores and shooting a couple of customers in one instance. No one except Lee and Derek know their names or how to contact them. Derek found a source of funds used to pay the contractors. We were never told the source of those funds.

We took great satisfaction in eliminating that drug king Ochoa in Paradise Valley. Most of our operations were directed at domestic violence. Here is some information about the crimes we have committed:

There followed a detailed description of eight operations undertaken by the Committee complete with dates, locations, methods, names of targets, and fragments of information that only someone familiar with the crimes would know.

I can't go on like this. I know if I attempt to quit the group, I will be "whacked" as they put it. And if I report it to the authorities, I will be exposed to prosecution for my part in it. I don't know what to do. My God! I made an anonymous call to the PD and suggested they investigate certain retired detectives. They interviewed Derek but found no evidence tying him to any of the incidents we conducted. He is very clever at planning the operations and careful of not leaving any evidence behind.

I will acknowledge that the people we punished had it coming. They were bad guys and if we hadn't intervened, their behavior would not cease. In a way, justice was served. But at the end of the day, we are criminals committing crimes against other criminals. It is only a matter of time until it must stop or we will all go to prison for it. I've confessed all this to Father Stephen and received absolution, so I think I'm okay with the Man upstairs.

If anything happens to me, I want Dana to forward this document to Detective Browning at the police department.

Philip J. Maguire

A handwritten note in large red letters was enclosed:

"THIS DOCUMENT WAS MAILED TO THE POLICE DEPARTMENT TODAY"

It was unsigned.

My God, we were right, Phil betrayed us and he made sure someone knew about it. This was sent either by his wife or someone he took into his confidence. This is the end of the line. Derek lowered his head and started to weep.

Two hours later, he climbed the stairs, entered the master bath, and started swallowing pills. Then he descended to the basement and started drinking gin straight from the bottle.

MARJORIE FOUND EMPTY prescription bottles of Oxycodone, Lunesta, and medications for diabetes and blood pressure in the lavatory basin of their bathroom. She also found a handwritten note on the vanity saying, "My dearest Marjorie and Ronnie, I'm so sorry. I can't go on with this, I hope you can come to understand. Maybe we can meet again someday. All my love, Daddy."

Oh, my God! She ran down the stairs into the basement and found her husband reclined on the couch as if asleep. An empty gin bottle lay on the floor by the couch. He was unresponsive and cold to the touch. She screamed, knelt on the floor in front him and fell on his chest weeping. Ten minutes later, Ronald discovered his parents in the basement, realized what had happened, and called 9-1-1.

DETECTIVES McAVOY AND BROWNING appeared at the door of the Overton's home the evening Derek was earlier found dead in his basement. Ronald opened the door and was asked if his father was home.

"You guys are a little late. My dad took his own life this morning and my mom and I are in shock. What do you want?"

"We're sorry to hear that. We won't trouble you further," said McAvoy as they retreated from the front porch.

"We need to get the coroner's report," said Browning as they walked to their car.

56
Aftermath

"Separate paths."

Represented by James O'Rourke, Marjorie sued the City of Phoenix and the individual officers who took part in the raid of their home for $2 million. The city eventually settled for $750 thousand, all of which came from public funds and none from the officers' personal accounts. Lawyer O'Rourke collected a $250 thousand fee, part of which financed a three-week vacation in the south of France for him and Amber, his current girlfriend. Detectives McAvoy and Browning were found to be "non-participants" and therefore not liable or responsible for damages to the Overtons. Instead, both were awarded commendations for meritorious service.

DEREK'S MEMORIAL SERVICE was attended by seventy-five people—relatives, former police colleagues including the chief and his assistant, and friends. Dana Maguire did not attend. Nor did John Wayne Barrett or David Baumann.

The *Committee* simply ceased to exist. The remaining two members drifted apart and did not encounter each other again.

David Baumann (Dave) – Initially investigated but not arrested, did not attend Derek's memorial, resigned from county attorney's staff, moved to Portland, Oregon, joined a thirty-lawyer firm, became partner after five years, met and married a fellow lawyer, began to suffer PTSD symptoms and sought psychiatric treatment.

John Wayne (J.W.) Barrett– Not investigated, did not attend Derek's memorial, resigned from Scottsdale security firm, remarried his former wife, moved to Oklahoma City, joined the police department and was promoted to chief of the homicide division after eight years. The *Daily Oklahoman* reported several unsolved cases of criminal suspects killed under mysterious circumstances.

Marjorie Overton – Investigated but not charged, remained with Scottsdale security firm six years, retired to Prescott, Arizona, sold the signed photo of Babe Ruth treasured by Derek for $4,100 on E-Bay. A pawn shop in Las Vegas previously offered a paltry $1,800 which she wisely declined. Ronald entered Arizona State University, did not graduate, and knocked around between dead-end jobs for several years before finding a decent job in automobile sales.

Janet Simmons – Investigated, but was not charged, attended Derek's memorial, married a former college classmate after three years, relocated to Lubbock, Texas, became a municipal librarian and a fan of Texas Tech athletics after her son walked on and earned a backup position as wide receiver on the Red Raider football team. He was awarded an athletic scholarship during his second year on the team, was drafted by the Cincinnati Bengals of the NFL in the sixteenth round, but did not make the team. He earned a degree in petroleum engineering three years later and found a lucrative job in with a major energy company in Houston.

Marcus and Deirdre Moretti – Indicted on two counts of first-degree murder unrelated to their contracts with the *Committee*, represented by James O'Rourke, pled to involuntary manslaughter, paid a fine of $10,000 each, sentenced to six years in prison in separate correctional facilities. Deirdre got on well with male prison authorities earning her special "privileges," appeared on televised production of "Women in Prison." Both paroled after four years, accessed their flush off-shore accounts, returned to their "consulting" business when their sentences were complete.

James O'Rourke – Became a nationally recognized criminal defense lawyer, defended numerous politicians accused of sex offenses and other crimes, contributed generously to the campaigns of Democratic and Republican politicians, married his third wife, stopped womanizing, expanded his firm to fifteen lawyers.

Detectives McAvoy and Browning – Promoted to rank of Lieutenant, remained with Phoenix Police Department until retirement, received multiple commendations for meritorious service.

Russ Milam and Ben Moskowitz – Not investigated, continued to develop profitable multi-use properties throughout Arizona and New Mexico, sought but did not find opportunities to fund extra-legal means of punishing wrongdoers. Through the skill of a nationally recognized plastic surgeon, Carlie Milam's face was restored to its former youthful beauty. She married her college boyfriend and became the mother of three children.

Detective Norman Wilkie – Sent condolence message to Marjorie Overton but did not attend Derek's memorial, promoted to Captain of Police, then to Assistant Chief of Police, frequently decorated for meritorious service.

Rolando (Big Man) Hayes – Killed in a drive-by shooting as a suspected informer on gang members James Arneson and Levone Barcroft. No arrests were made in connection with his homicide.

57
Postscript

Six years later.

On a cool dark evening in late November, wife abuser and suspected pedophile Bernard O'Neal emerged from a bar on the south side of Oklahoma City and was knee capped with a sawed off twelve-gauge shotgun. He went to the ground screaming with pain. Both knees were destroyed. The shooter hopped into a waiting SUV with a fake license plate and was quickly transported from the scene. No evidence was discovered to assist the criminal investigation. Bernie spent the rest of his life in a wheel chair, totally impotent to assault any woman or child again. The shotgun was wiped down and sawed into several pieces, each packed in newspapers, placed in trash bags, and deposited in different dumpsters.

Three days later in the same city, Malcolm Basinger, an unindicted serial rapist, was whacked as he was sitting in a barber's chair. A masked gunman entered the shop wearing ear protectors, walked up to Malcolm and pumped two .38-caliber slugs into his chest. Amid the noise, blood, and chaos, the gunman calmly walked out and climbed into a mini-van that had screeched to halt at the curb. Witnesses were unable to provide information about the vehicle as it sped off other than its color (dark). The *Association* could not understand why Malcolm was released from custody since he was a credible suspect in at least four rapes all occurring within a ten-block area of the city. The gun was destroyed, and together with the ear protectors, was deposited in several commercial dumpsters behind supermarkets carefully secured in plastic trash bags.

At a meeting in the basement of the barber shop shooter, the homeowner said, "Those operations went down pretty well. What's next?"

About the Author

Robert E. Key is a retired public manager and business owner. He holds a Bachelor's Degree from Texas Tech University, Lubbock, Texas, and a Master's Degree from the University of Colorado, Boulder, Colorado. He is the father of two adult children and has two grandchildren (the most beautiful, smartest kids on the planet), all living in Colorado. He is a first-time novelist living in Tucson, Arizona.

If you enjoyed this book, please consider posting a review on Amazon. Even if it's only a few lines, it will be very much appreciated. Here is a link you can use:

Thank you!

If you, or someone you know is a victim of domestic violence, call this hotline for help:

1-800-799-7233

Or, go to: www.thehotline.org

Author's Note: This is a work of fiction. I have the greatest respect for the Phoenix Police Department and the Maricopa County Attorney's office. Nothing herein is intended to call into question their excellent work in protecting the citizens of Maricopa County.

Acknowledgments

This book is dedicated to the memory of my high school English teacher, Nell Marie Wylie, (Miss Wylie), Lubbock High School, who taught the importance of grammar, spelling, punctuation, the need to use proper English, and the need to 'scrutinize' one's writing. I intended to thank her in writing for her contribution to my life and I greatly regret never having done so during her lifetime.

I was inspired by the novels of John Grisham and the intellectual genius of Charles Krauthammer. My thanks to both these literary giants. I am also indebted to Lt. Joe Kenda, retired homicide detective for the investigative skill dramatized on the TV program "Homicide Hunter" on the Investigate/Discover channel. I've never met him.

Thanks also to my editor, Emilie Vardaman for her careful attention to detail and to Debora K. Lewis for formatting and cover design.

Any and all errors are mine alone.

Made in the USA
San Bernardino, CA
07 January 2020